# Crocodile Mothers Eat Their Young

## Avi Morris

ALL THINGS
THAT MATTER
PRESS

ISBN 13: 9780990715801
Library of Congress Control Number: 2014948753

Cover design by All Things That Matter Press
Published in 2014 by All Things That Matter Press

This book is dedicated to two special young women who suffered and survived more in their young lives than I could ever have portrayed in a work of fiction

# Acknowledgments

The excitement I'm experiencing at the publication of *Crocodile Mothers Eat Their Young* would not have been possible without the support, help and caring of some people who I want to recognize. First and foremost is my wife Barbara, whose determination for us to become foster parents, and support for me to complete this novel, is only one example of this amazing woman's heart and determination. My good friend Marilyn Diaz, who is well qualified to judge the authenticity of matters in the novel relating to the foster care process, the justice system, and Hispanic culture, gave me valuable suggestions that found their way into the story. Brian Osborn, a friend for life, whose expertise with handling psychological problems facing school children is matched only by his willingness to laugh at my weak attempts at humor, gave me the assurance that my sense of the mind set of such children rings true. The greatest inspiration, as difficult as it was for them to live through, was from the actual experiences that two special real-life Miss Fs and Miss Zs had to endure. Somehow, they've survived and become terrific adults. That a novel like this is drawn from a harsh reality that innocent children suffer every day requires the acknowledgement of all the young Miss and Mister F, Z, A or Bs in the world and the wish that their number can be reduced to zero. Finally, to the public servants at state social agencies across the country who have the difficult task of trying to manage the often unmanageable, I don't envy you and appreciate your hard work.

~AM

# Author's Note

According to year 2011 statistics compiled by the U.S Department of Health and Human Services, almost six million children were referred to the various state children protective services in the United States. Approximately half of that number was reported to state authorities more than once. Of the total number of referrals, about 681,000 children were found to have been the direct victims of abuse and/or neglect. The remainder of the referrals included those who were not the direct victim, e.g. a sibling, a relatively few being false reports, and another large group where evidence of actual abuse could not be conclusively determined. The total of 681,000 includes 1570 fatalities. Of the six million referrals, approximately 225,000 resulted in new foster care placements, and another 900,000 children received some form of home protective oversight. As of September 2011, there were nearly 401,000 children in foster care, with slightly less than half being placed with non-relatives, another quarter being placed with relatives, and the remainder residing in such places as group homes, shelters and other institutions. Of the total cases: 78% involved neglect, 18% were physically abused, 9% sexually abused, and 8% psychologically abused. Some children suffered multiple forms of abuse. Typically, abuse is at the hands of someone the victim knows, with a biological parent being involved at least 75% of the time. Except for the 401,000 total children in foster care, these statistics are only a single year representation. It is believed that thousands of other cases of abuse and neglect go unreported every year.

# Prologue

"Childhood should be carefree, playing in the sun; not living a nightmare in the darkness of the soul."
~ Dave Pelzer, *A Child Called "It"*

"Dad, can I come in?"
"Sure, Tina," I answered from my bedroom.
When she opened the door, Valentina's face had that wide-eyed look of amazement that invariably unsettled me. After all, in most respects she appeared to be like any other fifteen-year-old, but then there was this part of her that made it seem so often as if she had just discovered some mysterious truth. This time, she didn't grasp the irony of her own disbelief.

"Dad, I was watching this animal show on TV. They said something I don't understand." She shook her head and repeated twice, "They said 'crocodile mothers eat their young'. I can't understand it. Crocodile mothers eat their young?"

***

Whenever my wife uses that little sweet voice and calls, "Hey, Honey," I know I'm in for some sort of wild idea. Usually, it isn't anything drastic and I've become accustomed to it after thirty-odd years of marriage. For the most part, it's only about some vacation plan or a way to surprise our three sons, all grown up and leaving us with an empty nest. So it wasn't with any sense of the improbable that I heard that familiar phrase shortly after we finished dinner one late fall evening. I'd felt throughout the meal that something was on her mind, that she was distracted, but I was wary enough not to pry. Besides, I'd had a difficult day at work, managing the legal division of a large corporation.

"Hey, Honey, I … um … want to discuss something with you," she half-mumbled as if the decibel level of her voice might affect my reaction.

Not yet focused, I replied, "Okay, what's up?"

"Well, you know how tough my new school can be, all the rough city stuff. Kids from families with problems we can only imagine. In just a few months, I've seen the state take a bunch of kids out of class and away from their families. The looks on those faces, I can't get them out of my head."

No wild vacation thoughts here. Now my antennae were humming. "Yeah, it really is sad."

"It's more than that, it's heartbreaking. I've been told that it's hard for the state to find temporary homes for the children while they're trying to locate a longer-term foster home."

By now, I knew what was coming.

"Hal, would you think about our becoming emergency foster parents? You know, just keep the kids a day or two until the Department of Families can find a placement?"

I can't say her question was completely out of the blue since we had hosted kids from tough environments for weeks at a time during summers, but I was much younger then. Besides, I was enjoying the empty nest and Roberta knew it. This was one idea I didn't dare joke about.

"Bobbie, I don't know. This is all kind of sudden. I can just imagine the kinds of problems we'd be facing."

Roberta's voice rose an octave, her eyes reflecting her resolve. "Quite an attitude, Mister Liberal. Anyway, I really only mean short-term arrangements. The state has a certification program and we can stipulate that it will only be for emergencies. There's a course starting in two weeks."

"Typical," I thought, "she's already plunged two steps ahead, ready to jump off the precipice without a backward glance."

"Bobbie, I know you're serious, but you're catching me cold. I'll think about it."

***

I'd barely stepped through the door the next night when Roberta started pressing me again. When she gets a bee in her bonnet, there's no stopping her.

"Okay, Bobbie, tell me about the certification course." She knew she had me. What the heck, a few nights with an unhappy kid couldn't be that difficult.

Roberta made the arrangements for the course and, as these things happen, I was drawn in. My wife made a point to the instructor throughout our education that we were only going to be certified for emergency, short-term placements. We received special information about how to handle various situations and were assured that we would never be obligated to shelter a child any longer than we wanted. Late that winter, we received our certification as foster parents. I figured, with any luck, the kids would be few and far between and I could just go on with life as I knew it.

# CHAPTER ONE

*March and May 2001*

Shaking the snow off my overcoat, I immediately felt the warmth of the fireplace and gave Roberta a peck on the lips. She grabbed hold of my hand with some purpose and only then did I notice how exhausted she looked.

"Bobbie, what's wrong?" I asked.

"Hal, it was a terrible day. I was visiting the guidance office when these two sisters were hauled in, crying hysterically, with the school policewoman and social worker right behind. I've never seen either of the girls before. They're Hispanic. One's about fourteen and the other thirteen, but they look more like seventeen or eighteen. It seems the older girl reported being beaten at home. The school called the state, you know, Department of Families. DOF took custody immediately, but the girls' mother showed up and created quite a scene. She left swearing like a soldier and, I gather, hurried to the elementary school next door. Before anyone could stop her, she took off with a younger daughter."

It had been a few months since we had received our foster care license and, privately, I was pleased that the state seemed to have forgotten about us. Now, fully expecting two teenage girls to be somewhere in my house, I paced the kitchen and motioned for Roberta to continue.

"I spent time helping to calm the girls. They didn't know me from Adam, but they seemed to want to talk. They're scared, and they seem like good kids. I talked to them for a while, especially the younger one, Valentina. I found out that they'd been in foster homes several times. They've been abused in every way imaginable. I'd love to string up their mother and her sick boyfriends. Anyhow, after several hours they were placed with a woman somewhere in the area."

I was a bit ashamed at the sense of relief I felt, knowing these girls wouldn't be my problem.

"That's a terrible situation, Bobbie. I'm sure they appreciated your comfort."

"I don't know, I just wish there was more I could do."

"Well, sounds like they'll have a decent place to live for a while."

\*\*\*

Springtime that year was hectic around our place. The wedding of the eldest of our three sons was just two months off, the first of the boys to be married. Jeff and his fiancée, Jane Gargan, lived down in Georgia and hadn't been back to Massachusetts for many months. While Jane's parents did almost all of the planning, we had plenty of preparations of our own to do, and adding to the family was the last thing on my mind. Then the call came. Of course I could only hear Roberta's end of the conversation, but I knew what it was and that there would be no resisting.

"Yes, this is Roberta Allen. Both girls? What happened?"

Even the see-saw Yankee–Red Sox game on TV couldn't distract me.

"I see," Bobbie said, "For how long? Uh … that's much longer than anything we'd planned on. I'll have to discuss it with my husband. Yes. I understand. I'll call back tonight."

"Okay, what's the story?" I asked, seeing a future without the Red Sox or golf come into focus.

"Hal, it's not working out for those two sisters I told you about. There are too many kids where they've been staying and they haven't adjusted very well."

"Great," I thought, wishing I could trash the damn foster license, and responded, "So why would they do any better here, and how long are we talking about anyway?"

"The man from the Department of Families explained that they'll do much better with a smaller number of people and they want to keep the girls together."

I let out a long breath and asked Roberta how long a time we were talking about.

"The state wants the older girl, Selena, to graduate with her middle school class, so they would be here until then and then on to a permanent placement."

"Roberta, that's six weeks, and you promised me only weekend emergencies. And the wedding's coming. Be real." I clicked off the TV and tossed the remote toward the couch. It landed a foot short and the battery compartment cover flew off, like the roof of a house in the path of a cyclone.

Roberta chose her quiet voice, her soft brown eyes pleading. "I know, I know, Harold, but they're such unhappy, nice kids. Bounced around, their mother taking off with the other sister for parts unknown, they need something to hold on to. I promise, six weeks and out. That's before Jeff's wedding."

"I must be out of my mind. What the heck will I do with two teenage girls around? I only know teenage boys. My house won't be my home any more. Damn!"

"So we'll do it? You're the best."

How she made the leap from my house not being my home anymore, to that being a statement of acceptance, I'll never understand. That's Roberta, and darn if she doesn't know me like a book. I supposed that six weeks wouldn't be too bad, would it?

\*\*\*

I don't remember being as nervous at the hospital when the boys were being delivered. Roberta spent an impatient half-hour looking out the front window and assuring me that these girls would be no problem. Finally, she announced that the state car had pulled up the drive. I stood behind her like a child seeking its mother's protection and we moved in tandem toward the entrance. Bobbie opened the door and the Department of Families case worker smiled at us and announced, "Mr. and Mrs. Allen, meet Valentina and Selena Diaz."

All I could hear was the quietest "Hi" that two teenage voices could possibly utter, coming from the mouths of the two most sad-eyed girls I could ever have imagined. The licensing course could never have done enough to prepare me for this moment, a moment when my nervousness vanished and my heart started to bleed. I'd confronted plenty of awkward moments during my years of law practice, but now, I couldn't find any words. Roberta did her best to make them feel welcome.

"Girls, come on in. I have pizza on the way and you can start to make yourselves at home."

"Yes, please, give me your things and come in," I managed to say.

Valentina, the younger sister, and quite a beauty, stepped from behind the caseworker and handed me a suitcase. "Wow, this is such a beautiful house. I've never seen a place like this." She had such a sweet voice, and her lack of a Spanish accent surprised me.

Selena handed me her things. A few inches shorter and a bit heavier than her sister, Selena looked tougher and not as pretty as her sister. She was a little withdrawn, only managing to thank me.

Turning to the prim young woman who had escorted the Diaz sisters, Bobbie said, "Hal, this is Mrs. Harwood, the girls' caseworker. We'll be having a lot to do with her."

I shook her hand and ushered the entourage into the family room. Selena and Valentina looked at their new surroundings and whispered something to each other, giggling afterward, then lapsed into silence. Bobbie and I had a ton of questions for Mrs. Harwood. It appeared from what we'd been told about the sisters, that we were getting involved in one of the more difficult situations the Department of Families was facing. Little in our experience with our own kids had prepared us for what we were about to face.

"Before we start with questions, I want to tour the house and the sleeping arrangements," Mrs. Harwood said.

Roberta answered, "They'll be upstairs. We have plenty of space and the girls can each have a room or they can stay together, whatever they want."

"I'll lead the way," I said, "Come on, girls."

When we reached the top of the stairs, the sisters looked at me hesitantly as I pointed out the various available rooms. I envisioned my sons, each standing in the doorway of his childhood retreat, unsuccessfully attempting to defend his territory from foreign invasion. Mrs. Harwood nodded her approval of our sleeping quarters, while Selena and Valentina explored. One of the three vacant bedrooms had twin beds and the others a single bed. After a brief discussion between the sisters, Selena came out of her shell and announced that they would take separate rooms, but maybe they would sleep in the same room from time to time, given that she had chosen the room with two beds.

"The girls can unpack while we talk downstairs," Mrs. Harwood commanded.

"Fine," Roberta said. "Hal, go down and grab the girls' things so they can start. Girls, use any empty drawers."

"We can handle our bags ourselves," Valentina volunteered. "We can do everything ourselves. No one helped us before, and we don't need help now."

I exchanged a glance with Roberta, wondering if this was a warning or just a statement of fact. We'd know soon enough. I told them to go ahead and we'd call them when the food arrived.

The sisters went to the first floor landing and began hauling their surprisingly large plastic, belongings-filled trash bags to their bedrooms. Then Mrs. Harwood took charge and hustled us back downstairs. When we were seated in the family room, what I thought would be one of the most important sessions of my life began. Unfortunately, it turned out Ms. Hardwood's determination to keep the evening rolling had more to do with her grumbling stomach than to any concern for imparting information to us.

Roberta started off by asking some questions about counseling programs. The caseworker answered them, glancing from time to time at her watch. I had many questions of my own, and hopped right in.

"Mrs. Harwood, these girls, they've been sexually abused. I don't think I should be alone with them. How should we handle that?"

"I need to be leaving soon for dinner, but ..."

God damn, I thought, I don't give a shit about her dinner.

"… anyway," she continued, "I agree that for now it would be wise for you to avoid being alone with the girls or give them any reason to misinterpret your intentions."

That didn't surprise me. It confirmed my own thinking, but it opened up many other questions and we'd need a lot of time with Mrs. Harwood before she left for the day. Here I was, a guy who only had sons of his own, suddenly confronted with these two girls, looking five years older than they were, and I would have to watch my step in my own house.

I asked a question about how boy-girl relationships should be handled.

"That's jumping a little ahead of things," she answered, and looked once more at her watch.

Roberta noticed the watch thing, but plunged ahead with a question about school.

"We'll be in touch about that. I really have to get home for dinner."

I'm not a violent person, but at that moment I wanted to give her a swift kick in the rear. If we ever needed support from the get go, this was it. I kept my cool, trying hard to ignore her, only because, for better or worse, Mrs. Harwood was our lifeline.

"Their mother is missing, but can they have contact with any other relatives?" Roberta asked.

Mrs. Harwood stood to leave and said she'd get back to us on that.

"I have lots more questions. This is new to us, and we are bailing DOF out by taking the girls, so if you can stay just for a while, I'd appreciate it," I said as calmly as I could muster.

"Look, I really have to leave for dinner. Call me in the next day or two if you need to."

Roberta rolled her eyes. Fiddling with a pen. I toyed with saying something nasty, but thought better of it. Obviously, our visitor could read our body language, but her stomach apparently took precedence over anything that might be troubling our ignorant minds. This was only the beginning with Mrs. Harwood.

***

Valentina, or Tina as she asked us to call her, and Selena arrived back downstairs in tandem. "Pizza here yet?" Tina asked.

"No, not yet, pretty soon," Roberta answered.

Selena wandered over to the picture window in the family room and looked in wonder at the back yard with its manicured green lawn leading to a dense stand of trees that separated our property from the neighbors to the rear.

"Can we go outside?" she asked.

"Sure," I replied, "let's take a look." I led the way onto the deck and out toward the woods.

"I never seen this kind of place before," street-wise Selena said. "Is this the country?"

I couldn't help laughing a little and even Tina smiled. "No, not exactly," I said, "this is what they call the suburbs."

"Yeah, Sellie, this isn't the country, no cows around here," Valentina added with an authoritative shake of her head.

Selena managed an embarrassed, warming smile, and said, "I know, but there's so many trees, so much grass, home got nothing like this."

"What home," Tina retorted, "we got no home. If you didn't say anything, we'd be with Ma."

"Shut up. You like being smashed like Ma did to us? You like those guys messin' with us? You like that?" Selena shouted.

Too mad to cry, Tina stamped the ground and snarled, "Shut your mouth, just shut up."

"Okay, girls, enough," I interrupted, while whatever hopeful thinking I'd entertained about the next few weeks evaporated.

Selena, her eyes reddening, kicked at an acorn and turned her back on her younger sister. Tina reached down and grabbed a fallen branch. She smacked it against her thigh and heaved it with a purpose into the woods.

Thankfully, Roberta stepped onto the deck to let us know that the food had arrived. The three of us trudged toward the house in silence. Our first evening together as a foster family had begun.

# CHAPTER TWO

*Spring 1990*

A few worshipers, as silent as the dim shadows caused by the bank of flickering devotional candles in old St. Ann's church, knelt in prayer, oblivious to the merriment in the street outside. There would be more time to rejoin the San Juan Club's San Jose Festival, but now it was time for some to reflect on the mercy of their God. Luz Diaz, twenty three and pregnant for the third time in five years, kept an eye on her fidgeting daughters Selena and Valentina, aged four and three, and slid her fingers along the thigh of Simon Texiera, the latest love of her life and the father of her unborn child. They sat in a rear pew, as far away as possible from the prayerful, mostly elderly, parishioners. Church hadn't been on Luz's agenda, but it seemed like the only chance to shut the girls up without having to forget about the festival altogether. Most days she couldn't deal with her kids and today was no exception. Given the fact that he'd taken up with Luz only a few years ago, Simon seemed to tolerate the girls' behavior much better than their natural parent. He saved his lady friend a lot of grief and limited the occasions when her frustrations boiled over into unpleasantness. Somehow, he was always able to control himself from hitting them, and Luz thought the girls would rather spend time with Simon than with her. For all they knew, Simon could have been their real father.

Luz looked around and then leaned closer to Simon. "I can't wait until we get home," she whispered in his ear and gave him a light lick on the lobe.

Simon himself checked to see if anyone would notice and then slid his hand under Luz's skirt. "No time like now," he answered, but quickly withdrew his hand when one of those devout old-timers walked up the aisle and gave him a disapproving stare.

Luz laughed, but quickly covered her mouth with her hand, trying not to seem obvious.

"Mami, what's the matter?" asked Selena.

"Just shut up, you see too much. You're supposed to be asking for forgiveness. Fold your hands and pray. And stop your sister from squirming, it's embarrassing me."

"Tina's not doing anything, Mami."

Luz glanced around again and then gave Selena a little shove. Selena reached to steady herself, bumping Valentina, who started to cry.

"Simon, let's get outta here," Luz muttered. "Wait until I get them home."

"Okay, okay, let's go outside. But calm down, I'll watch the girls and we can spend some more time at the festival."

No longer caring who was watching, Luz grabbed her daughters by the neck, forcing them to cry out, and made them stand. Turning to Simon, she spat, "All right, we'll stay, but so help me, if they ruin my day, they're gonna get it later."

Simon reached down to comfort little Tina while Luz pushed Selena toward the doors and out of sight of the gaping parishioners.

*** 

Outside St.Ann's on Main Street, a large number of the Hispanic population of Blue Hills, Massachusetts crowded the many temporary booths and regular shops opened especially for the annual springtime San Jose Festival. Simon held each girl by a hand while Luz stopped to talk to every other young woman on the street. On several corners of the eight-block business district surrounding the biggest community church, various local and big city bands played Latin rhythms that energized even the few Anglos daring enough to venture to the festival. Aromas of *empanadilla*, roast pig, and many other dishes gave the air a snap you could taste. The timing and purpose of the festival might seem strange to an outsider, but to the Spanish population of Blue Hills, it was a meaningful and bittersweet event.

Blue Hills is an unusual place. Basically a small town in the southeastern part of the state, not far from the ocean, it is still largely rural, but also part suburban, urban and largely Hispanic. Much of the Spanish population was drawn to the town during the big employment boom of the nineteen fifties resulting from the expansion of the textile plant in town. The company wanted cheap labor and found Latin America, and particularly Puerto Rico, to be a ready source. Luz's family had been in the first wave of immigrants, and the family of seven found a decrepit flat for an outrageous rent. That flat was where Luz, the second Diaz born in Blue Hills and the ninth family member, spent her first eleven years. Racial problems plaguing many places in the United States were largely absent from Blue Hills, but the new workers got the lowest paying jobs and the worst housing. Nevertheless, anchored by the new Spanish churches, particularly St.Ann's, which had formerly had a large Italian congregation now fleeing the urbanization of Blue Hills, there was a strong sense of community, undercut only by a troubling growth in the heroin trade.

Then, in the mid-1970's, problems with materials and high state corporate taxes brought an end to the good times at National Designs, Inc. At the beginning of the year, 1976, the company announced that it would be moving operations to North Carolina, effective by mid-April. If prospects for high income for the workers at the plant were minimal under normal circumstances, the news dashed whatever hopes most had for a better life and plunged the Hispanic community into collective depression. That is when the San Juan Communal Club, of which Luz Diaz's father and oldest brother were active members, decided to try and boost spirits by organizing a festival for March 31st in an attempt to inject spirit back into Blue Hills's Little San Juan neighborhood. The Mayor and Town Council gave enthusiastic support, if not much financial backing, and the first festival was born.

That first year, the festival seemed more like a funeral than a celebration, but the coming together of the unemployed workers, their families, and friends, provided comfort to them. When the San Juan Communal Club asked for volunteers the following year, there was a heartwarming response and the event as an annual attraction was secure. Although the festival came at a time when the remnants of winter often chilled the air, nobody would dream of changing the date because most people remembered and respected the original purpose of the event.

In 1990, there was none of the cold. In fact the day was warmer than normal, allowing for a brilliant display of flashy colors in the clothing of most of the celebrants, not the least of whom was Luz Diaz. Luz enjoyed nothing if not a good party and once outside of St. Ann's, she seemed to have forgotten her annoyance with the children. Simon watched her laugh and talk with other young mothers and admired the way her cleavage shifted as she swayed in her yellow halter top, her wide hips moving beneath her tight red, yellow, and orange skirt. He fantasized about what it would be like to take her right then and there in the street, but his attention was diverted, as it often was, by Tina.

Valentina was just getting the hang of putting sentences together, although the mixture of English and Spanish she heard at home complicated the process.

"Papi, Papi, I want ice."

Simon let go of Selena's hand to pick Tina up in his arms and gave her a long kiss on the cheek. "You want ice?" he laughed. "You mean you want ice-cream?"

Valentina shook her head, "Ice keem."

Simon hugged her again and put her down. "Okay, ice cream. You, too, Sellie? You want ice cream?"

"No Papi, I want *pollo por favor*."

"Chicken, always chicken," he laughed, "You had chicken for lunch. I think you're gonna have feathers. Okay, *pollo* and ice cream."

Luz had moved a little distance away where Simon spotted her talking with her eldest sister, Carmen, who worked at the furniture store behind them. A circus clown—actually Jorge Perez who owned the furniture store—stood beside them, juggling brightly colored balls, all the while encouraging revelers to visit his showroom. Carmen knew all about her sister's bad temper, but no amount of her efforts to get Luz to control herself ever made a difference.

Selena, Valentina and their papi walked over to Luz and Carmen. Simon interrupted the sisters' conversation.

"Hey baby, I'm just going up the block with my two sweeties for some food."

"Hey baby, I don't give a shit where you take them."

"What the hell's up your behind, I don't need no crap from you."

"Then you tell Carmen not to give me crap. I come over just to say hello and talk to Jorge and she starts pushin' me on how I been treating my little brats."

Carmen Santiago took her sister by the shoulder. "Why don't you just watch yourself in front of the girls? They're little kids, for Christ's sake."

"Butt out of my business. Just because you got a job and your husband is some hotshot teacher don't make you no better than me. You and these kids enjoy messin' up my fun. I just came to be nice. Forget that crap."

Luz turned and walked away, flashing her middle finger and ignoring Selena's tears. Tina didn't understand any of it and asked again for her "ice."

Simon looked down at the little girl, with her hand raised to take his, and thought to himself how lucky he was to have Valentina around. Luz was impossible sometimes and he needed someone else to make him happy. Indeed, Tina excited him in ways Luz never would.

***

It had taken Luz several weeks to get around to finding out where Simon came from. She hadn't really cared. When her boyfriend, the father of her two daughters, up and disappeared not long after Valentina's first birthday, she needed a man, couldn't see life without one. So she'd asked her mother and father to babysit the girls one night so she could go dancing with her girlfriends at one of the local clubs. The fact that she had not yet reached Massachusetts's legal age for drinking was no real problem at the Club Caribbean, but the dope would be more to her liking anyway. She'd spent the early part of the evening flirting with some guys she knew and getting high. Not so high that she didn't notice the unfamiliar face walk through the door.

The guy, maybe thirty or so, was medium height, handsome in the Latin way, muscular, and just what Luz needed. Her mind fast-forwarded to what pleasures the rest of the evening might bring. Luz swayed her hips, pointed at the stranger, circled her lips with her tongue, and began a slow dance in his direction. The man stared at her, then stepped forward, took her around the waist and the pair improvised a sensual dance, much too slow for the number the D.J. was playing. Moving to the center of the floor, Simon and Luz were in a world of their own, while the other couples stopped dancing, and formed a circle around them, hooting and clapping at the spectacle in front of them.

When the music stopped, Luz put her arms around her partner's neck and whispered, "*Me llamo Luz. Como se llama, senor?*"

"Luz. I like that name. My name is Simon."

"Well, Simon, I like how you dance. Is there anything else you do well?"

"A few things, I guess. Would you like to try some?"

"Right now, Simon?"

"Now, Luz."

The couple further introduced themselves in the back seat of Simon Texiera's old Ford sedan. Simon agreed that the relationship was promising and that Blue Hills was more interesting than he'd expected.

They spent a lot of time together during the next few months. Simon worked a few odd-jobs, but he spent most days sleeping and watching TV at Luz's small place. Aside from the physical aspects of their bond, Luz was impressed by Simon's willingness to help with Selena and Valentina. Anything to get some freedom from their crying was welcome, and when it came in the form of a fine male, all the better.

Although she'd learned that Simon had done a little time for some domestic abuse problem, that information didn't bother Luz. He had never been violent with her and besides, jails and the Diaz clan were no strangers. Her large family of uncles, siblings and cousins was notorious in Little San Juan for its fierce protection of a thriving marijuana trade that had branched into more serious drugs. Somehow, Luz's gentle father had resisted entering the family business and he'd struggled to make do with the modest income he'd had from the textile plant and other jobs. Not so some of his brood.

About two months after he arrived in Blue Hills, Simon moved in with Luz. She had found some part-time work and left Simon to help around the house. Whenever they were home together, he did what he could to take care of the children, including pushing Luz away when she went overboard in disciplining them. Much of the rest of the time, the lovers spent doing what they enjoyed most with each other.

***

Despite his frustration with Luz, Simon bought Selena and Valentina the treats they wanted and then wandered away from Main Street and the festival. His girlfriend's angry display made him anxious and he just wanted to get home, get the girls to nap, grab a beer and maybe sleep. Knowing Luz, she would stew for quite a while before coming back to the apartment.

Simon picked Sellie up in one arm and Tina in the other and hustled across busy Mountain Street and up the steps to the flat. Opening the door, he uttered an oath when the acrid stuffiness created by the warmth of the day wafted out of the living room and out into the hallway.

"Papi, I'm tired."

"I know, little Sellie. Time for your nap."

Simon walked the girls down the short hallway and into the tiny bedroom the sisters shared. Selena was now in a real bed and Valentina used the rickety crib next to the window. Simon helped Selena climb under her covers and set Tina in the crib. He opened the window to let some air in and walked out into the kitchen to get a beer. He waited a few minutes then went back into the little room and found Selena asleep as he had hoped.

Simon leaned over the crib and scrutinized Mountain Street. There was no sign of Luz. He pulled the shade down and said to himself, as if to excuse his intent, I guess I should see if the baby needs to be changed. He glanced over to make sure Selena was really asleep and when he was certain, he reached into Tina's crib. Quickly, he removed the toddler's clothes, picked up a baby wipe, and rubbed it slowly from her neck down to her hips. Breathing rapidly, Simon unbuckled his belt, then dropped his pants to the floor. In a full sweat, he pulled the sleeping child up and over the side rail of the crib and against his thighs. When he was fully aroused he pressed himself into the toddler. Valentina whimpered, Simon groaned, then opened his eyes when the child screamed out. Selena, as Simon had come to realize, was never wakened by her sister's crying. Today was no exception. When Simon finished, he backed away and wiped the beads of perspiration from his face. He took a long drink of his beer, pulled on his jeans, and stood over the crib where his victim was shaking, but no longer crying. Taking another baby wipe, he deftly cleaned and dressed her. He rocked her until she calmed, patted her on the head, and went out into the living room.

The place was always neat and clean, a mania of Luz's, and he carefully set his beer bottle on a paper towel on the table next to the couch. He put his feet up and drifted off to sleep, wakened about an hour later by the slamming of the door. Luz was in no better humor than hours earlier.

"I'd thought you'd calm down by now, Babe," Simon ventured and sat up.

"Ah, those people, my sister and her husband, piss me off. Where are the damn kids? I don't need any of their shit now."

"Went to sleep right away. I've just been resting."

"Yeah, well, good for them it was you and not me that took them home. Between them and Carmen, I've had it up to here," Luz said, pointing to the top of her head.

"Luz, baby, calm down. The kids ain't so bad. You need to get away from them anytime, just go take a walk. I'll take care of them. I handle them real good."

Luz took a sip of the warm beer left over in Simon's bottle and sat in his lap. A strand of her black hair fell across her forehead. Pressing her breasts against Simon's chest, she held his face and gave him a violent kiss on the mouth. Luz wiped her lips and told him, "Simon, you know something, those kids really are damn lucky you're around. Now, I'm going to make you lucky I'm around."

Simon put his arms around Luz's neck and drew his eyes close to hers. "Yeah baby, I don't know what I'd do without you."

# CHAPTER THREE

*May - July 2001*

Our initial weeks with Tina and Sellie actually went better than I expected. Certainly there were some rough spots, but the girls, disturbingly practiced at masking their misery, presented a normal teenage exterior. They seemed to be curious about everything, especially Valentina. Roberta and I nicknamed her "The Machine Gun." Morning to night, she peppered us with an endless barrage of rapid-fire questions. There was so much she had missed and so much she wanted to absorb.

I remember the first time I spent time alone with Tina. It was about ten days or so after the girls arrived and I was nervous. Even though Bobbie and I had made certain that I would not be left in the situation that even dear, dear Mrs. Harwood had counseled against, this particular day it couldn't be avoided. Bobbie had to take Selena for a late afternoon medical appointment—a female thing—and Tina had a heavy cold and had to stay in, so I was elected to come home early and keep her company. I was busying myself upstairs, keeping a safe distance from Tina who was watching television down in the family room when she yelled up, "Dad, can you come down?" It had been a jolt when the sisters first used the words "Mom" and "Dad" with Roberta and me, but I was getting used to it and reluctant to put the poor kids at a distance. Anyway, I yelled back that I'd be right there.

There wasn't much reason for the kid to trust any adult man, and I'd heard enough stories about abused girls making false accusations to be concerned for myself. Now, I had to put aside my reluctance to be in the same room alone with Tina and headed downstairs. As it turned out, I was the only one of the two of us who had such worries, at least when "The Machine Gun" was firing.

"Dad, can we talk for a little while?" she asked, sitting there on the floor, an empty tea cup beside her and her normally perfectly coifed mane of hair tangled in an uncombed web of curls.

"Sure. What's up?"

"I just have some questions about stuff."

"Okay, shoot."

"Dad, how come Jews don't like Jesus?"

If only the people at my office were so direct, there would never be any miscommunication. From Tina's perspective, my family was the only Jews she'd ever met, so we qualified as expert on the mysterious world of

Judaism, despite our lack of religious observance. I was sure she could hear the gulp when I plunged ahead with my answer.

"Valentina, how'd you get that idea?"

"Well, I told a friend at school that my new family is Jewish. She said you killed Jesus and don't believe he is God."

"Well, it's true Jews don't believe he is God or a savior. That's kind of the reason Jews are Jews and not Christians. But most Jews believe that Jesus was a great man and should be respected. I don't know about who killed him, but please, don't blame me; I'm not quite that old."

Valentina belly-laughed and said, "Daa-ad. I'm serious. Then who killed him?"

"Well, I'm not an expert, but I think it was the Romans with maybe some input from some people who were Jews."

It turned out Tina didn't know who the Romans were, so we spent a bit of time on that, and then why we Jews didn't buy the resurrection. That was a hard one since I really couldn't remember the resurrection coming up for discussion in my Hebrew school classes, so I made something up. I was about to tell her she had exhausted my limited knowledge of the subject when she jumped from the Virgin Mary to another famous parent, George Washington. I'd forgotten all my discomfort at being left alone with Tina and was beginning to relish the role of teacher.

"How come the British didn't like the Americans? This week in social studies, Mr. Hampton said something about them wanting our money and other stuff but I didn't understand. I thought our people came from England?" Tina was stretched out on the floor, her face propped between her hands, sniffing to clear her stuffy nose.

I leaned back in my recliner while I searched for a good answer. It struck me how concepts my own kids grasped easily were so hard for her. Bright as she was, there was one hole after another in her learning experience. Valentina knew it and was desperate to close those gaps.

Probably confusing her even more, I reached back in to my high school social studies days to try and explain. But it seems that the next question was the one that had truly been bugging her for several days. She opened her eyes wide in that amazed expression I would work so hard to have her eliminate and said, "Dad, I don't get how George Washington could be the Father of His Country. That's way too many people."

It was my turn to belly laugh, and luckily, Tina didn't embarrass easily.

"Sorry, I shouldn't laugh. Do you know what an *expression* is?" She nodded, but I'm not sure she really knew. "Anyway, he wasn't the real father of all those people, it's that he was such a great leader and the first head or President, that people felt like they were all his real children, so they called him the Father of the Country. It also means people thought he was one of the main reasons why America was born, like the daddy of a baby."

"I get it," she said, "just like I feel like you're my real father even though I know you're not."

I'm not sure if my dark complexion reddened, but I hoped Valentina wouldn't notice my discomfort. "I guess," was about all I could muster and quickly expounded on the Boston Tea Party, at which she announced she knew all about it. Tina raised her empty cup and said she was happy that the colonists had left some tea for her. We both laughed at that. It was the first time either of the girls had tried to joke.

Once we got American history out of the way, Tina got down to a subject much closer to my heart: all you ever wanted to know about baseball and the Boston Red Sox but were afraid to ask. She wasn't afraid to ask anything. I'm sure she could tell from our discussion that, for whatever twisted reason, Ted Williams held a place in my heart not reachable by any religious or political figure.

Just then, Tina said, "Hey Dad, wanna see something I drew before we came here? I think it's pretty good."

"Sure," I said, as Tina, who hadn't waited for an answer, scrambled to her feet and up the stairs. A moment later she reappeared and handed me the drawing.

"This is beautiful, it really is," I marveled at her talent, but was careful not to disclose how the theme startled me so from such a young kid. The spray of brilliant roses, somehow almost in darkness, beneath an angry sky, suggested just how much she longed for a happiness that seemed to be denied. It made me uncomfortable and sad. Wanting to hug her, I thought the better of it. I praised her talent again and turned the conversation back to lighter matters as quickly as I could.

Our three hours alone flew by and was interrupted only by the sound of the automatic garage door opener. I was exhausted.

\*\*\*

"Hal, I can't get Mrs. Harwood to return my calls," Roberta complained.

It was a few days after my home alone session with Tina and one of my usual Fridays off. Roberta had been trying to reach the caseworker for two days and was ready to go over her head. A seeming maze, we were just learning the Department of Families protocols and had no desire to make an enemy of our designated contact. The current problem was that Selena's night terrors and morning depressions of the past three days were too much for us to handle alone. Sellie wouldn't tell us anything specific about what was troubling her and Mrs. Harwood at least had direct access to Selena's psychiatrist.

"Go ahead and call her supervisor. I don't care about the DOF or their bureaucracy; I care about the girls and us."

"Right," Bobbie answered. She dialed the number and asked for Lydia Hernandez, Mrs. Harwood's boss. Mrs. Hernandez listened to Roberta for a moment and, I gathered from hearing one end of the conversation, she defended her subordinate and promised to have her call.

Roberta replaced the receiver. "How the hell can she protect that woman?"

"I do the same for my staff. Unified face to the public, kick ass behind closed doors. So long as we get what we want, I don't care."

"I suppose, but it just aggravates me."

I put my arms around Roberta and held her for a moment. The idealism of her desire to help the kids was being challenged by the real sadness of the situation.

About an hour later, Elaine Harwood called. Lucky for her I answered and not Roberta.

"Hello, Mr. Allen," the irritated voice said on the other end, "this is Mrs. Harwood and I really wish you would call me and not my supervisor if you need something."

"Well, Mrs. Harwood," I replied as politely as I could, "we would prefer that, too, if we could get a reply to our calls. We left several messages."

"I received your messages, but yours isn't the only case I have, you know."

I don't dislike many people, but I raised my voice and made sure she knew that I expected her to do something for Selena immediately. In none too pleasant a tone, Mrs. Harwood agreed to bring Sellie in to the psychiatrist and maybe there would need to be a change in her medication.

Shortly after we hung up, Mrs. Harwood called back and said she'd made an appointment for the following Monday. At least for this one time she had followed up quickly.

***

For almost four weeks, Selena had avoided anything resembling a family relationship. She'd seemed to be emerging from her shell, but then the depression took over. With only Sunday left to get through before Sellie's psychiatry appointment, Bobbie and I were doing what we could to distract her. Selena and Tina loved throwing a football, so I invited the two of them to go outside for a toss. Tina was all for it and helped me to convince her sister to get out of her pajamas and into a tee shirt and jeans.

Outside, Ollie Kintro, my taciturn neighbor, was preparing his garden for the mid-summer vegetables. What he thought about our houseguests I could only imagine because the only time he ever spoke to me was to tell me why he couldn't afford to repair his fence that had been slowly collapsing into my yard over several years. He watched the two Puerto Rican girls and me head for the clearing behind the oak grove, seemed to grunt something, and returned to his planting.

It was the third Sunday in May, and just the sort of spring day that makes that time of year in Massachusetts such a treasure. The PJM Rhododendron had blossomed pink and the grass and trees were in full green. Red-breasted robins had been around for a few weeks and shared airspace with the awakening honeybees. Walking through the alternating shadow and sunlight of the oaks, I realized how much I missed my usual weekend golf game, even if it meant spending too much time looking for wayward shots amidst the trees. I reached down for a fallen branch and swung it at an old acorn the squirrels had missed last fall, as if the rotted piece of wood was my erratic seven iron.

"Dad, come on, what are you doing?" Valentina called, suspending my imagined golf ball in mid flight. Her cold gone, Tina was as full of energy as her sister was withdrawn.

"Coming," I said and sprinted into the clearing, doing my best wide-receiver imitation. Valentina took the cue and heaved a perfect pass in my direction that I promptly dropped. The football bounced crazily toward Selena and stopped at her feet. She looked at me, then her sister, took one step back and gave the ball a whack with her right foot. The ball went sailing over what was left of Kintro's fence and landed just a few feet from Ollie, knocking over a rake. Selena put her hand over her mouth and laughed so hard I thought she would faint.

Apparently Ollie wasn't amused. "Dammit, you almost killed me and you could have ruined my garden," he yelled at us. He got up and heaved the ball back over the fence.

A weak "sorry" was all I could muster, and tried not to laugh myself.

Selena finally controlled herself. "Dad, I'm really sorry. I had to kick the ball."

"Don't worry about it," I answered.

"Yeah," Valentina chimed in, "it was really funny." She ran over and retrieved the ball from behind the largest tree in the grove and passed it to Selena.

"Catch, Dad," Selena commanded and set off a good fifteen minutes of making the old guy run, much to the delight of the sisters.

It was a relief to see Selena smile. It made her look younger and more relaxed. I congratulated myself for having brought her out of the doldrums, but I was premature. Tina threw a pass, watched Sellie make a sweet reception and shouted, "You go girl."

Selena turned to her sister and me, a tear escaping down her left cheek. "It's only a football. I gotta go inside," she whispered and handed me the ball. She ran up the deck stairs and went to her room. Tina headed after her but I told her to let it be. Roberta, who had been watching from the kitchen window, called out to Valentina to come in for lunch.

***

Before Tina and Sellie came to live with us, we'd been told in general terms about their past. We knew that both girls had been physically abused by their mother. Life in other foster homes had often been difficult. We also knew that there had been sexual abuse. It seems that each girl had been victimized by a different man, each connected to the girls' mother. They had the same real father who had had nothing to do with them once he'd abandoned them. Tina had been abused between the ages of two and eight. The predator had disappeared. Selena had been abused very recently, by a married, upstairs neighbor three times her age.

Tina's predator, who only much later she discovered was not her father, was the father of the youngest sister, Juanita.

DOF believed that Juanita had not been abused by Simon and it was obvious that she was the mother's clear favorite. When Luz Diaz disappeared from Blue Hills right after DOF had taken the older girls, there were reports that Luz was either in Florida or back in Puerto Rico. The police thought that Luz was in contact with her mother back in Blue Hills, but couldn't prove it, nor had they had any luck in finding Luz on their own.

It didn't really take a psychiatrist to figure out what was bothering Selena. No, the shrink only needed to determine how to get her out of it. I was no help and a conversation I overheard told me I was being exposed to a world both foreign and brutal.

A subdued trio of Bobbie, Tina, and me had poked at our dinner later the day of the football catch. Selena, who rarely let her mood get the better of her appetite, had stayed in her room all afternoon and evening, accepting only water and crackers for food. Tina went to her room to study as soon as the dishes were cleared. Shortly thereafter, despite Roberta's advice for me to give Selena space, I went up to check on her. Tina, I thought, would be in bed early per her routine. Instead, when I reached the top step, I found Valentina's door open and heard voices coming from Selena's room, even though no light shone through under the closed door. Heading down the hall to where I could hear the girls, I had an excuse prepared just in case they discovered me. I heard Tina, usually the more perceptive of the two, first.

"But why?"

"I don't know. I loved him."

"Selena, he is a bad man."

"I know, but I loved him and he told me he loved me."

"But you knew about him and Ma."

"I know. I don't care."

"If he loved you, why did he keep seeing Ma? Ray knew he can't be messing with you, and now where is he?"

"Well, when he gets out, he'll come for me. You'll see."

"Well, what are you going to tell the shrink tomorrow?"

"Valentina, don't be stupid. I'll tell him what I told the last jerk. I'll tell him I'm depressed about what Ray did to me and about Ma being gone. That's what I'm supposed to say. I don't want to talk about it no more. Tina, I don't get you. You're acting like you're happy here."

"It's not so bad. Better than that last place. You should be happier than me. You're the one who got us taken away."

"Yeah, well, I was tired of Ma's shit. If I wasn't doin' it with Ray, I woulda said somethin' sooner."

I heard Selena sniff a sarcastic laugh and she continued, "Yeah, Ma, she beat the crap outta him."

"So you don't like it here?" Tina asked.

"Mom and Dad are okay, but you know, no Spanish, no Spanish food. I'm glad I got you. We gotta be together, *mi hermana*."

"I love you Selena. But what if …"

Roberta's footsteps in the downstairs hall distracted me and I made a beeline for our bathroom before she could discover my spying. She must have seen the closed bathroom door, shaking her head, I imagined, that I was probably engrossed in reading my latest Grisham or suffering from an attack of my irritable bowel. Truth is, my stomach was churning, but it had nothing to do with my spastic colon. Anyway, I heard Roberta knock on Selena's door and tell the girls it was time to sleep. I waited a minute before I emerged. After some soul-searching, I decided I had to tell my wife what I'd heard and called for her to come into our room.

When I was done, Roberta asked me if I could be mistaken. I assured her that I was not. Both of us found it hard to relate to the girls sleeping in our home with the grimness of their young lives.

\*\*\*

May rolled into June and with it the end of the school year and the anticipation of three big events: Selena's middle school graduation; the sisters' departure for a new foster home once school was out; and Jeff and Jane's wedding on July Fourth. Each one required a special preparation and I hoped for the best.

Fortunately, Selena seemed to be over the worst of her depression. Both girls were handling schoolwork okay, especially Valentina. When the sisters first came to us, Mrs.Harwood had told us that they were both classified as learning disabled and enrolled as special education students. The reasons for their classification differed. In Selena's case, she had been born with some form of mild brain injury and had been saddled with a handicapped designation. Any reasonable person could see that the handicapped classification was a mistake because she was basically bright. However, conceptualization of abstract ideas was a problem and, at age fourteen, Sellie didn't know a penny from a quarter. Both girls had comprehension issues stemming from having little exposure to concepts that the schools assumed most children understood. Neither read for pleasure, nor had they ever been read to.

Tina's natural curiosity made her a willing student. Abstractions were a problem for her, too, but in her case it was partly an inability to comprehend stemming from a lack of exposure to basic vocabulary. This made her vulnerable to deception. It also resulted in her being amazed by some pretty obvious facts, stuff middle class kids knew at a much younger age. "Are you serious?" was Tina's mantra that often left Roberta and me shaking our own heads.

If there was any positive coming from their mother, it was that she insisted that the girls go to school and do their homework. Unfortunately, that was about all Luz had guided them to do. Any failure to do the work would result in severe physical punishment. Remarkably, the kids liked school, probably because it was the only escape they had from their mother and her men. We never had problems getting them to do their homework. Tina was a good student and her natural warmth and inquisitiveness charmed her teachers. Selena got by. We, especially Roberta, tried to get the girls interested in reading for fun. In the short time we knew them, we had some success with Tina, little with Sellie, and then something wonderful happened.

One night, no sooner had I come home from work than Selena jumped up from the kitchen table with a string of questions she rattled off a mile a minute. It was as if Tina had inhabited her sister's body.

"Whoa, slow down so I can understand. You speaking Spanish or something?" I teased.

"Dad, I gotta know about my people."

"You mean Puerto Ricans?"

"Not exactly. I mean the Indians. The Taino Indians. Kids were talking about them in school. They lived in Puerto Rico before any white men came. Part of me is Taino. I'm so excited."

"Well, I know you have a lot of questions, but I can't really answer them. I've heard of Tainos, but I don't know a thing about them."

"Okay, but I gotta know. I want to read about them. Can we go to the library?"

Roberta was standing by the refrigerator taking this all in. She was beaming. From behind Selena she gave me the "hurry up" motion with her hands.

I guess my smile was as wide as my wife's. "If your school work is done, I'll take you right after dinner."

"Oh Dad, thank you. I can't wait, I can't wait," she said and for the first time got up and gave me a hug.

It was heartwarming to see Selena interested in an intellectual pursuit. During dinner, the Diaz sisters switched roles, Sellie now a stream of chatter, Tina staring in disbelief. As soon as dinner was done, Roberta volunteered herself and Valentina to do the clean up. Selena dashed off to the car, ordering me to hurry. "Dad, please," she yelled from the driveway.

"Coming, coming," I shouted back, and grabbed my keys.

Selena stood by the car waiting for me to pop the lock. Ollie Kintro was in his front yard spreading some sort of chemical on his lawn. "Hey, he called to me," he never used my name, "do you mind not bein' so noisy at this hour."

I knew and he knew it wasn't late. All the while he stared at Selena and I knew just what was bothering him.

"Good evening to you, too," I said through a smile. "Talk later, and be sure to let me know when the fence will be fixed."

Sellie, who knew all about the fence story, gave a sly glance at Ollie who had turned his back, and stuck her tongue out. I decided not to admonish her. Following my lead, she hopped into the car and off we went. Ten minutes later, we arrived at the town library. As soon as the car stopped rolling, Selena jumped out and raced ahead through the big glass doors.

By the time I got inside, Sellie had already commandeered a librarian to help her find books about the Tainos. The woman entered the word into her computer search system and up popped about two dozen references, mostly in the same section of the library. She pointed us in the right direction and we headed for the stacks.

"Dad, help me pick a few?" Selena asked.

"Okay. Let's see if we can find two or three to start that aren't too long and maybe have some pictures."

"All right," she said, and reached for two thin volumes with colorful jackets. "What about these?"

I looked through them and both seemed fairly elementary and well illustrated. "They look fine," I answered.

"Dad, thanks, let's take them home."

Handing her my library card, I gave Sellie a little hug. She fairly sprinted to the desk. Selena hardly seemed connected to the girl-woman I'd overheard talking about a lover just a few weeks earlier. All the way home she said barely a word, already engrossed in finding out who she was.

*****

Tina was a diarist of sorts. For at least the last few years, she had been committing to paper recollections of the hurts in her life. With about two weeks left before the end of school, she decided to share her writing with Roberta and me. Actually, she shared first with her "Mom" who got permission to show the memoir to me. I had finally been able to get out for a round of Saturday golf with my old foursome and was feeling pretty good despite my typical up-and-down game. As usual, on the weekend the girls were still asleep. I put my clubs in the back closet and told Bobbie about one spectacular putt I'd sunk. It was clear she wasn't paying attention.

Roberta shrugged and said, "Hal, sit down, I want you to read some stuff Tina's written. She says it's all true."

I took the two pages that had been transposed to type on our computer and began to read, my Pebble Beach golf hat still shading my eyes. I knew most of the story, but the pain of it all was missing, until that moment.

"What did I do," the lament began, "to deserve this? I was a baby, a little girl. Was I bad? If nobody wanted me, why was I born? Even hiding under my blanket, Simon would find me. Why wouldn't my Mami protect me or believe me? I am junk. I have pain. My heart is bleeding and there is a cloud in my brain. Not even my pillows or my blankets or corners of the room protect me. At night, I still hear the door open and see a black shadow standing over me. Even when I begged him …" and on it went, elaborating in detail the horrors of her existence. The bare eloquence of it tore me up. I hated her mother and Simon even though I had never laid eyes on either. Rage doesn't say enough about what I felt.

"Bobbie, whatever happens, wherever the girls wind up, they can't ever be exposed to this sort of treatment again."

Roberta put an arm around my waist. "I wish there was a way they wouldn't have to leave. They seem content here."

"Bobbie, I know, but the wedding is coming and this is already more than we bargained for. We can stay in touch. They can even visit. I'm sure the state would want that."

"I know, I know. But it doesn't seem like enough. I can't quite understand why Valentina's writing didn't change your mind."

"Roberta, honey, don't think I wish I felt otherwise. I'm just not ready to be a full time father again, probably never will be."

Roberta closed her eyes and wept. Through her tears she sighed, "I know. I just wish—"

"I know, honey, I know."

\*\*\*

It was three days before Selena's graduation and DOF had yet to find a new placement for the sisters. The state wanted to keep the girls together, but it was proving difficult to find a home willing to take two teenagers. Knowing the girls' history, Mrs. Harwood focused on finding a place with few, if any, other children, but the prospects were bleak.

The inevitable happened. Lydia Hernandez called us that Monday evening.

"Hello, Mr. Allen?"

"Yes."

"This is Mrs. Hernandez of the Department of Families."

"Yes, hello," I answered, certain that this would be an unwelcome conversation.

"Hal, who's that?" Roberta called from upstairs where she'd had been helping Selena decide on her graduation outfit.

"Come down, please," I said and asked Mrs. Hernandez to wait until Bobbie picked up the other downstairs extension.

As soon as I'd explained to my wife who was on the line, her eyes pleaded with me, knowing what was coming, she picked up the family room phone.

"Mr. and Mrs. Allen, please call me Lydia."

"Fine," we answered at the same time. "And please, call us Hal and Roberta," I replied.

"Thanks. You're doing such a great job, and I've heard so much about you from Elaine Harwood, that I feel I know you."

I could only imagine how Mrs. Harwood portrayed us. We had to be the biggest pain in the ass DOF had to contend with, but we had the prime virtue of providing a good house and a stable home, so here we were, with the supplicant, Lydia Hernandez, laying it on us.

"We really appreciate all that you've done," she continued, "and have a very important question to ask. We are trying very hard to find a place for the girls, but we need more time. We won't make it by the Friday deadline. We would like you to consider keeping them until right after July fourth. It's only a few extra weeks and I'm sure something will open up once summer arrives."

I'm positive Roberta was silent only because she knew I wouldn't be crazy about accepting. After a few seconds, she said, diplomatically, "Please give us little while to discuss it and we'll call you back today."

"Thank you, Roberta, Hal. Certainly take the time you need."

When the call ended Roberta came into the kitchen.

"Well?"

"I don't know, Bobbie. It isn't the few extra weeks, but the timing is lousy. The wedding is coming and the girls haven't been invited. They haven't met Jeff and Jane, or even Joey and Eddie for that matter. We'll be busy as heck with the boys coming home. Besides, what makes you think DOF will have them out of here in two or three weeks?"

Roberta sat at the table with her hands folded together as if she were praying. "Harold, I agree with everything you said. But you know, and I know, that we aren't going to put them out if it means they have to stay in a shelter. If they have to stay home during the wedding, they're old enough. They're home alone after school and we can trust them. Who knows, maybe the Gargans will invite them. Maybe we can plant the seed."

I could hear the girls talking and laughing upstairs. One of the first things I'd noticed about them was how readily they accepted change. They'd been in five foster homes in between going back to their mother. From their perspective, I didn't know if it mattered one bit to them if they stayed with us or went elsewhere.

"Roberta, you're right, I can't put them out, but we have to give the state an ultimatum. They can have until the weekend after the wedding and then out. If they're placed earlier, fine. I feel like a damned ogre. I'll call Lydia."

"Keep your voice down, Hal. The kids will hear you."

"Sorry, it's just that—"

Robert put two fingers over her lips. "Shh. I know. You really have been a prince," she said and kissed my cheek. "I can't ask any more. Go and make the call."

***

We secured the expected agreement from DOF. What else could they do? They probably figured we were bluffing.

Bobbie bought a new dress for Selena that she wore to her school dance and to graduation. I took her to the dance, joined later by Roberta and Tina. Having been away from the student dance scene for a dozen years, I was taken aback, even put off, by the overt sexiness of the kids and that hysteria they called a "mosh pit". Selena had a great time, and overall, I did, too.

Sellie's graduation night was a working night for me, so Roberta took both girls to the Blue Hills Middle School. Normally, a graduation is an exciting event, what with the kids feeling grown up but intimidated by the unknown of the next of life's phases. I knew from something that Selena had said at dinner the night before that she missed having a mother and father to see her graduate. It turned out that she had an acceptable substitute, maybe even a preferred one. Bobbie reported that Grandpa Diaz had made an unexpected appearance at the graduation, accompanied by one of the girls' aunts. If Valentina and Selena truly loved any of their blood kin, it was their grandfather.

"He's a little bitty man, and very sweet," Roberta told me later that night.

The man seemed to have a magical effect on the girls because they glowed when they spoke of him. Hard to figure how he had a daughter like Luz. Supposedly, Grandpa Diaz's eight children were split between criminal types and a few honest, hard workers. Environment isn't everything, judging from Sellie, and especially Tina.

Jane and her family came through. Two days after Sellie's graduation, Jane called us from Georgia and told us her parents insisted on adding the girls to the invitation list and could adjust the seating easily. I'll never forget their excitement when Roberta told them. They had never been to a wedding. The big day was only two weeks away.

***

Valentina is a complete romantic. She also craves attention, that being a big reason why she doesn't do well in a home with lots of other kids. Nevertheless, she surprised Bobbie and me when she asked if she could write a poem to read at the wedding.

"Tina," I remember saying, "that's a nice thought, but you haven't even met Jeff and Jane."

"It doesn't matter, Dad," she said, "I feel like I know them, and besides, I just want to do it. Don't worry, I won't embarrass them."

"How about reading it at the rehearsal dinner when only the main wedding party will be there?"

Valentina played with one of her long curls and gave a pleading look at both of us.

"Hal, if she wants to read something at the wedding, I think it will be fine."

"Okay, if she wants to, and if Janie and Jeff say it's all right."

Tina let out a whoop, gave both of us a kiss, and dashed off straight to the computer. It wound up taking her a few days to complete, with help from Roberta on a few rough spots. In the meantime, Jane told us she'd be delighted if Valentina would read her poem at the wedding and was looking forward to meeting both girls when she and Jeff arrived at our home at the end of the week.

The rest of the week was hectic, mainly with making sure all the rehearsal dinner plans, that was our major responsibility, were set. Roberta went shopping with Valentina and Selena for a dress for Tina. Selena wanted to wear her graduation dress. My wife was in her glory. As much as she loved our boys, it was no secret that she envied her friends who had girls to shop with, and I believe she was having more fun than either Tina or Sellie. Every evening for three days they all disappeared, and from Tina's reports, went to every store in Massachusetts before coming home with just the right outfit on day three. Of course, it was something they'd seen the first night, but one has to be sure about these things, or so Bobbie always assures me. When they arrived home that last night, Tina disappeared upstairs and later came down into the living room wearing a striking white dress and a thousand watt smile.

"Dad, I'm gorgeous!"

"Who are you?" I asked. "Some movie star?"

"Daa-ad, stop. What do you think?"

"I think you look beautiful, a real young woman."

"Me and Sellie will look so gooood. Not as nice as Jane, but gooood."

Watching from the hallway, Selena and Roberta slapped five, then walked up to Tina and the three of them did an impromptu boogie. Poor Bobbie, she was beaming. She wanted the moment to last forever and I, the bad guy, stood in the way.

\*\*\*

That Sunday, a week before the wedding, the husband-and-wife-to-be made their appearance. Even though they had been living together for four years, for this week they would be staying at their respective parents' homes about sixty miles apart. Jane drove her dad's car up to our place just to meet the girls. I knew that our boys weren't crazy about Tina and Sellie living with us and sleeping in their old rooms, but they tried not to show it if one of the girls happened to answer the phone when they called. Jeff, the most easygoing of the three, was especially kind and Jane was naturally inclined toward the underdog, so the meeting went well, although even Tina was more restrained than usual.

By mid-week, our place looked like a boarding house. Joey was in from Manhattan and Eddie and Linda flew in from Los Angeles. There was a bit of uneasiness due to the sleeping arrangements. Sellie gave up her bed so that Eddie and Linda could each have a twin bed in Eddie's old room. That meant Sellie would have to use a sleeping bag on the floor in Tina's room. Joey had his old room—just as well because he would have carried on—and Jeff was displaced onto the sleeper couch in the family room. The use of the family room for sleeping disrupted the television viewing, especially aggravating to Joey because the Red Sox were on the west coast and on late at night, when Jeff wanted to sleep. We suggested they trade places, but Joey opted for his old bed. Once or twice that week, graciously out of hearing of the sisters, Jeffrey and Joseph dropped a comment evidencing their unhappiness over the presence of the girls in their home and the imposition on me and Roberta.

"They're not a burden," I lied on one occasion, "It's been fun being surrounded by females for a change. They're leaving in a week or so, so just forget about it." Anyway, they were nice enough to the girls.

***

All of the wedding party gathered for the rehearsal dinner on Saturday night. It turned out that the warm feelings generated would carry over to the wedding the next day. Valentina and Selena were fairly inconspicuous while Jeff and Jane took center stage. I was nervous since the last wedding I really cared about had been my own, over thirty years earlier. Despite my feelings of awkwardness, the evening went off fine and the big day lay straight ahead.

The wedding was at a country club near Jane's home and about an hour away from us. We would be heading down in two cars, with Joey, Ed and Linda in one car and me, Roberta, the groom and the girls in the other. It was July 4th and usually a beach day, so we decided to get an early start since there might be a lot of traffic headed in our direction toward the shore. The weather was shirt-drenching steamy, too, and overcast when we left. Before our little caravan got a mile from home, the skies opened up. Torrents of water made it almost impossible to see, so the absence of traffic in the bad weather was no real consolation. Up in front of us, Joey was doing his usual devil-may-care driving thing, making me all the more uneasy. In our car, Roberta and Jeff chatted about nothing in particular and the sisters sat quietly, perhaps contemplating their first wedding, or envying family happiness.

By the time we arrived at the club, the rain was easing and groups of golfers were congregated under an overhang, waiting for the signal to tee-off. The storms had only added to the oppressive heat, so the alternative decision to hold the wedding indoors was welcome.

The first hour we all spent with the photographer. Sellie and Tina took it all in, admiring the bridesmaids, ogling the ushers, handsome in their traditional black tuxedos. Then came the procession and the ceremony. Of course, it was beautiful, and Roberta's eyes glistened. Mine, too.

Once the recessional was over, the hundred seventy-five of us crowded into the reception room for drinks and hors d'oeuvres. When Jane and Jeff made an entrance, the guests cheered and then quieted. At that moment, Tina tapped me on the shoulder.

"Now, Dad?"

She fidgeted with the paper in her hand and I said, "I'll check with Jane and her mom and dad."

I walked over to where the Gargans and the newlyweds had congregated around the cheese table. After a brief conversation, I turned back to Tina and gave her the thumbs up.

Jane managed to get everyone's attention and called Sellie and Tina to the center of the room.

"Hi everyone. I want you all to meet Selena and Valentina Diaz who are staying with Jeff's parents. Tina has written something and we've asked her to read it. It's all yours, Tina."

I think if I was asked to do anything in front of a big group of strangers at age thirteen, I would barely have been able to speak. For Valentina, it seemed as natural as falling asleep.

"I hope everybody is having as much fun as me," she began. "I wrote a little poem for Jeff and Jane. I call it "Love."

*"Caring, laughing, holding hands,*
*And walking in the rain.*
*Love forever is their fate,*
*That is Jeff and Jane.*

*Sharing hours and days together,*
*Feeling joy, and never pain.*
*They join in love, their lives as one,*
*That is Jeff and Jane.*

*Don't we wish we had what they do,*
*Hearts forever to remain,*
*Tied in romance, love forever,*
*That is Jeff and Jane."*

There were no sounds for a moment, other than the soft swish of tissues dabbing wet cheeks, and then a burst of applause. Tina smiled a satisfied smile, and Roberta, Jeff, Jane and Sellie each gave her a big hug and kiss. I walked over and kissed her, too. Roberta shot me a look, but as touched as I was, there would be no changing my mind.

The rest of the day flew by. The girls were having a ball. They learned how to do the Jewish folk dance, the *horah*, and my boys and Bobbie's brothers made a point of dancing with them. Jeff even got the band to play the Macarena and Selena strutted her stuff. When the last of the guests finally left, we helped the Gargans to load up their car with the gifts. The heat was still oppressive in the early evening when we waved goodbye to my son and daughter-in-law as they headed off for their northern New England honeymoon.

For the entire drive back, Sellie and Tina laughed and sang and reminisced about their first wedding. The good mood prevailed as we walked into the family room. Then I noticed that the message light was blinking on our answering machine.

"That's strange," Roberta said, "since everyone knows about the wedding."

She pressed the button and the familiar high-pitched voice of Elaine Harwood began, "I know you'll be late from the wedding, but something came up late today and I need you to call first thing in the morning. We've found a place for the kids, and I'll be getting them sometime tomorrow. I haven't had much of a holiday."

Valentina looked from me to Roberta to Selena and burst into tears. Selena shrugged, as if to say, "No big deal."

"Mom, they can't do this," Tina cried.

"Honey, let's go upstairs and talk," Roberta said to me. Then she took each girl by a hand, and led them down the hall to start packing.

This is what I'd wanted, but not this way. I felt especially cruel. The fantasy of the wedding day was over.

***

On the day after the wedding, for better or worse, as it turned out, I had already planned to take the day to spend with the family before my boys scattered across the continent. When Eddie, Joey and Linda arrived home the night before, they had reacted little to the news of the Diaz sisters' departure. Now, mid-morning the next day, they were probably using their frequent late-rising pattern as a convenient cover to be absent at the moment of the girls' leaving.

We, rather Roberta, got Mrs. Harwood at about 8:30 that morning. From out of nowhere, two possible placements had turned up, but only one was willing to take both girls. Their new "home" would be in Glenwood, an old industrial town in the eastern part of Massachusetts. It has a significant minority population and is less than a half hour from Blue Hills. Mrs. Harwood assured us that the new foster parent had lots of experience. She was a deeply religious single mom with three kids of her own. When Roberta voiced a concern about placing the girls in a household with so many other children, the caseworker said the move was settled unless we wanted to become full time foster parents. Bobbie knew better and that was that, with the sisters to be picked up just after noon.

Selena kept busy packing, barely saying a word all that morning. Valentina chatted more than usual, her anxiety taking over. The weight of unexpressed sadness was more oppressive than even the relentless heat of the morning. Love and poetry one day, loss and uncertainty the next. I'd had a law school professor who delighted in reminding the students that *life is tough*, but I'm not sure he would have been so pithy with these girls. Privately I wavered, but would not yield.

The girls stacked their belongings in the front hall and sat down with Roberta and me for a last lunch, but none of us ate much except for Selena. The rest of the family stayed behind closed bedroom doors. It was an awkward scene at the table, finally broken by the Beethoven chimes of the front doorbell. That did it. Roberta and Valentina started to cry and Selena and I tried to comfort them as I moved away to open the door.

"Mrs. Harwood, please come in. We could use a little help."

"Yes, I can see. These things are never easy for any of us."

In one of her best performances, the caseworker spoke quietly with all of us and assured everyone that the new placement was with one of the better foster parents. She said DOF had decided that if the girls wanted us to remain in their lives, that would be all right. Sellie asked if there were Spanish people in the neighborhood and wasn't disappointed by the answer. I confess that it hurt that she didn't seem to care that she had to leave us.

Mrs. Harwood finished her pep talk, put an arm around Tina and said, "Let's load the car, we're expected soon."

When we were done, Roberta and I gave each girl a long hug and kiss. I handed them a little spending money and made a grand gesture of opening the car doors for them. Selena opted for the roominess of the back seat, and Tina buckled herself in next to Mrs. Harwood, who climbed in, started the car and backed out of the driveway. Before she could pull out all the way, Tina rolled down her window and started to scream, "Mom, help me, I don't want to leave you, I don't want to go. Come and get me."

The car rolled into the street and moved up the hill. Tina continued to scream, but the words faded as the car disappeared. Roberta gave me a look I'll never forget and ran inside. Sitting on his porch next door, Ollie Kintro scratched his head and yawned, and I swear he laughed.

*****

Later that day, Joey left for his grandmother's and then back to New York. Eddie and Linda had a week before heading to California. With things changing so unexpectedly fast, we hadn't made plans for anything in particular. A few hours after the girls left, Roberta dropped a New England travel guide next to me on the couch.

"Hal, I need to get out of here. Let's see if we can book some place on short notice. We can take Eddie and Linda."

"Good idea, let's try for Lake George. We've never been there. Maybe we'll get lucky with a hotel."

A few phone calls uncovered adjoining rooms available for three nights starting the next day in a hotel overlooking the lake. Hurried arrangements were made and the four of us got our vacation things together for an early morning departure for the four hour drive.

At eight the next morning, we packed the car and got the air-conditioning going. The Massachusetts heat was still unusually unbearable, expected to hit its highest in Glenwood at one hundred and five, according to the radio. Lucky for us, we would be leaving it all behind for the refreshing air of the lakes and mountains of New York State.

# CHAPTER FOUR

*1995*

Simon looked out across the project. An icy north wind burned his cheeks and scattered paper as it swirled across the dirt playground. There was one remaining swing on the rusted set that the gale caused to twist in aimless gyrations, clanging against a support leg. The noise accentuated Simon's anxiety. A year hiatus back to Puerto Rico had done nothing to chill his dislike of Blue Hills. The only advantage was that in Massachusetts, Luz was back at a steady job so he had more time alone with Valentina. He imagined that the older Tina got, the more she enjoyed the time alone with him. At eight, she was outgoing and pretty, although in his more honest moments, Simon admitted to himself that he seldom thought about her face.

The school bus was late this late March afternoon, as it had been all week. With the San Jose festival arriving in a week, the children were staying after school doing related projects. Even though Simon rarely contributed to the household income, Luz was grateful that he was there to wait for the girls to come home, the responsibility off her back. She had long-since ignored the stories Tina told her about Simon's abuse. More often than not, she would greet her daughter's allegations with a whack across the face. After all, she could see what a loving relationship her man had with their little girl, Juanita. Valentina was just jealous and wanted to make trouble. Selena never had similar complaints, so Tina had to be lying.

The sound of the school bus coming up the street to the drive near the play area broke Simon's reverie. He and two neighbor women were the only adults out to greet the children. Selena, Valentina and Juanita were among the first off the bus. Simon glanced over at Natalie Jimenez, the gossipy, rotund woman from Apartment 4B, and made a show of hugging his three charges. When Tina, the last of the sisters to endure his embrace, tried to squirm away, he laughed as loud as he could and held her even closer. "That should satisfy that nosy bitch," he thought.

"Papi, I'm tired. I want to sleep."

"Okay, Juanita, my little rose," Simon said. He released Tina and swooped his five year old kindergartner into the air and herded the others toward the narrow stairwell leading to apartment 5C, the three bedroom apartment they'd occupied for the last two years.

"I want to stay outside and play with Charlisse," piped up Selena.

"You know your mother doesn't want you outside, so don't bother me. She wants the apartment clean when she gets home."

"We are always cleaning. It's never dirty. I want to play. Why can't you clean instead of us?"

Simon thought about slapping her, but there was Mrs. Jiminez, just waiting to spread some shit about him throughout the project.

"Come on now, no arguing, Sellie. Just get upstairs."

Once they got inside, he poured Juanita a glass of juice, then hustled her off for her nap. Selena went down the hall and into her bedroom, the only place she ever felt safe.

Valentina munched on a cookie, looked warily at the man she knew as her father, and turned to go to the bedroom she shared with her older sister. She hoped that the quiet of the last few days signified a positive change from the nearly daily torture. She took two steps when a long arm reached around her waist and tossed her onto the little kitchen table. She started to struggle, but the man's grip on her throat was too much for her. Simon put all of the weight of his chest on the child while he unzipped his pants and yanked her underpants down. As in the countless times before, Tina tried to make her mind go elsewhere, but as usual, the pain interfered. For two minutes she endured until the man stopped and left her alone to suffer.

***

Dark visions swept incessantly through Tina's mind. She lay back on her bed, not listening to her sister's chatter about some boy she had a crush on. For weeks she had been making drawings that depicted her anguish, and the image of a new picture filled her mind. She was surrounded by devils while Simon laughed and her mother screamed at her. Nobody, not even Selena, knew about the drawings, so she would have to wait until she was alone to use her crayons. Alone was what she wanted to be, but that never happened, and Papi Simon was almost always around.

Selena, sitting up on the edge of her bed, motioned to her sister. "Hey, we gotta clean up now before Ma gets home."

"I don't feel like it. You and Juanita can do it without me."

"Hey, I don't feel like it neither. I don't want to get hit. Come on. I'll wake Juanita."

Tina scowled but stood up to tidy her small dresser, which in fact, had been tidied and undisturbed for several days. Selena stepped out in the hall to go into her mother's room where her youngest sister always napped. From the living room, she could hear Simon snoring, stretched out on the couch. She didn't dare wake him to help. Experience had taught her he wouldn't help anyway. She got her sister and they proceeded to finish straightening and dusting. After setting set the table for dinner, the girls occupied themselves quietly while they waited for Luz to return home. At about five they heard their mother's key in the door.

The three of them stood expectantly and in unison said, "Hola, Mami."

Luz put her lunch pail down, gave Juanita a kiss and ignored the older girls while she woke Simon. Simon shook himself awake and gave his girlfriend a pinch on the rump, making Sellie giggle and Tina look away. Then the usual ritual started with Luz inspecting the apartment.

Luz seemed satisfied with the living room and kitchen, so the girls started to relax. But when Luz walked into her bedroom where Juanita had been sleeping, she turned red-faced and started to scream.

"How many fuckin' times I gotta tell you. After Juanita naps, you gotta smooth out the blankets. You goddamn never learn."

Before their mother did anything, Selena and Valentina tried to run into their room, but Luz was too quick for them. She jumped in their way and slapped them both as hard as she could across the face.

Still out of control, Luz shouted, "I come home fucking exhausted and you leave this mess? I'm gonna make sure you never goddamn forget." She dragged the screaming girls by the hair to the kitchen, grabbed a broom and swung it as hard as she could across their backs, drawing blood from Sellie. "Now get in there and fix the bed. No goddamn supper."

Juanita lay sobbing in Simon's arms while Simon stared at his lover. He ran his fingers through his hair and moaned to himself that busybody Natalie Jiminez surely had heard the commotion.

***

Most of the litter from the festival had been cleared from the streets of Blue Hills and the routines of life in the neighborhood were back to normal. April rolled into May on the wings of a perfect spring and Luz and Simon even took the girls for a rare Sunday afternoon outing at Lilac Park. Typically, Juanita was the center of her parents' attention, enjoying pushes on the swing and swoops down the slide into her mother's arms. Her sisters sat on a bench by the duck pond, carefully adhering to Luz's admonition not to soil their clothes.

Out of earshot of the adults, Tina whispered to Selena, "I want to die. Simon does things to me every day. I can't get away. Ma doesn't believe me. You do, don't you, Sellie?"

"He never did nothing to me, so I don't know. I mean, I don't think you're lying, but I never actually saw him do nothing to you."

"What if you did? Would you tell Mami? She would probably hit you."

"Yeah. But I would tell if I saw him hurt you. Maybe Ma would believe you then. Ever since we found out that guy in Rhode Island is our real father, I don't trust Simon or Ma anyway. They could have told us."

Luz looked over at her daughters and scowled. "What are you two talkin' about? Boys probably. I goddamn told you to stay away from boys. They could do shit to you."

Tina kept herself from crying and glared at Simon.

"No Ma," Selena answered, "we were just talking about how we wish Grandma and Grandpa had come back from Puerto Rico."

"I don't believe you. But just stop. We're going home now."

***

"I got a call from my sister in Smithton. Her and Felix are living together now. She heard from my mother that her and my old man are moving back here from the island. Welfare sucks on the island," Luz announced to Simon.

"So, who gives a shit?"

"Shut your damn mouth, Simon. Isabel says they wanna live with her or me. Now do you give a shit?"

It was the Monday after the day in the park and the girls were in the kitchen doing the supper dishes. Up until now, it had been quiet in Apartment 5C.

"No goddamn way are they coming here. That place of Isabel's is much bigger than this, anyway."

"Simon, if my mother wants to come here, ain't no way I say no. She cooks and my father goes to the park with his old friends all day."

"Ain't gonna have no privacy, no space."

"Maybe you get a damn job and we manage the space. Anyway, they might wind up with Isabel. Bella says they'll be calling her or me this week."

From the kitchen, Valentina overheard the conversation and for the first time in a long time, she felt hope. With more people in the house, Simon would have to leave her alone. Besides, she loved her grandparents.

The conversation was interrupted by a knock on the door. Simon undid the chain, opened the door and threw his arms in the air. "This is all we need," he growled.

"This is no pleasure for me, believe me," Luz's sister Carmen said when she stepped into the apartment.

Luz turned her back on Carmen and snapped, "Why did you come here without calling me?"

"I was driving by. I haven't seen the girls in a while and I miss them. You, too."

"Cut the crap. You don't miss me and I don't miss you."

"I'm sorry you feel that way but—"

"But nothing. Me and Isabel and all our brothers feel like you act like some queen or some shit like that. Like we embarrass you."

Carmen shifted from side to side and shook her head. "It's not like that," she lied. In fact, what brought her to the flat was a suggestion from a schoolteacher friend at the elementary school that Tina had not been her usual outgoing self for weeks, but the child wouldn't volunteer what, if anything, was bothering her. Carmen, always distrustful of her younger sibling, and outright loathing Simon who seemed just too smooth, wanted to see things for herself. She had no idea what she might find or what she would do if there were anything seriously wrong.

"Luz, no, I really wanted to see you. You guys didn't even stop to see me during the festival."

"Aunt Carmen, I wanted to see you," Tina said and ran to her aunt.

"Well why didn't you, sweetheart?"

"Mami said it was too late. We didn't have time."

Luz turned crimson, but before she could explode, Carmen said, "I understand. But I'm here today, just wondering how my nieces are."

"Aunt Carmen, Aunt Carmen, come see what I made in art," chimed in Selena.

"Okay, okay," Carmen replied, relieved that she would not appear to be focusing on the middle daughter.

"Don't take too long," Luz warned, "we gotta eat."

"I'll be out of your hair in a couple of minutes. Just let me visit the kids and I won't bother my dear sister."

Carmen disappeared into the small room where the older sisters slept, Selena leading the way, Tina trailing behind, and Luz giving her sister the finger as soon as her back was turned. Carmen spent a few minutes praising Selena's artwork, then sent her to the kitchen on the pretext that she wanted a glass of water.

Speaking softly and rapidly, Carmen quizzed Tina on how she was feeling.

"Okay, I guess, but sometimes not so good."

"Why? I mean not feeling good sometimes."

"Tia Carmen, if I tell, promise you won't hit me or tell Mami."

"I would never hit you, sweetheart. What is it?"

Tina chewed a fingernail, paused a moment and said quietly, "Sometimes, Simon hurts me."

Carmen scowled, "What do you mean? Does he beat you?"

"No, he never beats me. He touches me."

Aunt Carmen was beside herself. "How? What does he do?"

A tear leaked down the little girl's cheek. "He puts himself inside of me."

"Oh my Lord!"

Carmen enfolded her arms around her niece. "I'll do my best to make him stop. Does your mother know?"

"Aunt Carmen, I told her, but she doesn't believe me. Please, please don't say anything."

At the sound of Selena coming back down the hall, Carmen pressed her lips to Valentina's cheek and assured her that she would not tell Luz, but said she would try to make things better.

A moment later in the living room, Carmen put on her best face. "Luz, I loved seeing the kids. I'd love to come more often."

"Maybe when I ain't here. You know Ma and Papi are coming back. If they stay here, you can come. Just go now."

Carmen hugged each of the three girls and turned to leave. She couldn't bear to look at Simon and promised herself not to waste a minute in doing something about the bastard.

***

Late the same night, Simon lifted his head off the pillow. Luz was asleep beside him, the sum total of her five boilermakers assuring she would stay that way. The clock said 2:15 a.m. He shifted as quietly as he could and maneuvered until his feet touched the floor. He smiled at the slumbering form of Juanita who had come from her own room and was lying next to her mother as had become her custom. Simon took his familiar path out of the room, across the hall, and into the darkness of the older daughters' bedroom.

"Fine," he thought, seeing that Selena seemed to be in a deep sleep. For years he had followed the routine and for years the sobs of an abused girl and the groans of an aroused man had failed to awaken the older child. Fact was, he really didn't worry about it.

His boxers already falling below his knees, Simon leaned over Valentina. He moved swiftly to pull back her covers and yank her little nightgown above her waist. He made a move toward her when out of the corner of his eye he thought he saw something move. He turned to see Selena trying to grab his arm. Before she could do anything, Simon cupped a hand over her mouth.

"Keep your mouth shut or I'll kill you," Simon snarled. "Curious are you? I'll give you something to see." He pulled Selena by her hair alongside Tina's bed, pushed the weeping younger sister down and raped her, oblivious to the nightmare of her fright, pain and tears.

It was too much for the sisters and they wailed so loud that even Luz's hangover couldn't prevent her from hearing. With Juanita close behind, she stumbled into the next room and turned on the light in time to see her lover threatening her daughters, his shorts still around his ankles.

"Goddamn. Simon, get the fuck out of this room. Oh Jesus, what am I gonna do? Juanita, get back in my room. Valentina, stop screaming. Stop it, stop it! Selena, what the hell?"

Luz made a move to punch Simon, but he grabbed her first and said, "Calm down, I can explain. This isn't the end of the world."

"You son of a bitch, you're freaking hurting my arm. You better get your shit together and get out before I call the cops. You bastard, I'm gonna call them anyway."

"Don't call nobody," Simon ordered, "you'd be in as much trouble as me."

The alcoholic haze was lifting from Luz's brain and as it did, her selfishness started to overcome any anger she felt. She started to swing at Simon again, but then just turned away, causing both of the daughters to shield themselves. But Luz was done fighting. Through tightened lips, Luz sputtered, "Okay, I won't call nobody, but you do this again and I'll kill you. Maybe you move out and we just see each other. We figure this out. Leave now before I change my mind."

Tina and Sellie continued to cry. For once, Luz tried to calm them down. "Girls, I ain't going to let Simon do this again. We just be quiet about it and everybody will be okay."

"Mami, Papi was wrong, I didn't want to watch and Tina was scared."

"Damn, Sellie, shut up. It don't make no difference now. Papi isn't going to do it again."

Luz pushed Simon out of the bedroom. Her body shaking, Juanita peered from her mother's bed into the hall where her mother and father stood. She didn't understand why her Mami was telling her Papi he'd better leave. Luz turned toward Simon and threw up her arms in desperation. I don't look for this trouble, don't deserve it, she thought. She hustled Simon away and made sure the kids at least had the lights out, then went into the kitchen to pour herself a soothing drink.

***

"Look ma'am", the desk sergeant answered, "I'm sorry, but we can't do anything unless you tell me your name."

"You can't just do nothing. Please. Anything," Carmen begged.

The officer took a sip of his black coffee, first cup of the morning, and spoke back into the receiver. "Well, I believe the Department of Families might go on an anonymous tip. We just can't do that."

Carmen hung up the phone in the booth around the corner from her place and ripped through the blue pages of the phone book searching for DOF's phone number. After a sleepless night, she had decided that a faceless tip would be a good way for her notify the authorities about Tina and whatever else might be happening at her sister's hell hole. Hoping that the state would be more receptive than the cops, she punched the buttons and waited for someone to answer.

"Department of Families. How may I direct your call?"

"I think a little girl is being abused. I need to talk to someone."

"Hold on. I'm transferring you to Mrs. Hernandez."

Carmen almost lost her nerve in the few seconds she had to wait, but before she could change her mind, the line opened again and a voice said "Can I help? I'm a supervisor here, Lydia Hernandez."

"Look, I can't say who I am or how I know these things, but a little girl is probably being molested by a man in her house."

Carmen began to shake, her voice a torrent of rage. "I mean raped. He's raping her."

Lydia Hernandez tried to calm the caller. "I understand. I promise you, we take these situations seriously and deal with them right away. I would prefer to have your name, but give me the child's name and where she lives or her school."

"Oh, thank you. Please do something. Her name is Valentina Diaz. She goes to Blue Hills Elementary. I don't want to say where she lives. I'm afraid her mother will figure out who called."

"Ma'am, I can't promise anything other than we can work with the school to see if there is anything they know. Maybe you're mistaken, at least we hope so."

"I am not mistaken," Carmen replied, "Please do something immediately."

***

The caseworker sat in the nurse's office at Blue Hills Elementary. He waited outside the examination room while the nurse examined the little girl. Valentina Diaz had made it easy. When she was called to the principal's office, her first time, she got scared and blurted something about it wasn't her fault, that she'd done nothing wrong. She scarcely noticed the young DOF case worker in the plaid sport coat sitting next to the principal, Mr. LeVine. When the principal asked what she meant, she became hysterical and spilled out a jumble of statements about her Papi hurting her. After she calmed enough to explain more clearly, the DOF worker asked the principal to accompany him with Valentina to the school nurse who would examine her as best she was permitted. Any internal examinations would have to await a physician.

After several minutes, the door to the examination room swung open and the nurse stepped out, leaving Tina behind to dress.

"Mr. LeVine, I think that child has been sexually assaulted, and very recently. She's bruised and I'm sure there's blood on her thigh. She needs to be examined at the medical center by a doctor right away."

Without pausing, the young man from DOF pulled out his cell phone and direct-dialed to Lydia Hernandez. "Ms. Hernandez, the nurse at Blue Hills Elementary says that the Diaz girl has definitely been abused and wants her taken to the hospital to be examined further. I want authority to remove her and the other children from the home. I also want to ask the police to have the mother and her boyfriend arrested. They live at Apartment 5C down in the housing project."

After a brief discussion, Ms. Hernandez said she would get the required authorization and in the meantime, Principal LeVine would keep Valentina with him in his office. The DOF man asked to have the older sister brought to the office as well. The youngest daughter was believed to still be with her mother.

Frightened, Tina followed Mr. LeVine to the office. She cried quietly and jumped up to throw her arms around Selena when her sister came in. The caseworker explained what was about to happen and now both girls were in a panic.

A short while later, Ms. Hernandez called and directed that Valentina be brought to the medical center and that she would have Selena brought to the DOF office to be joined later by her sister. In the meantime, DOF filed a complaint with the police and a squad car was dispatched to the apartment. Later, a doctor at the medical center confirmed the school nurse's evaluation, and a distraught and confused Tina was sent to join Selena.

\*\*\*

Luz had been chain smoking and drinking ever since her discovery the night before. She hated Simon, but she needed him. When he had left in the dark, early hours before dawn, he said he'd go to sleep at a shelter for a few days, probably hang out at the San Pedro bar. She'd called in sick and kept Juanita home. Now the kids weren't on the bus and she was having trouble getting a straight answer from the school except that the girls were safe. She paced the floor, waiting for someone to tell her where her kids were, and kept her eye on the street beyond the basketball court. When she spotted a squad car slowing to a stop with another car close behind, and saw two officers walk across the play area toward her building, she raced for the phone and quickly dialed the San Pedro's number.

"Roberto, is Simon there? This is Luz. Hurry."

"Hang on, he's right here, a little drunk."

The phone clattered and then a thick voice said, "Hey babe, you miss me, huh."

"Simon shut up. I don't have time. I can't explain it all right now, but I think the cops know about you and Tina. They just pulled up. You better get out of Blue Hills fast."

She looked out the window again and saw a small car pull up and a gray-haired woman step out.

"Leave now, Simon."

"What the fuck? All right, I'm gone. I'll let you know where I'm at," Simon shouted and slammed down the receiver.

Luz thought about running herself, but it was too late. Besides, she didn't see where she had done anything wrong. When the two officers knocked on the door, she let them in and was shocked when they read her rights and locked handcuffs around her wrists. The gray-haired woman stepped in behind the officers and took Juanita by the hand.

Luz screamed, "What the hell are you doing?"

Juanita started bawling.

"You'll be safe now," the caseworker said to Juanita.

"I want my Mami," the five year old cried.

Without saying another word, the woman led the girl out of the apartment and to her car while the police pulled Luz down the stairs and into the cruiser.

***

The DOF procedures were handled expeditiously. Selena, Tina, and Juanita were placed separately in temporary foster care. The Family Court had given DOF custody and the agency set out to find a place where the girls could remain together. In the meantime, the local prosecutor was reviewing the situation to decide what charges to file against the mother. Simon himself had disappeared, but the prosecutor promised herself that this case would remain open as long as possible.

Exhausting all possibilities, DOF found that there were no foster families willing to take the three girls together. Reluctantly, the authorities decided to take the offer from Luz Diaz's sister Isabel, in Smithton, to house the girls. She had assured them that the young man who visited her frequently, Felix Williams, did not live with her and that he had a responsible job as a security guard. The facts seemed to check, Felix had only a few traffic infractions, so the sisters seemed to be headed to a stable situation.

A few months after her little daughters moved in with Isabel, Luz was out on bond awaiting trial on neglect and other charges. She received a message from Roberto of the San Pedro that Simon was well and living with a new name in rural Puerto Rico. For his and her own good, he asked Luz not to try and find him. She told Roberto to let Simon know it was okay for now, with her trial coming, but she couldn't promise not to try to find him. She didn't mention that a guy who moved into her building had become very friendly and his wife wasn't around most of the time. While Simon was never far from her thoughts, the neighbor was never far from her bed.

# CHAPTER FIVE

*August – December 2001*

DOF was as good as its word, but only, as it turned out, if we behaved ourselves. Roberta and I, mostly Roberta, had pretty regular contact with Tina and Sellie at the Glenwood foster home. I was pleased that things appeared to be going reasonably well for the girls. Perhaps I was more pleased for myself than I was for them, an admission I could make only much later. The new foster mom, already referred to as such by Tina and Sellie, was pleasant to us at first whenever she happened to answer the phone when we called. Mrs. Gaylord was deeply religious and hard working. Her own kids, two girls, ages sixteen and fourteen, and a boy, six, provided some companionship for the new members of the household, even though the Diaz girls' quest for attention sometimes spilled over into arguments with their new foster siblings.

It was not much more than a month after the girls were placed with Mrs. Gaylord that the sisters, especially Tina, divulged some troubling developments to us. She complained, "After that miserable experience living with Aunt Isabel, I thought that bad foster homes were in the past. It's not so good here."

Of the things she revealed, two circumstances in particular stuck out. First, Valentina was regularly required to babysit the boy while Mrs. Gaylord went to work. Babysitting under those circumstances not only violated the State's foster care guidelines, but in Tina's case, also provided a painful reminder of the days when her mother virtually made her a slave within her own home. Second, Mrs. Gaylord's devotion to her fundamentalist religious beliefs resulted in her suggesting to the girls that they were somehow to blame for the evil in their lives. The last thing the two of those young victims needed to hear was that the devil resided in their hearts and it clearly troubled them to be told so.

It troubled me, too. I told Bobbie I was going to find out why our old caseworker friend was willing to tolerate these conditions. Something Tina had said made the circumstances all the more ludicrous and I was sure DOF wouldn't stand for the charade. Tina told us that the excuse for her babysitting was that she was "tutoring" the boy. Interesting, that a kid with Tina's learning difficulties was tutoring, and even more interesting that this period of instruction lasted five to six hours a day with no other supervision.

On a Monday morning in late August, I decided to go to work late. I had harbored many negative thoughts about Elaine Harwood, but never in a million years would I have expected what I heard, even from her. The conversation is burned into my brain almost verbatim.

"Sorry to trouble you, Mrs. Harwood, but it can't wait. Thank God you agreed to let us continue our contact with the girls or we never would have found out."

"Found out what?"

"A couple of things. Mrs. Gaylord is virtually telling the girls that they're possessed by Satan and that is why bad things happen to them. I know we were told directly during our licensing course that we weren't supposed to impose our religion on kids coming into our home. The girls are upset about it. You need to get Mrs. Gaylord to stop."

"I can assure you that I know how to handle my job without outside interference, Mr. Allen. You said there were a couple of things. What else? I need to be finishing up some reports."

I wondered what good I was doing, but plunged ahead. "Mrs. Gaylord is having Tina babysit her son while she works. Supposedly the deal is that Tina is tutoring the kid. Pretty outrageous."

There was a moment of silence and I'm sure the voice I heard next was coming through clenched teeth.

"Outrageous, is it? Well, I okayed it. There is nothing at all wrong with tutoring the child for the rest of the summer. I think you and Mrs. Allen have to mind your own business."

"You have got to be kidding. You approved this arrangement? Even if Tina could actually tutor the kid, it certainly wouldn't be for more than an hour or less. This completely violates DOF rules, not to mention, goddamn it, that it shoves the horror of poor Tina's enslaved life with her mother right back down her throat. I thought you people are supposed to help these kids!" Unexpectedly, I was shouting, but I didn't care.

"Expert are you? Well maybe I need to reconsider allowing you and your wife to have anything whatsoever to do with the girls. Look at the trouble you're causing. You can't even control your temper. I have a mind to get your license revoked," she retorted, clearly emphasizing the word *your.* "And for your information, Rosa Gaylord is one of our best foster mothers and now, because of your meddling, I'll have to investigate the lady. Rest assured that I'll be talking about you with Ms. Hernandez. Good-bye."

Before I could say another word, the phone went silent.

***

A short while later, I reported back to Roberta. She'd never seemed so down.

"Hal, this is crazy. My God, what next? Now I wonder about this Wednesday," she said.

"Why? What's happening then?"

"I guess I didn't tell you. Mrs. Hernandez approved my bringing Tina for a check-up with the doctor she was seeing when she lived here. I'm getting her from Mrs. Gaylord day after tomorrow."

I could feel my face color. "Bobbie, we just shouldn't be that involved. Moral support is enough."

"Well, this is no, big deal. Anyway, I'm going ahead. Harwood's boss approved it."

***

Early the next evening, a thunderstorm dumped sheets of rain across the highway as I drove home. I'd almost arrived when Strawberry Fields Forever chimed on my cell phone. It was the Wednesday following my conversation with Elaine Harwood and I'd forgotten about Roberta's medical mission with Tina, but my wife's voice in the earpiece jolted my memory.

"Come to the hospital right now. I took Valentina for her examination and the doctor ordered her in. She is so depressed the doctor's concerned she'll harm herself."

"Jesus Christ," I said, "I'll be right there."

When I arrived at the small community hospital, I was directed into the emergency ward where I found Roberta sitting in a hallway next to Valentina who was resting, eyes-closed, on a gurney.

The first words out of Bobbie's mouth were to the effect that as soon as Tina got into the car, she could see by the withdrawn, unusually vacant look in her eyes how desperate the child was. Moreover, without any prodding from Roberta, the doctor at the clinic where she'd had her examination had concluded that Tina should be hospitalized and ordered an ambulance.

Bobbie reached out to me and I put my arms around her. "What next?" I asked.

"Well, the hospital social worker is on the way and DOF is sending a caseworker. Luckily, Harwood is off doing something else, so it will be someone new."

Valentina opened her eyes. "Good, I don't want that woman," she whispered before appearing to drift off.

"Hal, one more thing. I encountered Mrs. Gaylord and she gave me an earful. She thinks we're going to cause her to lose her license. I'm afraid I lost my temper and told her a thing or two about how she's mistreating Tina. Maybe I shouldn't have, but I told her I thought she didn't care at all about helping Tina, just wanted the money. You know something, I'm glad I did."

I nodded, and reassured her that the woman had it coming. We stopped talking and just stood there looking at the sleeping young girl who had made such an impact on our lives.

Before long, the hospital social worker appeared, accompanied by a young man who introduced himself as Jim Covain of DOF. He seemed pleasant enough, and businesslike. He asked us to wait in the Social Services office while he and Mrs. Buck, the social worker, spoke with a doctor and Tina.

About a half hour later, the pair arrived in the cluttered office. It was now about nine and dark outside, the thunderstorm long gone. The grandmotherly Mrs. Buck, grey hair pulled up in a bun and tortoise shell glasses hanging from a chain across her chest, offered us coffee, which Roberta accepted. Mr. Covain, all five foot six of him, waved off coffee for himself and began.

"First things first. We quite agree that Valentina is deeply depressed. I don't understand why nobody noticed before today. We'll be looking into that. She'll be kept here for one or two nights for some rest and the beginning of anti-depressant medication. I've cleared all this with my supervisor. She's alerted Elaine Harwood. Which brings me to the next point."

The caseworker, who'd been standing until then, pulled a chair next to us, as if to soften what he was about to say. He leaned forward and said in as sympathetic a voice as he could muster, "I also have to tell you that Mrs. Gaylord will now have her license investigated. In addition, Mrs. Harwood has gone straight to our Regional Director with a very strong recommendation that you should have no further contact with the girls. You'll be advised about that very soon. She claims that she had no knowledge of your taking Valentina to the doctor."

"We most certainly had permission, direct from Lydia Hernandez. This is insane." Roberta pounded her fist so hard on Mrs. Buck's desk that a vase with fresh cut tulips tipped over, spilling water and flowers, then rolled off the desk and smashed into pieces on the floor.

Bobbie began shaking. "I'm so sorry. Let me clean this. This whole thing, we meant to do right, it's a nightmare."

Mrs. Buck grabbed several napkins from her desk and began soaking up the water, telling Roberta to stay put and collect herself.

"I'll clean up after you leave. Look, I know this is hard, but you are doing the very best you know how and the child knows it."

"My God, poor Tina," Roberta said almost as if she needed to remind herself where we were at the moment.

Without saying another word, she jumped from her chair and out the door to check on Valentina, but there were only two nurses attending to a new arrival. Tina and her gurney were no longer in sight.

Jim Covain and I walked my wife away from the hall and back into Mrs. Buck's office. Roberta threw her arms wide, grasping for words, then just sank into her seat.

"You know, this won't be the end of this, not by a long shot," I said. "No way is that kid going to be abandoned now. No way."

Both Covain and Buck shrugged, more out of helplessness than indifference, I thought, while Bobbie wiped the trickle of tears from her cheeks.

***

There's an old saying that goes, "Smile, things could be worse, so I smiled, and sure enough things got worse." I wasn't smiling at all, but things certainly got worse, and it didn't take very long. In fact, it was while Bobbie and I were clearing the dinner dishes that night when the phone rang. Our caller ID displayed that the caller was from DOF back in Blue Hills and it certainly wasn't going to be a social call.

"I'll get it," I said, but Bobbie hurried into the family room to get on another extension.

It was Lydia Hernandez and after a curt hello, she dropped the shoe.

"This isn't working," she said, "and based on Elaine Harwood's recommendation, the State has determined that you should have no further contact with Selina and Valentina. We acknowledge the positive influence you have had on their lives and commend you for it. Now, you must leave it up to the professionals to look after their welfare."

"May I say," Roberta said in a voice so soft she that she hid her anger even from me, "that the professionals, and I mean one in particular, haven't—"

"Please let me finish," Ms. Hernandez interrupted. "I understand that this is hurtful to you, and if it is any consolation, I have removed Mrs. Harwood from the case and have assigned one of our best young men. He'll begin his investigation tomorrow and if warranted, he will remove the girls from the Gaylord home."

"Ms. Hernandez," I said, "we don't agree in the least with your decision. So far as we know, there have been no other responsible role models in these girls' lives."

"You know," Roberta growled, "I'm not taking this lying down. Whose damn welfare are you protecting? DOF? Your own? Incompetent Elaine Harwood? That Gaylord woman? We're going to find a way to fight you and we'll win, come hell or high water. Those kids are going to find they have some real friends in this world."

"If you want to make this difficult on everyone, I guess that's your choice. Don't you think it would be better if you just cool off and back away? I'm doing my best for those girls, believe me."

Lydia Hernandez sounded dispirited, not at all combative, almost like she hoped we'd fight.

Bobbie didn't notice. "We'll see about that," she said. "We'll be talking to the girls' lawyer and their *guardian ad litem*, and our state legislator. In the meantime, you had better get Rosa Gaylord straightened out."

"Look, I feel bad about all of this, but my hands are tied," Ms. Hernandez replied. "I really can't talk any longer. Please think about this a bit more before you do anything. All we want is for those kids to have a good place to stay."

"Wrong," Bobbie retorted, "I want a lot more. I want them to have the good life that they deserve."

\*\*\*

Diane Paquin, the *guardian ad litem* who was appointed by the court to represent the girls' interests, was sympathetic to our concern, but she felt she had no alternative to offer so long as the girls were in an acceptable environment. We'd always had a good relationship with Diane, although sporadic, and she favored our continuing contact with Tina and Sellie. About a week after our discussion with Ms. Hernandez, Diane informed us that DOF was almost done with its investigation of Ms. Gaylord and was likely to be deciding to remove the girls. "But under the circumstances," she told us by phone on a Wednesday night, "you know, no contact and all, I can't tell you where they're going except that they are being separated. I can't elaborate, but I agree that they need to be apart."

We hadn't been able to reach the girls' Family Court appointed lawyer who'd been away on a summer vacation. A few days after our call from Mrs. Paquin, the lawyer finally returned our call. We'd had many discussions with Steve Baron during our period of care for the girls. They were always cordial, usually ending with his ambiguous promise to look into whatever our issues were. Anyway, on this evening, Steve was of no more help than anybody else. "You've been great, best thing ever happened to those kids, but DOF is in bounds here, never had to allow contact in the first place. Maybe someone like your State Rep can help, but I wouldn't count your chickens."

\*\*\*

In early September, the news from Diane Paquin was reassuring. The kids had been placed and were doing reasonably well. I was hoping that Roberta might take this as good enough and drop the idea of contact. But the return call from our State Representative Nancy Carver regarding the message Bobbie had left with her office, guaranteed that our fight would proceed. Her regular hours for constituent meetings at our library were resuming for the fall and we arranged to see her Thursday, two nights away.

The next day, before the meeting with Representative Carver was to occur, I was in the den going over some work material while Bobbie was doing the dinner dishes. The phone rang and a few moments later Bobbie yelled for me to pick up my extension. She added that I would be surprised. I guess so.

"Dad, hi, it's Valentina," the soft voice said, as if I wouldn't have recognized it.

"Hal, listen to this. Go ahead honey."

"Okay. I'm out in Donaldstown with a lady and three kids. She's all right, but those kids are driving me nuts."

I don't know why, but I found myself reminding her that we weren't allowed to contact her, that we could get into trouble.

"How are you calling us, paying for the call, I mean?"

"Dad, I had to talk to you guys. I used the calling card number mom gave me when I was with you. I gotta get out of here. I wish I could come back to you."

"Harold," Roberta said, "I already told Tina that coming back here probably wasn't going to happen, at least not now."

Whatever *at least not now* means, I thought, then added, "Hang in there, Tina, we're doing what we can to get the State to let us contact you. Hopefully that will work out and maybe you can even visit. What about Selena?"

"Like I just told Ma, we were getting on each other's nerves at Mrs. Gaylord's. Probably better we were separated, even though I miss her and we're allowed to talk. She's in another place in Glenwood, same high school. Hey, I hear someone coming. Gotta go. Please help, okay?"

***

There were actually many more people at the library than I expected for a week night so we had to park behind Town Hall, seventy five yards away. As we wound our way through three rows of cars, Roberta was rehearsing her pitch to Nancy Carver. I was daydreaming when I literally bumped into the paunchy form of Ollie Kintro , who had appeared from behind his dented pickup truck, second only to Kintro's fence as the neighborhood eyesore.

"What are you blind or something?" he sniffed. "Coulda killed me. Say, Allen, havin' any more of them, uh, house guests?"

"What business is it of yours," I retorted, all the while wondering what a sort like this guy would be doing at a library.

"Can't hardly have nobody out in my yard with kids like that around, if you know what I mean."

"No, I don't know what you mean," I lied. "As a matter of fact we're planning to have five new kids next week and I'll have them outside all day long," I shouted. "What the hell are you doing at the library anyway?"

Bobbie, seemingly half-amused, half-mortified, quickened her pace toward the library.

"Well, now, that ain't none of your business, is it," Kintro sneered, "but for your information, we just had a meeting in there to get going to stop the damn Town Council from spendin' my hard-earned money from being taxed any more just to build a new middle school. Bigger school, more kids, more scum coming here. Liked it lots better when this town was just a bunch of farms. Didn't have no do-gooders like you bringin' all types around. Now get outta my way. You're blockin' the door to my truck."

Kintro pushed past me and I hustled to catch up to Roberta who was standing near the library entrance.

"Harold, I was sure he was going to punch you. Anyway, I'm proud of what you said." With a twinkle she added, "Five kids, for real? Okay, I'd settle for one or two."

Once inside, I could see from the many empty reading room seats that most of the cars in the lot had been there for the middle school meeting in the library community room. Representative Carver used a small room near the entrance to meet with her constituents. A window in the door allowed us to see that she was already there, alone and busy writing. Bobbie knocked on the door and Nancy looked up, smiled and waved us in.

Nancy Carver, a slim bundle of energy, had been in the State House for fifteen years. I knew her slightly, my wife a bit more, but only because our respective youngest sons had been pals in high school. I had never bothered much with my legislators; usually saw them only as a source of endless election year junk mail.

For about fifteen minutes, Bobbie conducted a virtual monologue, detailing just about everything about her and our history with Valentina and Selena. I interrupted to interject a point here or there as infrequently as possible because I could tell that Nancy Carver seemed to be engrossed and I didn't want to distract her.

When Roberta was finished, the legislator let out a breath. "Whew, I've heard a lot of sad stories in my years in office, but this one is right up there. Tell me what you'd like me to do."

"Representative Carver, just convince DOF to let us resume contact with the girls," I said, "that is, assuming that's what they both want."

"You know," she replied, "sometimes I think DOF has a death wish. They seem to fall all over themselves to screw up. I get so many complaints. In my head I know they have a hard job. In my heart, I know they can do lots better. Please call me Nancy. We've known each other long enough to drop the formalities."

"Fine, Nancy. And yeah, sometimes it seems they spend more time in CYA, using the kids' confidentiality as a shield for their bureaucratic behinds, than they do helping."

"Well, be that as it may, Hal, let's do something about these two children. I can't promise the result, but let me try a few things and I'll get back to you very soon."

She shook my hand, much more firmly than one would expect from such a slight person, and put her arm around Roberta.

"I wish there were more people like you," she said. "Sometimes I delude myself into thinking that we elected officials are out in front, fighting the fight for the people. But the truth is, you and others like you are the real heroes, taking the body punches and without the power lunches. Trust me, I'll do my best."

\*\*\*

Like most cities and towns in the world, Blue Hills is nothing more than a series of small villages thrown together for convenience. Like any small village, little goes on within the smaller community without the knowledge of just about everyone. And so, even though almost six weeks had passed since our meeting with Nancy Carver with nothing more than a series of phone message exchanges and conversations with legislative staffers, Roberta's job in Blue Hills enabled us to be well aware of the general facts of the circumstances of both Valentina and Selena. Tina, we knew, had been moved from her foster home in Donaldstown to a so-called "therapeutic" foster home in Hillview, placed with a family supposedly better equipped to handle her many emotional and educational issues. Selena remained with the family in Glenwood and was progressing through high school, albeit not without difficulty. There was a suggestion that fourteen year old Tina was attracted to older men, and that even the therapeutic home was toying with having her placed in a supervised group shelter. Roberta constantly fretted about the situation and not a day, perhaps an hour, passed without Tina's fate being the main topic of conversation.

Then, a few weeks before Thanksgiving, we received a voice message from Representative Carver's office that after much arm-twisting, DOF, in the person of the District Supervisor for the agency's Glenwood-Blue Hills District would meet with us all at the State Capitol Building in five days, on a Tuesday afternoon. I made the arrangements to leave work early that day and join Roberta and Nancy for the 3:30 meeting.

***

The second floor of the Gothic state capitol building was filled with a steady stream of earnest young legislative staff and an occasional politician. We sat on a slightly worn bench with a 1970's aspect to it outside of the bustling office Nancy Carver shared with another legislator. Roberta had a tight grip on my arm and was commenting on how nervous she felt, when she was interrupted by a perky young woman who introduced herself as Mindy, aide to Representative Carver. She ushered us into a nearby meeting room where Nancy was seated at the end of a long table with a pale, puckish faced, sandy haired man of about fifty sitting in a chair along the side just to her right.

"Roberta, Hal, so glad we could arrange this meeting," she stood, shook each of our hands and continued, "This is Ronald Magnuson, Glenwood District Supervisor for DOF, Lydia Hernandez's boss."

Mr. Magnuson rose and extended a hand, his six foot five frame surprising me under that boyish face.

"I'm always so pleased to meet such dedicated foster parents," he assured us, sounding so sincere that he almost disarmed my skepticism. "Representative Carver has been filling me in on your own family. Sounds as if Diaz girls were lucky to have spent time with you before they had to move on."

"Thanks," Roberta said and I echoed her, more wary now of his intentions.

Nancy must have noticed the look on my face. "No need to hash out the whole background," she started as we settled into our chairs. "Mr. Magnuson and I have already had a very frank discussion and I believe you will be pleased."

"First of all, please call me Ron. I'm not much for titles. I want to elaborate on what I began to say. You two really are a shining example of what we at DOF want from our foster families. A hotel can provide a roof over someone's head, but not care and consideration. There's absolutely no doubt that you two exemplify the best we can offer these unfortunate kids."

Bobbie began to say something, her eyes moistening for what must have been the hundredth time since we embarked down this path, but Ron kept talking.

"Now that isn't to say you've done everything right, or at least gone about everything exactly the way some might prefer, but at least you were obviously always looking out for Selena's and Valentina's best interests. I hope I can say the same about my own staff. Please accept my word that I'm going to review that very carefully."

"It's not that we think the staff weren't trying," I was surprised to hear myself say, "but—"

"Please Hal, I appreciate what you mean, but there is no need," he continued, "Here is what I've decided and this will be confirmed in a letter from me to you and Nancy. Contact may be resumed between you and the girls, but only to the extent that they agree. Since we don't want to interfere with their relationship with their current foster families, phone contact must be handled so as not to be disruptive. Personal visits will also be as agreed to by the girls, with specific prior approval by DOF, and be limited to no more than a few occasions a month with any exceptions requiring prior approval. We reserve the right to suspend this arrangement at any time that in our judgment it is no longer in the best interests of the girls or their current foster families. Is that understood?"

"Yes, yes, yes, God bless you," Roberta said, still teary and smiling all at once, "and God bless you Nancy. We can't thank you enough."

"Yes, well you have yourselves, and certainly Nancy, to thank. I've already informed Lydia Hernandez and their caseworker, Jim Covain, of the decision. Now, I do have to get back to Glenwood. It was my pleasure to meet you, even if I did all the talking," he smiled.

After he'd left the room, Nancy embraced us both. "I'd like to meet the girls sometime, anytime."

"You bet," I said. "We can't thank you enough."

\*\*\*

Three days later we got a call from Jim Covain. The word we got was not unexpected. Valentina was anxious to hear from us. Selena wanted to think about it for a while. The news wasn't that good in general. Tina's foster mother at the therapeutic home had finally decided she couldn't handle her anymore. The kid had indeed been trying to see a twenty-nine year old man. Covain suspected that the girl was seeking a father figure as much as a boy friend, but a visit from the local police had scared the man away. In the absence of immediate other foster care, Tina was about to be moved into what was meant to be a temporary arrangement in a State-owned group shelter in Hillview. When Roberta hung up the phone and turned to me with those pleading eyes that had only one question in mind, I shook my head no. "Not yet anyway. It's meant to be temporary, so let's just see how it goes."

# CHAPTER SIX

*1996 and summer 1998*

"Valentina, finish your lunch. We need to clean up before Uncle Felix comes over."

Nine year old Tina licked the remains of the chicken wing from her fingers and shook her head, her luxurious curls bouncing across her shoulders. "Felix is not my uncle and I don't like him."

"You watch your damn mouth. You don't hear Selena say nothing bad about him," Isabel Diaz scolded her niece.

For the several months she'd been taking care of her sister's kids and it was wearing her out, much more trouble than she'd bargained for. Her only child, Ernesto, was never a problem, even took after his Aunt Carmen in the classroom. First year of high school and a member of this club and that team.

"Yeah, Tina, I think Felix is okay," chimed in Sellie who was standing by the sink drying her dishes.

"Hah, you like any guy," Tina snorted, "now you growing boobs and all, you think you're really something."

Selena tossed the towel at her sister. "You're just jealous," she retorted, and she was right.

Fact was, that the absence of a gorgeous face seemed to go unnoticed by the average eleven or twelve year old boy in Smithton, burgeoning breasts commanding most of their attention. On that score, Selena, almost eleven, was at the head of the class, a fact not unnoticed by Felix Williams, fourteen years her senior and ten years Isabel's junior. Not that either mattered to him after a long shift in his new night security position at the aircraft engine plant. A little female companionship and a stiff drink was all he needed.

A few minutes later, he stepped up the creaky front steps of the first floor porch of the aging two-family house. Felix, once Isabel's live-in lover, had moved out to his brother's place when the DOF placement of the kids seemed imminent. The move was pretty much in name only, because there was scarcely a night when Felix didn't stay with Isabel. Isabel, having heard Felix coming, opened the door for him and threw her arms around his waist. He kissed her, turned and winked at Selena who was standing in the kitchen doorway and tossed his jacket on a rocking chair, revealing the badge and nametag on his uniform shirt.

"Hey, Mama, how about that tequila and another kiss."

"Hey, boy, I ain't your mama." Isabel grinned, "The kiss comes first, then the drink."

Felix looked over at Selena again, and when he had turned back, Tina caught her sister's eye and stuck out her tongue, pretending to wretch. Selena frowned, then stifled a giggle.

Isabel gave her boyfriend a long, moist kiss on the mouth before going to a cabinet and returning with a half-empty fifth of tequila, worm and all. Felix twisted the sticky cap off and took a swallow. Wiping his lips, he took a bite of yesterday's pizza that Isabel had re-heated and put in front of him. He took another drink from the bottle, belched, and devoured the rest of the first slice. He noticed a drawing on the table, Tina's most recent effort. Roses and violets, as usual, dominated the scene, a hint of sunshine reflecting off a particularly dark crimson rose, the ray struggling through an otherwise dark and ominous background of clouds.

"Man, you're good girl," he said to Tina, "but this is some seriously depressing shit. You know, I been thinking, maybe I brighten your day. Maybe I move in full time," Felix suddenly announced. He took a long swig, got up, and stumbled against his chair.

Selena and Valentina stopped their chatter. Little sister Juanita, who had just come into the kitchen, stopped still.

"You know that's a problem with the girls here, "Isabel answered. "Nothing I'd like better than you being here, but man, with DOF coming around, I get into big time trouble. I worry now you stay here too much."

"Hey, I know we can pull it off. The girls, they love me. Nothing they'd like better than having me around all the time." He blew a kiss at the sisters and finished off the tequila.

"Felix, you don't know what you're saying. It's the booze. You been drinking too much lately. You're gonna lose your job. You gotta lay off."

"Shit, the only thing I'm going to lay is you," Felix leered, "and DOF can kiss by ass."

"Why don't you just shut up, you damn drunk," Tina shouted.

Selena gasped and grabbed her sister.

"Leave me alone," Tina screamed, just as Felix slapped her across her face.

"You smart mouth little bitch, I'm gonna show you a little game we used to play on my street with wise-asses."

Isabel made a move to intercede, but Felix shoved her and warned her not to get in his way.

"Gonna tell me to shut up? We'll see if you do that again," he growled and twisted Tina's wrist. "You come with me."

He yanked her into the living room and forced her to the floor.

"Isabel, you go right now and get me a bunch of pins from your sewing kit, a cardboard box and three or four sharp knives."

Isabel and her nieces were all crying. "I'm not going to let you hurt her. You're drunk. She didn't do anything that bad," Isabel pleaded.

"Ain't no kid going to tell me to shut up. I'm not going to touch her. Just get me the stuff," he shouted.

Felix kept a hold on Tina's arm until his girlfriend came back into the living room after a few moments. He told all the others to get out then turned to his petrified captive.

"Get under there," he ordered," motioning toward an end table near the couch, "and get on your hands and knees."

"But I won't be able to move. I'll be squeezed under there," she said, her voice quaking.

"You catch on real fast. Now go."

While Tina hunched under the table, Felix made two cardboard strips from pieces he tore from the box. He shoved more than a dozen pins through one piece, close enough together so a small hand couldn't fit between. He took four knives and thrust them through the other piece.

"Now, little big mouth, have fun with this. Maybe you'll be the one to shut-up next time."

Valentina, hysterical and already aching after just a few minutes under the table, watched in horror as Felix placed the board with the pins on the floor in front of her so that if she reached out, her hands would be impaled. She couldn't turn, but she heard Felix moving something behind her, then felt the slightest sensation of something grazing her buttocks.

"So, we're done, and I haven't touched you," he said. "In case you're wondering what's behind you, the board with the knives is propped right behind you. You move back, and you won't be sitting down for a long time. Now think about how to talk to me and don't bother asking me if you can get out of there. You'll get out when I'm good and ready."

Felix turned and went out of Valentina's sight. She heard low conversation coming from the kitchen and saw both of her sisters' feet go by as they headed toward the front yard. She dared not to try to look up when her aunt came into the room a few minutes later, and instead of being comforted, she heard Isabel say that maybe discipline was what she needed.

*** 

The monotonous whir of the electric fan Isabel had placed in front of Tina to provide some measure of relief almost caused her to doze off. She forced herself to stay awake, afraid of slipping forward or backward. Her tears had stopped, but excruciating terror remained. All she could think was that her whole body was in misery. Valentina had been left in her tortured position for almost two hours. Isabel was afraid to defy her lover and Felix had gone to sleep.

Valentina was startled and almost banged her head when the front door slammed and a voice screamed, "What the hell! Who did this to you?"

Before she could answer, her cousin Ernesto threw the knife-laden cardboard aside and pulled Tina out from under her prison.

Tina's body heaved and she seemed to shrivel, clinging with all her young might to her savior.

"Felix, he did it. I didn't do anything bad. I hate him."

"Stay here," Ernesto ordered his young cousin, just as Isabel came into the room.

"Ma, I'm going to kill him. How could you let him do this? Hasn't the kid gone through enough? Where is the bastard?"

"I tried to stop him," Isabel lied, "but he was out of control. He would have hurt everyone. He's not a bad man. Just had too much to drink."

"Answer me, Ma, where is he?" Ernesto swung his fist at the couch.

"You got a problem, kid?" a voice snarled from the bedroom hallway. "C'mon tough guy, I'll beat the shit out of you."

Ernesto turned toward Felix, who was only slightly less drunk than before, and before anyone could react, he grabbed a knife from the cardboard and slashed at the tormentor, barely missing an arm.

Felix dove for the floor and yelled for Ernesto to stop. Isabel grabbed her son from behind and held him back before he could make another thrust. The children shrieked while Felix crawled on his hands and knees toward the front door. In his haste and stupor, his right palm landed squarely on the cardboard with the pins and he howled in pain, little droplets of blood spotting the floor in his wake.

"Stay away from me," Felix yelled, "you're crazy. I'm leaving."

"Damn you, you'd damn well better get out," Ernesto screamed.

Felix scrambled to his feet, Isabel trailing after him. She yelled at him not to leave her, all the while keeping an eye on her son who had turned to consoling the kids, being satisfied that Felix wouldn't be around anymore.

"Hey, if I don't get respect, I'm not comin' back here," he slurred, "specially if Ernesto is around."

Before Felix could reach his car, a police cruiser, siren wailing, came around the corner and blocked the driveway. A burly, well-muscled red-haired officer stepped out of the passenger side. His rangy, African American partner climbed out of the driver side. The first officer announced that they'd received a complaint about a disturbance and asked what was going on.

"Just a little argument," Isabel said, "everyone's calmed down."

"How'd that happen?" the driver asked, pointing to the blood dripping across Felix's arm.

"Just a little accident, no big deal," Felix answered, his head much clearer now.

"No big deal, huh," Ernesto shouted from the doorway. "You might want to see this, officers."

Isabel glared at her son, furious at what she knew would happen.

While the burly policeman kept an eye on Felix and Isabel, his partner followed Ernesto into the house. The three young girls stood on the porch and peered into the living room. They watched as Ernesto showed the cop the blood-stained home-made pin cushion and the improvised knife rack, one blade lying on the floor where Ernesto had dropped it. Tina shook when Ernesto gestured toward the end table, as he described the scene he witnessed when he opened the front door.

The officer went back outside, had his partner arrest Felix, read him his rights and then made a call to the local DOF office.

"We ought to arrest you, too," the driver said to Isabel, "just for allowing that creep in the house with the kids, and that might just happen after we investigate further. For now, the state will handle you and the children."

Waiting until two officials from DOF arrived, the policemen moved Felix into their cruiser and drove away.

The DOF interview didn't last very long and the distraught sisters were bundled up with their belongings to be brought to the DOF office to stay until a place could be found for them to live. It was almost dinner time. A young caseworker disappeared and returned a short while later with some fast food burgers, fries and sodas for the sisters. Another worker had been busy going through her lists of emergency foster parents, hoping to house the girls together for at least a short time, but she wasn't having much luck. Because the local supervisor was out on a call, it was certain that the kids would have to sleep on cots kept for that purpose in the DOF office. Worn out, after Tina and Juanita stopped eating following a only few bites and Sellie had finished her meal, the three of them lay down on the cots and fell sound asleep.

\*\*\*

Juanita was the first to waken and she crawled alongside Tina, whose eyes fluttered open and then gave her young sister an embrace.

"Tina, what's going to happen to us? I'm scared they're going to send us to some strangers and we won't be together."

Valentina stroked Juanita's hair and told her everything would work out, that they had to be strong.

Aroused from a deep sleep, Selena lifted her head and started to complain as if she'd forgotten where they were, then propped herself up on an elbow.

"Hey, you guys, we stick together. Not Isabel, not Felix, not Simon gonna break us up."

"What about Ma? Just because she's been good during her visits at DOF doesn't mean she's changed," Tina said. "She did a good job of breaking us up."

Protesting, Selena argued, "I think she's changed. She's sorry. She doesn't get that mad at us anymore."

Valentina, still trying to comfort Juanita, thought for a moment about what Selena had said.

"I don't know, maybe. I don't trust her, but what are the chances they would let her take us back?"

"If they can't find nobody, then maybe they'll give her another chance. I hope so. I hated Smithton. All my friends are in Blue Hills."

"Yeah," Tina answered, "but don't forget, Ma never let us go out with friends. Only time we saw them was in class. I don't know."

Juanita shifted in Tina's arms. "Ma never hit me. She was good to me. I miss being with her."

"You were little. You still are. It was different for you," Tina said. "Really, I don't know."

***

A little over an hour after Tina, Sellie and Juanita got out of the cots, the complete day shift arrived at the office, including the field office director. From a day shift caseworker, whose name none of them could pronounce, they learned that the supervisor was in discussion with the Blue Hills DOF director to try and decide on a placement. They sat for a few more hours and could see through a small window in her door that the supervisor was in frequent animated conversations on the phone. Almost an hour passed before the sisters heard a familiar voice from somewhere near the entrance. The three scrambled to their feet as Juanita led the way in a dash through the hall where Juanita jumped into Luz Diaz's arms.

***

Valentina no longer screamed when a lizard skittered across the dirt path that ran between the small house and the little cove. It had taken her several weeks to adjust to the palpable differences between life in Smithton or, for that matter Blue Hills, and the place that didn't even have a dot on a map but was known locally as San Ramon de la Playa. A little over four months after DOF, with few options, had granted Luz Diaz custody of her three girls, she picked up stakes and moved them to the place her father described so lovingly on the south shore of Puerto Rico. It seemed to the girls that the move had softened their mother and even though they missed the pace of city life, they agreed that the trade was worth it. Besides, school attendance was acceptably hit or miss, and not just because the trek to the little regional school was arduous along the rutted road from San Ramon. Schooling just wasn't important to the inhabitants of this sparsely settled area.

Tall trees along the shore shaded parts of the cove from the worst of the local heat and Tina looked forward to the dip in the shallow waters that Luz now allowed her to take without supervision. All the girls had taken to the water like fish and Tina had become a strong, if self taught, swimmer. Although it never occurred to her consciously, it was a fact that the swims in the warm water were the only times when she never thought about the terrible things that had dominated her young life.

Today, Tina pulled off the plain white tee shirt that covered the brightly flowered bathing suit that she was starting to fill out in a womanly way, and dove into the water. As usual, she opened her eyes and admired the soft sandy bottom that was clearly visible through the clean turquoise ripples of the cove. She thought the only problem with the clear water was that it gave no reflection, and it made her favorite sport of mirror gazing impossible. Tina swam back and forth near the shore for a while then sat on her favorite spot in the sand, letting the heat evaporate the water on her body and enjoying the feel of her long, wet hair on her shoulders. The squawk of birds in the trees above her had become comforting background noise. It wasn't long before she slept, the kind of deep, refreshing sleep it had taken her a very long time to achieve.

*** 

Dinner time later that day was a clamorous affair. Luz greeted her children with the news that her mother and father would be joining them for a few weeks before making their long-anticipated move back to the mainland. Isabel had agreed to take them in and Grandpa had insisted on making the difficult trip from San Juan to see the island family before leaving for Massachusetts. Very few events were totally sweet for the young sisters, and this would be no different. Their grandparents were the only relatives, Ernesto and Aunt Carmen excepted, who had never brought pain into their lives, and nobody made them laugh like their beloved *abuelo*. While *Nani* and *Abuelo* hadn't been to see them often since the girls' arrival on the island, the visits were welcomed and now those were about to end.

Small as their place was, some things don't change, and Luz insisted that her brood keep the house military-clean. She never had to ask the kids more than once to put things in order since the failure to do so met with punishments any military court would have considered inhumane. As soon as the last vestiges of dinner had been cleared and cleaned, Selena led her sisters in a sweep of the four rooms to make sure that when their grandparents arrived the next day, all would be in order. They gave a collective and silent sigh of relief when Luz gave a rare word of praise for their efforts, and then settled down to various quiet activities until it was bedtime.

*** 

About an hour or so after the raucous welcome the next day, the family sat around the kitchen table, finishing their lunch. Grandpa Diaz rubbed his hands together, took a sip of strong coffee, then cleared his throat.

"Did I ever tell you I was a slave?"

Tina and Sellie laughed.

"Only every time we see you," Tina smiled.

"I don't care. I want to hear it again," Juanita chirped.

"Of course, of course, I'll tell," *Abuelo* Diaz said and he leaned forward to share the dark stories of his past as a teenager in a province not far from where the clan now sat huddled around the kitchen table.

"Oh that story, it only scares the kids, and I think you make most of it up," Grandma scolded, but the little man with a thousand wrinkles just waved his wife off and started the story his grandchildren could recite by heart.

"This is the true story of my life; nothing I say is make believe."

"Why you want to tell it, anyway?" his wife asked.

"So maybe people understand, it's not a way to live, to be treated bad. Maybe they don't treat anyone else bad."

Valentina tried not to look at her mother, who pretended not to listen to her father, as Grandpa Diaz began the familiar story.

"I was only fourteen, and my mami and papi were dead, killed in that terrible storm. One of my sisters, too. The rich man who owned the sugar cane plantation, he lost some help, but no matter, he was a bad man and all he cared about was his business. He had slaves before, and now, with my mami and papi gone, I had nobody to protect me. His foreman found me looking for food a few weeks after the storm. He hit me with a club, cut my chin open. I passed out and next thing I know, I'm in this mud hut, flies crawling in my cut, and a big man with a knife standing over me and this other boy who I didn't know. Turned out to be Pablo San Remo. He became the biggest drug dealer in all of Puerto Rico, maybe the Caribbean, finally killed by the Colombians."

"Anyway, they never let me out of their sight for the next three years. They beat me if I worked too slow. I cut cane, hauled the stuff to carts to push to the mill. They only fed me water and rice, sometimes fruit so I wouldn't get sick. I never learned to read. That's why I am proud of you young ones. Just work, sweat, get soaked, be beaten. Made me tough."

"But nice, too," Selena said, throwing her arms around his neck.

Grandpa laughed and hugged back.

"Well, anyway, I never thought I would get away from that place. But God would not let me and Pablo and the others suffer forever. Bugs started to destroy the crops, for which we were beaten, and then another bad hurricane came that destroyed most of the plantation. The owner killed himself one night and during the confusion, most of us ran away. I hid and ran for weeks until I reached San Juan. I found some work, married your grandma, had kids. We lived from hand to mouth while I saved some money to get to New York. And then the job at the mill in Blue Hills."

"Grandpa, nobody will ever make me a slave," Tina declared, "Nobody has the right to do that."

"No. No they don't, little jewel. No they don't."

*** 

Soon after her grandfather had finished the familiar tale, Tina took him by the hand and led him down to the cove. The old man listened while his granddaughter spoke quietly about how her life had been and how it was better here, now.

Grandpa Diaz looked down, absent-mindedly rearranging the dirt with the heel of his shoe. "Yes, it's better here," he agreed, and decided not to remind her that there are bad people everywhere.

A whistle of wind through the palms and a spatter of rain signaled an approaching downpour, and the old man and Tina hurried back toward the house where Sellie and Juanita were waiting for their own private time with *Abuelo*. Before going inside, he motioned for Tina to stop.

"So, will you miss me?"

"*Abuelo*, you know I will. I love you more than anything."

Grandpa Diaz took Valentina's hand and squeezed it gently, reassuringly, and motioned back at the cove. "This place, it's so calm and beautiful, I wish I could stay here. But I'm getting old and I don't breathe too good. Your Grandma needs help, too. The mainland is better for us now. You're lucky to be here, but I will miss you, too. But tomorrow we head for San Juan and the day after, just like that, we'll be with Isabel. I miss her, you know."

"Well, I don't miss her too much, but I really miss Ernesto. He writes me funny letters sometimes, but nothing too personal. Ma reads them all."

Grandpa didn't tell Tina how relieved he was that the family had moved to the island. He thought Luz would behave better and so far so good. The girls seemed relaxed and there were no men around to bother them. If Luz reading a few letters was the worst of it, they could all be hopeful. And somehow, she hadn't gotten into the drug business like too many of her siblings, the eldest boy already behind bars and one awaiting trial.

"*Abuelo*, I think Ma won't stay here a long time. Maybe I'll see you again soon."

Scooping Tina into his arms and kissing her hair, he answered, "Yes, at least for a visit. Now it's time to say good-bye to your sisters."

\*\*\*

About a month after the elder Diaz couple had moved back to Massachusetts, just before supper on another blustery, sticky, rainy Puerto Rico day, there was a knock on the rattling screen door at the front of the little house, the oddly comfortable house that had become the first place any of the four female occupants could call a peaceful home.

"Who could be coming here?" Luz wondered aloud. "I'll answer it."

The sisters peered from behind their mother and instantly recognized the face, even though it was now covered by several months of wiry black growth.

Tina screamed and bolted through the kitchen to the bedroom she shared with Selena.

"Papi, Papi," Juanita celebrated.

"What are you doing here?" Sellie sneered.

"Yeah, what the hell are you doing here?" Luz sputtered, not sure whether she wanted to hug or kill Simon Texiera.

Simon pulled Juanita up into his arms and his daughter reciprocated with an unrelenting squeeze around his neck.

"Look, baby, I heard you were here and I ain't staying long, so don't worry."

"How'd you find us?" Luz demanded.

"I was in San Juan and this guy I know knows your old man. The old guy was flapping his mouth to him about visiting you up here. I guess he knew I missed you, Luz, so he told me. Look, that daughter of yours, she caused all my problems. Don't believe all she and the other one tell you. That's all I come here to say. Man, I do miss you."

"Simon, I know what I saw," Luz said and swung her fist.

Simon caught Luz's arm in mid-air, grabbed her by the hair and pulled her lips toward his. He crushed his mouth on hers, and she barely resisted before giving in altogether.

"Ma, what the hell are you doing?" Selena shouted.

Luz pulled away from the embrace and shuddered. "Simon, I don't understand nothin'. You shouldn't have come here. Please leave, right now."

"See, baby, you want me just like I want you. I'm leaving, but you'll come looking for me, with or without your girls."

Simon winked at Juanita, then scooped her up. "I love you baby. Papi will be coming around again sometime. Now back to Mama. Adios, Luz."

Tina heard the screen door swing shut and peered into the kitchen. "Mami, I hate him. I hate him," she cried.

"Just be quiet and finish putting the dishes on the table. I got stuff to think about."

# CHAPTER SEVEN

*Spring - 2003*

A few weeks, occasionally up to two months, was the duration of stay for a kid in the Hillview state youth shelter. With barely enough space in a room for a marginal wardrobe, and school classes day-in and day-out in the cinderblock, one room basement school, the young residents rarely had the opportunity to vent their adolescent energy. Placement in a foster home or other more permanent arrangements normally came swiftly. In some rare cases, the older teens were hard to place. Tina was such a case, now in mid-April finishing her third month. Tina kept us up to date with constant tales of discontent on the one hand, and camaraderie on the other with one girl about her age. Her new friend had already overcome a drug addiction but, like Tina, was difficult to place.

Despite Roberta's constant prodding, I refused to give in to the possibility of Tina becoming a permanent resident in our home. Besides, DOF had been true to its commitment. We, and sometimes Bobbie alone, had seen Tina almost every weekend and she had even been allowed to spend a few weekends at our house. Once, Selena, with whom Valentina had some contact, asked if she could join her sister for one weekend. Both DOF and Sellie's foster family had agreed. Unfortunately, all the day of that visit, the sisters did little more than bicker. It was evident that the kids were being overwhelmed by the bleakness of their lives. Instead of relying on each other for support as they had for so long, now they seemed to be competing with one another over who had it harder. In truth, there was little to choose between one form of desolation and another. That spring weekend turned out to be the last time the girls would see each other until events almost a year later would thrust them together.

Most of our weekend visits with Valentina were, in fact, delightful. I marveled at how Tina appeared to behave like an average teenager, whatever that might mean. Appearances can be deceiving. During one of the visits on a particularly warm day in late March, a week after Selena's visit, we were all outside on the deck. Tina amused herself quietly for a time, watching a half dozen squirrels compete for the choicest spots for new nests in our generous supply of oak trees. Usually, when we were all together, Tina addressed Roberta, but this time, she chose me.

"Dad," she said, "what is it like to be as free as those squirrels? I mean, to live where you want, see the sky, the grass, the trees all the time? I hate that place. I mean, the people who run the shelter are mostly okay, but man, I feel like I'm in prison and I didn't do anything wrong."

I glanced over at Roberta. I thought back to that first conversation alone with Tina where simple jokes about George Washington had been enough to satisfy her. This time, I answered as best I could.

"No, Tina, you didn't. You didn't do a darn thing wrong. Maybe something will work out soon."

"Dad, I don't think I can wait. I'm just so unhappy. Without you guys, I just don't know."

Then, it all gushed out. Tina started to quiver, leaned forward, her head face down on the deck table and cried in waves of pure desperation. For a moment, she seemed to hold her breath, then covered her head with her forearms as if trying to make herself invisible.

Roberta stared at me, lips drawn tight, while she stroked Tina's shivering back. My own eyes dampened and I, in turn, ran my fingers gently across my wife's neck. Roberta shifted away from my touch. After several minutes, Tina lifted her head. Half laughing, half crying, she tried to apologize.

"There's nothing to apologize for, sweetheart," Bobbie whispered.

Tina nodded her head and said, "I know, but I shouldn't cry like that. It just came out."

"Tina, I understand, and I'm certain Dad does, too. You're entitled to be frustrated. Something will work out soon. How about going upstairs and getting some rest? We'll eat dinner and then maybe stop for ice cream on the way back to the shelter."

"Okay, Mom, but will you stay with me for a little while?"

"Of course I will. I'll stay with you just as long as you want."

\*\*\*

I pride myself on being a pretty logical guy. Give me a legal problem to solve, and I can hack away the weeds to uncover the flowers just about every time. So why was I resisting so hard? Under the circumstances, the only proper answer to Tina's situation was beating me over the head, and I just wanted it to go away. Roberta came back downstairs after seeing Tina off to bed and gave me that look that I'll never forget, I knew what was coming, yet I didn't feel quite ready.

"For God's sake, Hal, we have to get her out of there. She's falling apart. I'm afraid she's going to hurt herself. Almost as bad, she just told me her mommy dearest is back in the state and is making noises to get Tina back. She must be plain out of people to abuse. How the heck she dared crawl out of her hole and without worrying about being arrested herself is beyond me. I gather she had fled down to Florida, but came back with the little sister when she learned she wasn't facing arrest." Indeed, Jim Covain later confirmed to us that now seventeen year old Selena had refused to press charges and the State's Attorney closed the file.

So there were still things Tina would share with Roberta and not me. I thought maybe she was playing us off against each other, but that seemed too devious for her. Having Luz back wasn't exactly news I welcomed for Tina's sake, but on the other hand, maybe if she had a chance to prove she had turned a corner, Bobbie would let the situation play out for a time. Anyway, I just shook my head to acknowledge the news.

"Hal, that woman is no good."

"Well, maybe she's changed," I said, "but we have no control anyway."

"Look, I'm going to speak with Diane Paquin. Just so we can see what the options are. I don't want to wait to see what Luz is going to do, not a day longer if I can help it. I am not going to see that child suffer any more."

The proper answer shouted at me all the more. But, sometimes, I suppose my hearing isn't so great.

"Bobbie, I'm not quite ready to make the move you want. I need a little more time. Fine, if you want to speak to Diane, or Steve Baron. I'll join you. But, and this is my bottom line, I'll agree to make a case for us to take Tina in only if everyone, Diane, Steve, Jim Covain, Lydia Hernandez, all agree that there is no other imminent solution. But then only for so long as it takes for DOF to find another family."

Of course, I understood that the chances for finding another home were small, and I still can't explain exactly why I made that last effort to resist.

The new look in Roberta's eyes told me that maybe I'd given as much of the right answer as she could have hoped for. She squeezed me and said she knew I would come through. I still felt small. I gave her a hug back and grunted that Valentina was due back at Hillview by noon the next day.

*** 

It was near ten at night on the Wednesday after that weekend when our phone rang. It wasn't that unusual, Eddie often called from California around that time. Roberta picked up the receiver, said "Yes? Oh my God no. No she isn't here. I spoke with her yesterday about seeing her again. Please let me know as soon as you find her."

"Bobbie, what's happened to Tina?"

"She's run away. She was at dinner and now she's disappeared. It's dark. I'm scared. And dammit, I'm mad, too."

I was afraid, too. I hadn't realized until then just how much I'd come to love that kid. Bobbie and I held each other for a moment. All we could do was wait and worry.

*** 

Thursday was a working day for both of us, which was just as well. Meetings occupied me for most of the morning and Roberta, of course, was busy with her classes. My thoughts kept drifting to Tina, praying that she would be found soon. I was angry with her, too. What was left of any effort to concentrate on business was rapidly losing the battle when, at about 11 o'clock, my secretary interrupted my latest meeting to tell me I had an urgent call from Roberta. I could feel my heart racing as I hurried from the conference room and into my office where I picked up my outside line.

Without waiting for Bobbie to say anything, I screamed, "Is she all right?"

"Yes, thank God, yes."

"Tell me."

"First off, Hal, DOF wants us to consider taking her in starting tonight. The shelter doesn't want her and anyway, she's had enough there."

I think that I let that slide for the moment, don't quite recall. I wanted details.

"Bobbie, what happened? Where was she? How did they find her?"

"Hal, you won't believe this. According to Lydia Hernandez who called me, Tina took off through the woods without any particular destination in mind. Sort of funny, apparently she stayed in the woods to keep away from any bad guys who might be driving by. Lydia said she got pretty scratched up and dirty in the brush. Anyway, I guess she was near enough to the main road that sometime near midnight, she spotted a gas station that was still open. Get ready for this, Tina went to the station to call her mother, of all people, to come get her."

"You've got to be goddamned kidding."

"Wait, it gets more interesting. So she told the attendant some story about having been lost and he let her use the phone to call Luz. Maybe the woman's got some sense now, I don't know, but she told Tina to wait. Instead of showing up herself, she had the police get her. They tried to take her back to the shelter, but they refused to let her in. The police wound up having DOF get her. I guess she was pretty steamed at her mother at first, but I'm told she's calmed down. That's about all I know from Lydia. Of course, except that the shelter is refusing to keep Tina any longer and there is no place else to go, at least not now."

It didn't matter. I had made up my mind.

"Roberta, okay, Tina can come stay with us, but there is something you have to agree to first. We drop our regular foster care license and get classified as special case for Tina alone."

"Hal, you know what that means. We can't take any other kids. I'd prefer that we sit down and—"

"Bobbie, stop—"

Before I could finish she continued, "...talk. But you've done just about everything I could ever have wished, so if that's what you want, that's what it will be. Shall I call Lydia? There'll be a lot of things to discuss."

As relieved as I could be under the circumstances, I agreed, "Yeah, go ahead. I'll try and make it home a little early. I never, ever thought I'd be starting a second family after turning fifty. I need my head examined."

"But not your heart, Sweetheart, not your heart."

***

Maybe my memory isn't clear, but I think that as soon as Tina got out of Jim Covain's state car and walked with her bulging trash bag up our front walk, all of my doubts disappeared. It felt like a true homecoming. The tears, so many tears these days, which at first trickled from Bobbie's eyes, flowed steadily the more that Valentina's beaming smile widened. When Tina stepped into the front hall, she dropped the bag and gave me a crushing hug.

"Thank you, thank you, thank you so much, Dad, Mom," Tina said as she loosened her hold. "I promise, I will do anything you want. You saved me. You're the only people I can trust."

"Sh, sh," Bobbie said, pressing her index finger across her lips. She embraced our "daughter" and told her everything was going to be fine. In silence, she held Tina's hands for a moment, then said, "Okay, time to get down to business. Go upstairs and pick whatever room you want. I'll get that bag emptied and start a wash."

I'm afraid we'd forgotten all about Jim Covain who was taking this all in with his hand still in place on the front door knob. He cleared his throat and told us that before he left, there would be a number of things to discuss and hoped we would afford him the time he needed. Bobbie and I exchanged glances. We couldn't believe Jim Covain and dear Mrs. Harwood worked at the same place.

"Absolutely," I said, and offered to get him coffee, which he accepted.

Roberta led him to the family room where we commenced to have a reality check. If I thought bringing up our boys was a challenge, it soon became clear that they'd been a piece of cake compared to things we were likely to face with Tina. I leaned forward, trying to absorb everything Jim was telling us. Bobbie wrote a detailed list as we chatted, and we frequently interrupted with questions that he answered in detail. At one point, Tina came back downstairs and Jim asked her to leave us alone for a little while. He invited her come back when we were finished to ask whatever was on her mind.

There were so many things needing an answer, things that hadn't seemed necessary during Tina's original stay. Would her mother and sisters be involved? Should I avoid being alone with Tina? What about counseling? How would she fit in at school? How much could we depend on support from DOF during rough times? What about dating and going to parties? How should we handle discipline? In my own mind, one question popped up constantly: Am I crazy?

School was a real issue. Valentina had always gone to schools with a heavy Spanish speaking population. In her new school in our lovely little suburb, Tina might be the only Hispanic in her classes. In fact, almost the whole school population was Caucasian. Jim told us that the way the system worked, Tina's home school district would have to pay for any of Tina's special needs and that she would have a surrogate parent appointed, that is, someone to make sure her educational needs were properly addressed. We could sit in at planning conferences, one to be held no more than a week from now, but all of the education decisions would be up to the new guidance department, the liaison from Tina's original school system, the surrogate and DOF.

As far as social life went, Jim suggested that we let things play out normally, just the way we would with any of our own kids. If ethnicity became an issue, we'd just have to see how that went. He said that counseling could address some of those issues, as well as once and for all getting Tina to talk about the things in her life that had been unspeakable so far. DOF would pay for all the counseling necessary.

The sound of Tina running downstairs again brought our discussion to a temporary halt. How a kid in her situation could light up a room was beyond me, but here she was, walking into that room of people who might be changing her entire life for better or worse and she said with the broadest smile, "Hey you guys, hurry up, I'm hungry."

Jim couldn't help grinning but said, "Just a few more minutes and I'll be out of here, I promise. Then you can stuff yourself silly."

"Okay", she answered, "but it better be quick. I am starving."

After she'd gone back upstairs, Jim shook his head, "Don't let that façade fool you. She's scared to death that she'll blow it again. There's one last thing I need to tell you. We've received word that Simon Texiera has been located and arrested in Puerto Rico and will probably be brought back to Massachusetts. Tina doesn't need to know for now, and Luz won't know for a while either. Depending on what we learn, both Simon and Luz may face some jail time and Tina and her sisters might have to testify against them. If that happens, she'll need more emotional support than ever."

"Thank God," Roberta said. "I'm just glad that monster's been caught. He makes my skin crawl. Don't worry, we'll give Tina all the help she needs. Will her life ever be normal?"

"Normal, I don't know. Difficult, for sure. Anyway, let's get her down here before she wastes away."

***

In the first few days after her return, Tina slid right into life with us. If she was worried about how we felt, she hid it well. She volunteered to help prepare dinners, our gain as it turned out. Food was one of her great talents, both creating and eating. Amazingly, unlike my sons, and me, too, I suppose, Tina never left a mess behind, although Bobbie and I thought that was probably as much a habit born of fear of her mother's neatness obsession than anything else. Valentina was anxious to settle in at her new school and never seemed openly to be bothered by the fact that indeed she was the only Hispanic student at the high school. As it turned out, school was the one place where none of the hard facts of her life ever encroached.

***

A week after our new daughter started school, DOF organized the first of what was to be three planning meetings centered on her curriculum. Roberta and I were invited to sit in, but primarily to be spectators. The chair of the meeting was actually the curriculum director from Blue Hills. As Tina's home school district, Blue Hills remained responsible for Tina's progress and, in fact, for awarding her a degree even if she were to complete school in some other town. I recognized some of the other people at the table from my boys' days at the school, but there were a few that were new to me. There was the vice-principal Joseph Hospidar, looking anxious to be over and done before the first idea was exchanged, the guidance chair, Miss Angelo, who had always been the first to call and congratulate us when one of my sons had achieved the latest in their string of academic awards, and a special education teacher who later introduced herself as June Hotchkiss.

Representing the state and Tina's interest were Jim Covain, Diane Paquin, and her surrogate parent, an elderly gentleman whose real purpose was at the time and to this day, a mystery to me.

One by one, they said their set pieces, with the exception of the surrogate, who I imagined did not, nor ever would, know as much about Valentina as I did. After giving their individual evaluations, the group got down to the business of setting up Tina's curriculum. They went round and round for almost forty-five minutes, beating to death one option or another. There never was much doubt that Tina would have to go into some sort of special education program, as bright as she was, all because of her shaky educational history and as a result of a lack of knowledge and ignorance of so many things.

As these experts went about shaping her future, it occurred to me that young Tina had no control over her life now, and in fact, never had. Her life was happening to her, instead of being lived by her, as if she were merely some mute rock, forced to accept whatever the elements threw at her, until she simply eroded into history.

"That's going to end." The thought tumbled out of my mouth. Everyone at the table was staring at me. "Sorry, I was just thinking about something. Didn't mean to think out loud. Anyway, I was wondering where we, I mean Roberta and I, fit in. I mean, do we have any say in how she is progressing? Are we entitled to school conferences?"

"Certainly you are," Jim Colvain answered, "it's just that you need to let us know what, where, when. You know the drill, so we can decide if we need to be there. Listen, you two are as competent as any foster parents we have, and we value your judgment. But, like it or not, we, DOF I mean, still has to make the calls on Tina's future, including how issues at school are handled. But believe me, you'll have as much freedom as we can permit."

For a moment, I thought the surrogate was going to object, but Miss Angelo, the person we knew best at the table, volunteered that there couldn't be a finer set of parents to bring proper perspective to Tina's situation. Bobbie grinned at me, and I relaxed for the first time in a long time.

***

When Tina and Sellie had first come to stay with us, I hadn't really considered it to be any sort of long term arrangement. I knew this would be different. We'd be living with a girl, a teen-aged girl at that, who had more negative history and future obstacles to overcome than we could ever have envisioned. The first few days at high school went well according to both Tina and her teachers, whom Roberta had phoned several times. Monday of the second week brought news that one girl in her special ed classes was making fun of Tina's accent, slight as it was. Tina had gone to push her, but fortunately the girls were separated before anyone got hurt and a stern lecture to both of them seemed to calm things down. It turned out, however, that the girl had told her boyfriend who spent a great part of the following day taunting Tina, enlisting some of his buddies to join in the fun. From what we learned, Tina handled them well, better than one could have expected. I guess she realized after the incident from the day before that she had to figure out a way to survive in her new environment, just as she had been accustomed to doing so many times before.

We might never have known about the problem if Bobbie hadn't heard Tina laughing out loud in her room shortly before dinner. When Bobbie inquired, Tina, still giggling, said she was just thinking about how she'd been teased and that the look on those guys' faces was worth it. After hearing Tina's story, Bobbie laughed, too, and called me up to hear Tina's tale of what had happened.

"Dad," she said, "I was getting sick and tired of the teasing, but I didn't want to get into no trouble." She suppressed another smile and made a gesture as if she was patting herself on the back. "So, I was walking out to the bus after school when these four guys who'd been harassing me showed up and started again. I looked from one to the other, gave them my sweetest smile, and in my best Spanish, I told them that, and I'm sorry for my language, their penises were smaller than a straight pin, their balls were like little peas and their brains were made out of shit. When they asked me what I'd said, I told them that I had said I knew that they were really good guys and that I could teach them some neat Spanish stuff if we could be *amigos*. I think using the Spanish word did the trick. They were so surprised that they said maybe I was kind of cool and they were sorry. One of them was staring at me like he has a crush or something. I think his name is Josh. I hope they never find out what I really said." In her typical way, she finished by declaring that maybe they weren't so bad after all, just a little ignorant.

Of course, I'd been tempted to laugh, too, but instead just told her that I was pleased that she had figured out a way to make lemonade out of lemons. Under the circumstances, I assured her that her use of rather specific descriptive language, albeit in Spanish, was okay, so long as it was limited to such circumstances. No longer able to hold back, I laughed, causing a chain reaction and we roared until our sides ached.

Sometimes, actually more often than I'd have ever expected, Tina would succeed in ways I couldn't have really expected. From my viewpoint, she continued to exhibit that wonderful, maddening combination of street smarts and ignorance of the world at large that she'd shown from the first time we'd met over two years ago. Discovering ideas that seemed so fundamental as to require no special insights, still caused Valentina, with her eyes and mouth wide open in disbelief, to wonder, are you serious?

She had joined the Glee Club and was enthusiastic about her studies, with English and Art being her favorite subjects. As always, she was a torrent of questions about everything and did a great deal of writing and artwork whenever she wasn't raiding the refrigerator. Roberta and I swelled with pride when Tina brought home her first teacher's report that showed excellent progress in all of her academics, along with an envelope containing a private note to us from Miss Hotchkiss that read:

"What a jewel. Valentina is a leader, both in her studies and among her peers. They look up to her. Some kids create resentment. Students warm to her. She is doing as well as one might expect overall, but her ability to write and express herself surpasses any student I've ever had. She doesn't know yet, but I nominated her for school Student of the Month and I've just been informed that she's been selected. I am so pleased for her and both of you as well."

What a moment. I think of it often. The only thing that she didn't seem to be doing well, even though kids liked her, was making many real friends.

***

When Tina first arrived back at our home, among the many things we had had to arrange with the help of Jim Covain was both a complete physical evaluation, which showed Tina to be a totally healthy young woman, and a regular regime of psychological counseling. And there was the issue of how and when Tina could or should have contact with her family. Family connections would become the principal issue in her counseling sessions.

Valentina had so many unresolved issues. She was wary of men and she craved men. Her mother scared her, but Tina loved her anyway. Tina missed her sisters, but Sellie in particular drove her crazy. She appreciated Bobbie and me, but she felt strange away from the Hispanic community. DOF had arranged for her to meet with a psychologist in a nearby town who specialized in teen counseling. The woman's name was Renee Bronislaw and, fortunately, Tina seemed to like and trust her. Roberta was shuttling Tina to and from the sessions and had met the psychologist. Bobbie liked her, too, although she thought the woman very young.

According to what Tina was willing to share with us, the initial focus was on Tina's relationship with Luz. Apparently, Jim Covain had to decide if and when Tina could have supervised visits with her mom. From what we knew, Selena was already meeting with Luz. I guess I understood why some sort of reconciliation was being considered, but the idea that DOF might ever consider a permanent restoration of parental rights seemed outrageous. After the second of the weekly sessions, Tina wanted to sit down with us to talk about her feelings about Luz.

I thought it would be pretty awkward, but Bobbie insisted that it was up to Valentina, so as we sat around the dinner table the evening after the second session, Tina, almost too unemotionally, told us some things that made me feel like a babe in the woods.

"Mrs. Bronislaw asked me how I felt about my mother. I knew she would ask, but it made me think and even cry a little, because I try so hard not to think about her. When I think about her I get so mixed up, so confused. She's done so many bad things to me, or let so many bad things happen to me. But she's my mom and I love her."

I know how I felt when she said that, but I held my tongue.

"So," she continued, "at first I didn't know what to say. It makes me nervous when Mrs. Bronislaw doesn't say anything, like, you know, it's so quiet and I feel like I gotta say something. She just waits for me. I just said, 'I think I hate her, but I want to see her.' I don't know why that came out. I don't really hate her. She's even done some really good things. When she took us to live in Puerto Rico, she was good almost all the time. Just, she got such a bad temper and she's, you know, weak with guys. Guys. Why aren't the guys my Ma meets satisfied with her, like you guys are with each other? Well, anyway, Mrs. Bronislaw was still quiet, just gave me a Kleenex. I really didn't want to say any more, but finally I said that maybe I didn't hate her so much, but I really didn't trust her. Does that make sense to you guys?"

Roberta shook her head and told her she thought it made a lot of sense.

Tina smiled a little and went on. "Anyway, I wound up talking about a lot of stuff, good and bad about my mom. Things I never told anybody. Oh, DOF knows some of it, but I never told anyone else."

Without batting any eye, Tina told us about being examined by the school nurse after Simon had committed the last rape and how humiliating it had been. She shook a little when she told the horror story about her Aunt Isabel's boyfriend torturing her for hours by leaving her trapped under a table surrounded by sharp instruments. She glowed, as she always did when it came to her cousin, when she recounted Ernesto Diaz's rescue. She told us of countless beatings of her and Sellie by Luz with any hard object available for offenses *so serious* as not cleaning a small drip spot on the kitchen floor or not making a bed quite fast enough. And she talked of the endless nights of Simon disturbing her childhood sleep while Luz lay drunk in bed in the room next door, never believing Tina's complaints about Simon until the night Simon was forced to flee.

I could see Bobbie struggle to hold herself together, as did I, but Valentina remained absolutely detached.

"Mom and Dad, Mrs. Bronislaw finally opened her mouth. She asked me how it made me feel to tell about all of those terrible things. I cried a little more, but it's funny, I actually felt relieved. Not better, just glad not to be holding it in. So, anyway, we decided that next time we might talk about how I feel about seeing my mom. She said after we talk, maybe the week after that, before my session, you guys can come and talk about some stuff. I think someone from DOF has to be there, too, probably Jim."

That didn't surprise us because Jim Covain had told us to expect to meet with him and the psychologist occasionally. "Fine," I said while Roberta reached toward Tina to rub her shoulder.

Tina smiled again, then simply broke out laughing as if she couldn't believe she had shared so much of her misery. She suddenly noticed that, unusual for her, she hadn't eaten any of the dinner, and grabbed a now rather cold baked chicken breast without using a fork and knife, and took a large bite.

***

"Hey Dad," Tina tapped me on the shoulder while I was watching the news after dinner, "I want to play softball. You know, for the high school team. Tryouts are in a few days."

As usual, the girl was full of surprises. "Well," I said, "have you ever played before? You know, almost all of the kids playing for the high school team have been playing organized softball for several years. And the pitchers are fast."

"Yeah? Really fast?"

"Yeah. Really fast. And the ball they use really isn't soft, it's actually very hard."

"I don't care, I want to play."

"Tell you what. I think the high school team is too hard for you to make. But let's see if there isn't a less difficult league around town for you to play in. If there is, I can help you practice hitting and catching and understand some of the rules that maybe you don't know so well."

Valentina shrugged and told me that she wasn't afraid to try out, but agreed to see if there was an easier level around town.

The next day she called me at the office, very excited that indeed, there was an organized minor league that was much more suited to beginners. My evenings and weekends were being mapped for me. I supposed that Bobbie was standing nearby, feeling rather justified and superior at that moment.

\*\*\*

Monday the next week was a full day for Tina. Immediately after school, she had her counseling session and then, following dinner, was the first try out for the girls softball league over at the Shade Tree Elementary School.

That morning, Tina was nervous on both accounts.

"Ma, I don't know what I'm gonna say about meeting with my mom. I think she hates me, you know, for her maybe getting into trouble. What should I do?"

And then, in true Valentina fashion, without skipping a beat, she frowned and said, "Dad, what if I'm not good enough to make the team?"

"Don't worry about the team," I said, "it's mostly for new players. And as far as you and your mom are concerned, you'll have plenty of time to figure out with Mrs. Bronislaw what'll work best for you and your mother."

Avoiding my glance, Roberta looked down and toyed with her eggs.

\*\*\*

It couldn't have been clearer when Tina walked through the door that the counseling session had troubled her. She was tense and went straight to her room and didn't come out until she was called down to dinner.

When she came into the kitchen, she had no real expression in her eyes, but was clutching the baseball glove I'd given her the day before.

"C'mon, Dad, let's eat and go," she said, and quietly ate all the food on her plate.

When we'd finished, Tina gave us a weak smile, walked toward Bobbie and gave her a long hug. "Maybe we'll talk later," she whispered.

"Whatever you want," Bobbie answered.

Tina picked up the glove and motioned for me to follow her to the car. "C'mon, Dad," her light went on again, "let's show them what I can do."

On the way over to the school, Tina was back to asking all sorts of questions about softball. I explained that it was basically the same as baseball, to which she replied that she didn't know a thing about playing baseball except that home runs were good. So we talked about the different bases, balls and strikes, the different fielding positions and other basic stuff that she was trying very hard to absorb. In the little time we'd had since she had expressed her desire to play, I'd discovered that she could manage to catch the ball once in a while, had a very strong, almost masculine throwing arm, if totally erratic, and a bat that seemed to be more hole than aluminum. This shaped up to be an interesting adventure.

Valentina was literally on the edge of her car seat when we pulled into our parking space. Without a backward glance, she had me running after her toward the gym where sign ups and a little bit of warm ups were to take place. The coaches of the four teams comprising the league were standing in a corner, eyeing the erstwhile prospects, wondering, I suppose, which of these girls could carry them to rec league softball coaching glory. I admit that I was surprised and pleased that two of the coaches were women. There was a table with sign-up cards and other sheets to be filled out by doctors, and another table with assorted goodies, milk and punch. Tina nudged me and said that she knew a few of the girls, although not very well.

Most of the rather short evening was comprised of the coaches and other league officials talking about organization, try outs, sportsmanship, and other start up issues. They made it clear, much to Tina's relief, that the try-outs were only to see what the skills of each kid were so that they could try and balance the teams. But everybody who tried out would be on a team and every player was guaranteed to play at least a few innings a game and have at least one at bat a game. They announced the actual tryout times and adjourned for refreshments.

A rather tall, sweet-faced girl came walking toward Tina and me where we stood sipping punch under one of the basketball hoops. In a rather sing-song voice she extended a hand toward Tina and bubbled, "Hiee, I'm Kristin. You're the new girl, right? I think you're nice, at least you have a nice smile, so maybe we can be friends, and hang out or something." She took a deep breath and went on, "I mean, you don't have to if you don't want to, but you being new maybe I thought it would be cool."

Then, it seemed she noticed me for the first time, looked back at Tina and in a definitive tone declared, "Hey, your dad, he's cute, you look just like him," at which I'm sure I blushed and Tina just burst out laughing.

Tina being Tina, simply reached out her arms, and gave the surprised, and obviously pleased Kristin, a big hug. I can't say I was disappointed. Even though I didn't know the kid, and while she certainly seemed ditzy, she was totally refreshing and likable.

"Maybe, we can be on the same team. Heyee, what's your name? I forgot to ask."

Valentina laughed again and said "I'm Valentina, but you can call me Tina. That would be cool if we can be on the same team. Do you know how to play? I'm learning."

"Nope, never played much except a few times in recess. I'm pretty good beating my little sister in Wiffle ball, but she's only eight, so maybe that doesn't count."

A heavy-set man came toward us, shaking his head, but smiling.

"I see my girl has cornered you."

"Not at all," I answered, introducing myself, "she's a nice kid."

"Daddy," Kristin said, "Tina and me are going to be on the same team."

"It's 'Tina and I', and how do you know?"

"I just know. But gotta go. Got homework. English grammar, ha ha, Daddy. Bye,Tina."

We watched as Kristin floated away in the same way she had entered our lives.

\*\*\*

Tina tossed her glove on the couch before beginning. She had held herself together during the softball meeting, and as she emphasized during the ride home, she was happy as could be to have met Kristin. Now, other realities took over.

Ever since Tina had come back to live with us, Bobbie worried about the day that Tina would officially be able to see Luz. Sitting in the recliner, she fidgeted with her bracelet and motioned for Tina to sit near her. I sat on the far end of the couch.

"So, is there anything you want to share, sweetheart?"

"Mom," Tina began, "Mrs. Bronislaw was disappointed you guys couldn't make it today, but she's happy that you're coming next time. I was kind of scared without you because I thought she was going to push me to see my mom. And she did. Well, not push exactly, but she said that the only way to see if going back to her made sense, was to face her and talk about the things that bother me. Do you think Jim Covain would let her get me back?"

Bobbie leaned toward Tina and replied, "Do you want to go back? I think they won't have you do anything you don't want to do."

"Mom, I don't know. I'm still mixed up."

I thought to myself how strange the whole scene was, with Tina calling Roberta "Mom" so naturally.

"I want to have a family that loves each other. I got hurt so much with her. But she's my mom. I love you guys, but—"

"You don't have to say anything more," I interrupted. "You know, when we come to the next session, we'll help you figure out the best way to handle this. We know that visits with your mother are going to happen, and we'll do our best to help you get through it. It probably won't be as hard as you think."

"I guess. Just the last time I was with her was so bad, especially for Selena."

Roberta came over to the couch and sat between me and Tina. "Whatever happens, we will always be here whenever you want. Everything will work out."

Tina looked at us both and rubbed her eyes.

"It just makes me tired," she said. She sighed, gave us each a hug and went to her room for the night.

# CHAPTER EIGHT

*Winter 2000 and Spring 2001*

As seen from afar, the little knot of people standing in front of the local Burger King next to the DOF office might have been any tight-knit family in the midst of a joyous reunion. Luz Diaz squeezed her beloved Juanita and held her up for everyone to see. Tina and Sellie took turns hugging their little sister while their grandmother and grandfather wept. It had been almost a year since they had all been together; having been separated again not long after Luz had had enough of the quiet life on the island and returned to the States.

Behaving as best she could during the latest DOF intervention, Luz was able to convince the state officials that she should be reunited with her brood once again. Her on again, off again affair with the married man in the apartment above hers had been discreet enough not to attract attention. But, nine months after her girls had been removed following two drug and alcohol sprees, Luz was deemed to have complied with all of the court requirements. Valentina and Selena were returned to her in due course. Grandma had also moved in to supervise, and her estranged husband, Grandpa Diaz, came to visit often from his home with daughter Isabel in Smithton. The reunification with young Juanita was the last step in the recreation of Luz's family.

Grandma Diaz, always the stern one in the family, took Tina and Sellie aside.

"Girls, you see your Mami is happy now. It's gonna be hard, but we gotta help her. That girl, she's always been crazy, but she loves you. Maybe she don't know the best way, but she always been trying."

"She's been okay since we been back," Sellie said, "I guess she's trying, now that there's no more Simon."

"I love her, but I still get a little scared when I do something wrong," Tina offered, "but I think she is trying, too."

Grandma nodded and walked back toward Luz and Juanita. Grandpa Diaz winked toward Tina. *"Te amo,"* he said. Tina replied in kind. Her Grandpa always made her feel special. She would always love him more than anybody.

\*\*\*

Sellie checked to make sure nobody was awake. Grandma was snoring on the sofa and Luz had been in her room for a few hours already. She opened the door to the room Tina and Juanita shared in their three bedroom government assisted apartment and could see that they were both fast asleep. Quietly, she walked down the hall, into the kitchen and out the back door. She waited a moment on the middle landing where she could see the door to the second floor apartment. After a few minutes, the door opened, creaking enough to almost make her lose her nerve, and out stepped Ray Hicks, Luz's off and on lover, and at age 34, already the father of six children mothered by four different women.

"Hey baby," he whispered to Sellie, not yet turned fifteen, "you ready?"

It never particularly mattered to Ray that despite looking almost eighteen, his neighbor was not yet in high school. She was already well-endowed and clearly knew her way around. And that hot body was in love with him.

"C'mon, behind the dumpster," he directed, pulling her along.

It wasn't long before they were rolling on the ground, fondling one another and moving from one stage in their earthy adventure to another and to an ultimate climax.

Selena felt herself shaking, wanting even more, and her mate was more than willing. They spent almost two hours together before Ray said that they'd better get back inside before they were missed.

\*\*\*

"Hey Sellie," Tina said to her sister, "where were you?"

"What do you mean?"

"I mean last night. I woke up to get some water and I couldn't hear you, so I opened your door and you weren't there, or anywhere."

Sellie gave her younger sister a hard stare and then checked to make sure the rest of the Diaz women hadn't returned from the market even though she already knew that she and Tina were alone in the apartment.

"Why were you spying on me? What do you mean you couldn't hear me?"

Tina shrugged, "You always snore real loud, I can hear you through the door. I was worried I couldn't hear you. I wasn't spying."

"Well, it ain't none of your business where I was. I was around."

Now Tina was very curious, "Around where? It was like two thirty. You know Ma makes us stay in after ten."

Now Sellie's emotions got the best of her. She'd been aching to share how she felt about Ray with someone, and Tina was always her first choice.

"You gotta promise me you won't tell nobody. I could get in big trouble."

Now Tina was more than curious. "What is it, Sellie? Tell me."

"First promise."

"I promise I won't tell."

"Okay. I love Ray."

Tina laughed, "So you got a crush. He is handsome. But where were you?"

Sellie thought twice about continuing, but it was killing her.

"I was outside with Ray. We were doing it."

"What, are you dreaming?" Valentina yelled, "Why would he do that with you? You know he and Ma fool around, and you are way too young."

"Tina, be quiet. I ain't dreaming. I love him and he loves me. He don't love Ma. He told me so. Besides," she added with a purpose, "you weren't too young for Simon."

Tina stood up and whacked her sister across the mouth. "That is not the same and you know it. I hate you," she shouted.

Sellie started to retaliate, but stopped herself. 'I'm, I'm sorry," she said. "I know Simon was a bum, but Ray is different. He loves me and I love him."

"Don't be so dumb. He's using you. He should be arrested. I think I should tell someone. You're gonna get pregnant."

Sellie screamed and cried all at once, "You promised you wouldn't tell. He says he loves me and I can tell he means it. You tell anyone and I tell Ma he's been doing you."

"That's a lie," Tina yelled back.

"I don't care, you just keep your mouth shut, or I'll tell Ma anyway about you. She'll beat you so bad, she don't care about no truth."

Tina took one step toward her sister, then turned and ran outside.

***

The Diaz family had settled into a routine that pretty much kept them all peaceful and mostly out of each other's way. Luz had a full time job at a local factory. Grandma did most of the cooking, something she was much better suited for than her daughter. Selena and Valentina were off at middle school and Juanita was in half-day sessions at the overcrowded elementary school. Grandpa Diaz visited every few weeks with Aunt Isabel and occasionally cousin Ernesto visited as well. Aunt Carmen even came by a few times, although she and Luz maintained a wary distance.

Good neighbor Ray spent his time entertaining Luz and Sellie, although Sellie was becoming more of a chore than a few hours pleasure warranted. About six weeks after Sellie's confession to Tina, Ray decided that the young girl's now constant worry about their relationship was too much to handle, and that her more experienced mother was more to his liking anyway. He decided to break it off.

Sellie's sobbing woke the whole apartment.

Luz came out of her room, rubbing her eyes, with Grandma and the other girls trailing into the dark kitchen.

"What's wrong with you, Selena, can't you see it's three in the morning? Where the hell have you been? You got dirt on you and you're shaking like a sick dog."

"I hate him," Sellie yelled.

"Hate who, and where have you been?" Luz demanded.

Tina was now fully awake and couldn't believe what was happening. She wanted to be anywhere but in that room.

"Ray. I hate him. I hate him so much."

Grandma, grasping that something very bad was about to happen hustled Juanita out of the room. Luz gestured toward Tina to get out of there, too.

"What about Ray?" Luz spit the words out slowly.

Sellie trembled uncontrollably. "I love him, but he says he don't love me no more."

"What the hell do you mean, he don't love you no more? Are you out of your mind, some kid crush you got?"

Selena commenced to tell her mother the whole story. For once, Luz didn't react right away, too stunned, and hurt and jealous and mad. When she finally collected herself, she did the only thing she really knew how to do. She shoved her daughter to the floor as hard as she could, gave her a kick in the side, and bolted out the kitchen door and up the stairs.

Tina rushed back to comfort her sister. But, after what seemed like minutes of banging on a door, they could hear Luz flailing away at Ray, could hear Ray's latest wife beating on Luz, and then after apparently gleaning enough from Luz's ranting to understand what was happening, joining her neighbor in pounding on Ray. Adding to the chaos was the two of his kids living with Ray hollering in the background.

In the meantime, Grandma Diaz had dialed 911 and before the commotion had subsided, the bruised combatants felt themselves being hurled to the ground and cuffed.

One of the officers lifted Luz, black eye and split lip oozing blood, and she tried to rush back at Ray who was kneeling on the upper landing with his arms secured behind him. Before anyone could stop her, Sellie ran into the hall and tried to join her mother's futile attempt at resuming the attack on Ray. They were both restrained, but Ray's wife broke through and kicked her husband in the back, sending him face forward into the floor boards. The two officers regained control and proceeded to march Luz, Ray and his wife away. All the while Ray protested that he was only defending himself and Luz raged that Ray had raped her daughter. One of the cops gave Ray a little push. "You sorry bastard. We'll make damn sure your fun days are done for a long while," he growled. And this without knowing of Ray's liaison with the older Diaz female.

After the cruisers had departed with the prisoners, it was left to Grandma to calm the family. Tina felt a new identity with her older sister, even though unlike Tina, Sellie had asked for it. Grandma's thoughts wandered to whether or not the kids could be kept together with her if Luz had to be sent away, and she wasn't sure she could manage two young teens and the perpetual motion Juanita.

***

The day after the brawl, a young DOF worker arrived at the Diaz apartment. She was well aware of the family history and was prepared to remove the children. Grandma Diaz allowed her in with the greeting, "These kids ain't gonna be separated again. Their momma has been good, and besides, I can take care of them," a conclusion she'd reached at that instant.

The young caseworker paused for a moment to consider this unexpected offer. "Is it Mrs. Diaz?" and she went on without waiting for an answer, "Mrs. Diaz, with the history of this family, and your daughter's inattention to Sellie's conduct, it is unlikely that the children will be allowed to stay here even with you in the home with your daughter. At the moment, we're seeking suitable placements, but the kids can stay here with you until Luz is released. She's being arraigned later today and I wouldn't doubt that she'll be free soon after the hearing. If there hasn't been a placement by then, we will remove the children and make temporary arrangements for them."

Grandma Diaz started to cry. She protested that the kids couldn't take any more moving around and that she was sure Luz would behave.

"Well, her behavior has not exactly been exemplary, even if she can't exactly be blamed for her daughter's problem."

"But she been good," Grandma said, realizing that the worker didn't seem to know that Luz was having her own affair with Ray.

"I'm sorry, but removal is the only option. I'm going to call for transportation for the kids which will be here as soon as possible."

"You guys, you think you got all the answers. I'm tellin' you, Luz been good to them girls. You think you wouldn't attack a man you just found out raped your girl? Some kinda mother you would be."

The caseworker looked down at the floor, turned away and pulled out her cell phone.

*** 

Subdued as it was, the Diaz household was ecstatic that they wouldn't be broken up. Early that morning, three days after the brawl and Luz's release on bond early the next day, the family court judge had found that while Luz's handling of the news about her daughter was deplorable, it did not signify the sort of bad parenting that justified removal of the children, and that based on her recent history, she seemed to have met all of the conditions DOF had set for her when last reunited with her daughters. The bruise in the relationship between Sellie and Luz regarding the competition for Ray's attention had been reduced to an unspoken truce. The whole family focused on the court's favorable determination, even though they would still be subject to frequent, unannounced DOF monitoring. Luz had been let off with a wrist slap on her breach of the peace charge. For several weeks, relative calm prevailed in the small apartment, with Luz only occasionally snapping at the two older girls.

Toward the end of the second week in March, with excitement in the neighborhood building toward the annual festival, there were a few flurries and a breezy chill dampening the streets of Blue Hills. Luz arrived home from her factory job shortly after Valentina and Selena came home from school. Grandma Diaz was busy showing Juanita how to peel plantain.

"Goddam I'm tired. My boss was a pain in the ass. Do this, do that. Can't do nothin' for himself, the lazy bastard."

Grandma Diaz turned from the counter. "Watch your language. You want these kids to talk like you?"

"Leave me alone. I'll say whatever the fuck I want to say."

Grandma Diaz stepped closer to her daughter. "You been drinking? I thought you quit?"

"Mind your own business. I just stopped for a few drinks on the way home. That damn boss pissed me off."

Luz walked away and past the bedroom where Tina and Sellie had put their books down.

"What the goddamn hell is this mess. I told you not to make a mess. Why you got those coats on the bed, and get them books on the table."

"But Ma," protested Selena, "we just got home. We were about to clean up."

"I goddamn don't need none of your back talk and I goddamn told you to put that shit away right away. You know what you need?" Luz screamed. "You need a fucking lesson."

Luz made a move toward the old wooden chair that stood beside Selena's bed.

Tina started to wail and pleaded, "No Ma, don't, Ma don't."

Luz shoved Tina away and grabbed the chair. Sellie saw what was about to happen and turned and dove toward her bed, but not fast enough to avoid the blow of the chair smashing into her back. She shrieked in pain, but Luz told her to shut up and started to raise the chair again when suddenly the chair was yanked from her.

"Luz, what are you doing," Grandma Diaz yelled and slapped her daughter across her face hard enough to stun Luz.

Luz shook it off, glared at her two daughters and her mother, and Juanita bawling in the hallway just outside the room. Luz stormed out of the room and slammed the door to her own bedroom.

*\*\**

Sellie and Tina lay on Sellie's bed holding each other.

"Tina, I thought this would never happen again; that Ma had changed. My back, it's hurting so bad, I can't take this no more. I gotta tell someone. I'm afraid she's gonna kill us."

"Oh please, don't tell anyone. They'll take us away again. I feel like I'm dead."

"Then why you wanna live like this? She gets so outta control. I really thought she was different, but she ain't."

"I'm afraid, Sellie, I'm just afraid."

*\*\**

The two girls sat in the school office totally stunned. Luz Diaz had stormed in and out, heading toward the elementary school next door. She was about to disappear for a time. One of the teachers, a woman the girls had seen around but didn't know, happened to be in the office at the time. She saw the distressed students and walked over to see if she could do anything. Tina in particular poured her heart out and talked about awaiting still another foster placement by the State. When the teacher turned to leave, she gave Tina a hug. Tina thought the teacher was very nice, but had enough on her mind not to think twice about it. She had no way of knowing just how important Roberta Allen would soon become in her life.

# CHAPTER NINE

*Late Spring 2003*

It was just a few days after the softball tryouts had begun that Tina pulled another surprise out of a hat. A boy, as in a possible boyfriend. As in, "Help Roberta, how are we supposed to handle this boy friend? The DOF manual said nothing about boyfriends. Josh. Ominous sounding Josh. Sex-crazed Josh. "Can Josh come over?"

"Now Hal," scolded Roberta with a laugh, "you're being ridiculous. I'm sure he's just a kid with a crush. But, I'm a little nervous, too, especially given her history. It's probably a good idea that we meet him."

"Yeah, maybe. I never thought … it never even occurred to me, that this might happen, at least not so soon. Kind of dumb of me. She's so pretty, there are probably lots of boys interested in her."

"He's a junior, Hal. Almost two years older. And the prom is right around the corner. Hmm, I always wanted to help a daughter pick out a high school prom dress."

Tina emerged from her room and joined us downstairs. Roberta told her that we'd been discussing her request to have Josh come over on the weekend and that it would be okay. She flashed that great smile and thanked us.

"I'm nervous," she said, "but he's really nice. I like him. He was part of that group I told off in Spanish that day. We'll just talk or go for a walk or something. Maybe after softball practice on Saturday or on Sunday."

Roberta said that either would be fine. Tina smiled again, turned and virtually bounced back up stairs.

\*\*\*

The other new person in Tina's life, Kristin, was a true godsend. As offbeat as she was, she was just as sweet and kind. She and Tina wound up on the same team, the Cardinals. So at each tryout, and now team practice, the same scenario played out. Kristin was always there before us. Tina would walk to the fence behind the bench and Kristin would greet her. "Hieee, Tinaaa. We are a great team. We're gonna be the champs." After which she would give Tina a hug and twirl her around. Valentina would always belly laugh and the two of them would spend the next minute or so giggling before their coach, Lou Spinelli, called the squad to attention.

I had spent a bit of time getting Tina used to catching the ball—judging fly balls was still an extreme challenge—and batting. When she connected she was very strong, but the "when" was not very often. Witnessing team practices ranged between funny and excruciating. Tina was actually in the middle as far as ability went, an ominous sign for the team's future. Kristin was a pretty good hitter and could judge the ball in the air as well as any of the girls. A stocky blond named Yvette was the obvious star, regularly hitting the ball hard and with great hands and instincts on defense. I had no doubt that the next year she would be suiting up for the high school team.

About half way through Saturday morning practice, Tina called me over to the fence near her spot on the bench. "Dad, where's the bathroom? I need it bad."

The softball league used the town Little League fields. There's a refreshment stand with a restroom in back. But during practices, the stand is closed and I suspected that the restroom was locked.

"Give me a sec and I'll check," I replied. I hurried down the small hill near the stand and tried the restroom door. Locked, as I expected. I climbed the hill back toward the bench.

"Sorry, Tina, it's locked. Practice will be over soon. Can't you hold it?"

Tina roared loud enough for the whole bench to stare at us. "Dad, I don't have to go to the bathroom."

"Then why do—"

"Dad," she said through the laughing, tears streaming down her cheeks, "it's a girl thing."

I don't know how many shades of red I turned. I mean, I had three sons. When my kids needed the Little League bathroom, it was always to, well, go to the bathroom. I had a lot to learn about having a teenage daughter. First a boyfriend and now this, all in the same week.

"It can't wait?" I asked, basically pleading.

"I have bad cramps Dad."

I motioned for Coach Spinelli. He trotted over and as I explained the problem, he just grinned and reached into his pocket. "They give us all a key that fits the equipment room and the *john*."

I don't know who was more relieved, me or Tina, but she took the key, grabbed her small tote bag and hustled to the restroom. When she returned, she gave me another laugh as if to let me know how much I had to learn. Kristin spotted her as she walked back place back to the bench and shouted "Tinaaa, way to go girl." Rolling her eyes, Tina settled down next to her friend.

*\*\*\**

Saturday turned out to be the big day. Josh was coming over before supper and the two kids were going to watch TV together and just hang out. Josh, thankfully, had to be home for some family thing by dinnertime. His mother was dropping him off, and I would have to bring him home. No driver's license yet, which was actually a relief for me.

At about 2:30 the doorbell rang. Tina scrambled down the stairs. "I'll get it," she said.

All traces of Valentina's softball practice had been showered off and the soiled practice sweats exchanged for a simple blue skirt and polo top that I felt revealed both too much leg and too much womanliness. Tina opened the door to a slim, tall, very young looking boy wearing black-rimmed glasses, jeans, a T-shirt that looked like it might have said "Pink Floyd," except that most of the lettering had worn off, and a hair cut that was short on the sides and a rather full dirty blond on top.

Roberta and I hung back in the hall, maybe a little too obviously curious. "Mom and Dad, this is Josh Johnstone."

"Hello Josh," Bobbie greeted the boy.

"Hello Josh," I said and extended my hand, which Josh took in a much firmer grip than I had expected. It actually impressed me.

"Hi," he said, "nice to meet you."

Polite, I thought and his voice was deep and strong, if a little surprising coming out of such a thin, young-looking face. Maybe he was okay, for a boy after my daughter.

"Mr. Allen," the voice said, "Tina's told me what a great dad you are, I wish mine were still alive. I couldn't wait to meet you. And Mrs. Allen, she can't stop talking about you."

Okay, so now I'm totally disarmed. Mature, polite, charming. Tina clearly had good taste in men, and he clearly had good taste in women.

"Sorry about your dad," I answered.

"It's okay. He was in the army. He was killed in the Gulf War. I was pretty young, so I don't really remember him, but he was a hero."

I could only nod. Roberta motioned to me and said to the kids, "Well, we have some things to do upstairs. The TV is all yours."

Tina pointed Josh toward the family room and I had my first true butterflies as the father of a teenage girl.

\*\*\*

Between school, Josh and softball, punctuated with visits from effervescent Kristin, most of Tina's life was pretty normal. But, as Bobbie often reminded me, maybe never sure about my attitude, difficulties in our foster daughter's life were rarely far beneath the surface. The day had arrived when all three of us were to join Jim Covain in meeting with Mrs. Bronislaw. Our role was to listen and provide support. Jim had decided that we should meet first with him and the psychologist without Tina, and then she would be called in. What the standard protocol was, we had no idea, and were about to learn that we were being accorded an unusual privilege, if it can be called that, to be a part of the decision on how, not whether, our foster child should be meeting with her natural mother.

Tina sat quietly throughout the short drive to Mrs. Bronislaw's office. Bobbie thought I was being more critical than usual about the way my fellow drivers were handling their responsibility. I had no idea why I should feel so edgy, but I couldn't wait to get this done and behind us.

When we arrived, Jim Covain was already there, and had met briefly with Mrs. Bronislaw. He greeted Tina with a smile and assured her that everything would work out okay.

Mrs. Bronislaw, prematurely graying, wearing a smart dark blue suit, with long, gold and blue bangled earrings with necklace to match, and gold-rimmed glasses, jumped right into it.

"Tina is one of the most remarkable kids I've met. She's wise, but innocent, warm, but wary, and nurturing, but dying to be nurtured. The only reason I asked that you two come along today, and that I convinced the State to allow you here, is that you are about the only people in the world that that girl trusts completely. I'm not certain how much she trusts me, but from what Jim tells me about the mother, the time is right for them to see each other, and Tina needs whatever reinforcement is available."

Bobbie volunteered, "Obviously we'll help. But I can tell you how deeply conflicted she is. Hal and I are probably as nervous as she is."

"Well, most kids in her position feel strange," Jim Covain said, "but our mission is to see if reunification is possible, and these sort of meetings are one of the few ways we have to test the water."

"And," added Mrs. Bronislaw, "Tina really needs to see her mom if for no other reason than to see and judge for herself if her mother's home should be her home. Being in and out of that home so often is pretty much normal to Tina, but she's old enough now to appreciate how abnormal that really is. And she is more wary about Luz. Another big factor for her will be Selena. I don't know if you heard this, but Selena has reached the age when she can legally terminate her relationship with DOF and she is opting to do so. She's going back home to mom."

"No, we didn't know. That's hard to believe after all Luz did to her," Bobbie said.

"That's how it is for these kids. The pressure will build for Tina to join her two sisters with mom. I've seen it over and over again. For now,

DOF can prevent it, but when Valentina is of age, she can choose for herself."

Roberta was holding herself together, although I knew how hard it was for her to imagine any safe relationship for Tina with her mother.

Jim understood and reassured us both that for now, there was little chance of a permanent reunion. "But now, we need to call Tina in. What we are going to tell her is that I'll take her to our offices next Friday after school and she will meet with Luz together with me in the room for a short time, no more than a half hour. Ultimately, if things work out, she can see her once a week for a longer time, and they can visit each other at their homes."

"You mean our house?" Roberta said in disbelief.

"Yes, that's the idea," Jim replied.

"No way, not that woman in my house," Roberta declared.

"Look, we would only want you to agree to that once it's clear that Luz and Tina can deal with one another in the way that we all hope for. I, or someone from DOF, would always be along. But that's down the road away."

Roberta looked at me and then at the other two. "Quite far away she said, "and I hope we will have a lot to say about it. But right now, yes, we will be supportive. What choice do we have?"

"Okay then," the psychologist said, "Jim, please bring her in."

He opened the door and Tina stepped in, visibly nervous. I smiled at her in a rather silly effort to calm her. She pulled the last empty chair in the room as close to Roberta as she could.

"Tina, we've told Mr. and Mrs. Allen that we've arranged for you to go with Jim to DOF at the end of the week to meet with your mom. They told me how mixed your emotions are, as you and I have also discussed, but that they understand why you and your mom should meet at this time. They agree that the time is right."

"That's right, Tina," I said, "and we believe you've been getting yourself ready for a while."

"Right," Bobbie said and gave Tina a reassuring pat on the hand. "And Jim will be right there with you."

"You'll see, it won't be as terrifying as you imagine. I've been through these sorts of meetings many times," Jim said.

Tina yawned, maybe out of tension, or maybe she was just burned out. Then, in a voice not quite so sweet as I was accustomed to, she spoke as if she was by herself, practicing.

"She is my mother. I know how to talk to her. I know her tricks. I cannot be tricked any more. I will do this. I will get through this. She will see that I am not a little girl any more. She cannot control me. I will be the one who makes the decisions."

She stopped, almost embarrassed by her monologue, and said to us all, "Okay. I'm ready."

***

The Thursday evening before the meeting between Luz and Tina was the first game of the softball season. I had to drive Tina over early for warm-ups. She got her customary greeting from Kristin and jogged out to left field to shag some fly balls, or I should say tried to shag some fly balls. Luckily, she couldn't get close enough to any of them to jeopardize her head. But she kept trying, encouraged by coach Spinelli. A few minutes before the game started, Bobbie arrived and soon thereafter, Josh and a few of his buddies showed up, too. Tina gave him a wave and then took her place in the order for some batting practice.

Bobbie pointed out that our girl had her game face on. Whether it was wanting to do well in front of us and her boy friend, getting her nerves controlled over the meeting with Luz, or just plain not wanting to embarrass herself, she was so intent that I had to laugh. But it paid off at the plate. Somehow, in two of her three at bats, she hit the ball hard, even chugging into second base in the fourth inning with a double. The smile was worth everything. She even managed to knock a ball down in the outfield, a major advance. Budding star Yvette slammed a game-winning homer, scoring Kristin in front of her, to pull the game out for the Cardinals as darkness closed in. Tina was ecstatic, having forgotten about other things for the moment. I did get a little uncomfortable when Josh gave her a hug, sweaty uniform and all, but I don't think Tina even noticed.

***

According to what Valentina told us afterward, the meeting was anti-climactic. Jim Covain had sat silently throughout the reunion of mother and daughter in a dingy small interview room at the DOF regional office. Luz apparently behaved herself and avoided any controversial topics. If Tina had expected an expression of love, it hadn't happened. Not at this first meeting. Luz had filled her in on her sisters and Grandma. She told Tina that Grandpa Diaz was not well, and wanted to see her. Jim Covain had told her after the meeting that he would try and arrange a date for her to see her grandpa.

Back at home, Tina went to her room for a while and then came down just before dinner. Clearly, she wanted to say something and seemed to be trying to choose her words carefully. Finally, she cleared her throat and asked us to sit down. The three of us sat at the kitchen table while Tina spoke.

"I wanted so much for Ma to tell me she loves me. I felt small, and I wanted to tell her I love her, but I made up my mind that she has to tell me first. Maybe that's stupid, but that's the way I want it. It was so weird, like talking to a stranger. But I learned something. I can handle this. At least I think I can. I know that I'm not ready to go back to her and I don't think she's ready for me. I think she's having issues with Selena coming back. Some family, huh?"

Taking a deep breath, she leaned back from the table, not really expecting a response. Nobody was hungry.

# CHAPTER TEN

*Summer 2003*

Luz had been in a frenzy for days. Word was out, the way things get around in a small town, that Simon was in custody and back in the state. She still had a thing for the guy on the one hand, but was afraid that she'd face trial herself and wished Simon had been better at hiding. Grandma Diaz kept out of her way as much as possible. Sellie had a job at the supermarket and Juanita was away during most of the daylight hours at the crafts camp that the city ran for underprivileged kids. So for the most part, Luz was left to herself. It was a good thing, too, because Luz was back at her breaking point.

There were other issues stressing the family as well. Grandpa Diaz had decided to return to Puerto Rico to, as he put it so often, "breathe the air I was born to breathe until I can't breathe no more." It drove Luz and Grandma crazy every time he said the damn thing and they were glad that Isabel was the one who had to put up with him most of the time. He kept pushing them to see his beloved Valentina before he left.

"Papi, I can't do nothing about that, like I told you a thousand times," Luz yelled into the phone a few days after getting the news about her former lover's arrest. "I got big stuff on my mind. You want to see Valentina, you call her. Maybe those rich people she's livin' off of now can help you. Go ask them." She slammed the receiver down just as hard as she wanted to punch her annoying father.

Luz lit a cigarette and paced the kitchen. The smoke hung in the thick air of the hot afternoon. A little fan on the counter wasn't much help in place of the broken window air-conditioner.

"Ma," she yelled toward the living room, "I got to get out of here. I need to think. Wait for the kids. I'll be back later."

\*\*\*

Once outside, Luz grabbed her lipstick from her bag and applied a fresh coat. She tousled her hair to look like what she remembered it had looked like a dozen or so years ago. While she couldn't do too much about the extra pounds that covered her once perfect shape, she thought she still looked pretty good. She walked down to the bus stop and boarded the bus for the center of town, disembarking at the police station stop and headed inside.

"Can I help you ma'am," the desk officer asked, a little warily because he knew exactly who was facing him.

"You got a prisoner here, Simon Texiera, I want to see him."

"I don't think so, ma'am, only one guy in the tank right now."

"You're lying," Luz shouted, "I got a right to see him, he's my husband."

"Please ma'am, calm down. We do not have a Simon Texiera here. You say he's your husband," he said, but knew very well that Luz and Simon had never married. "Why do you think he's here?"

"Don't lie to me. I know he was arrested and brought back to the state," she continued to shout.

The officer scratched his head and leaned forward. "Look, I'm really not supposed to say anything, but believe me he isn't here in Blue Hills. Nobody will know where he is being kept until the State's Attorney gives the word. If there's a trial, it probably won't be in Blue Hills, either."

Luz put both hands on the counter. "Okay, say I believe you. Who's this attorney? Can I at least talk to him?"

Now that the woman had gained some control, the officer told her that he couldn't promise anything, but if she would leave her number, he would call after checking to see if someone from the prosecutor's office was willing to speak with her. Luz scribbled her number on the sheet of paper the man had given her, turned and walked out the door.

After taking a few steps, she lifted her fist toward her mouth and bit her hand as hard as she could, drawing some blood. Then she wiped every trace of lipstick off of her lips before heading to a bar on the next block.

*\*\*\**

Jim Covain had just given the news to the Allens that Tina's grandfather had come forward expressing an interest in seeing Tina before he left for his return to the island. It would be sometime in the next month. The Allens told him they were thrilled on the one hand, knowing how much Valentina loved her grandfather, and saddened on the other hand that he apparently might be leaving her life for good.

The only hitch was that the meeting would be on a weekend when nobody from DOF was available. He asked the Allens if they would be willing to drive Tina to Smithton so she could spend the day with Grandpa Diaz and then pick her up after several hours at a restaurant. When the Allens questioned him about the wisdom of letting Tina go on her own for an unsupervised day with her grandfather, Covain told them that after a long discussion with the grandfather, DOF decided it would be okay.

"He's pretty harmless, Roberta, and he has no way to take her away. We'll help you to pick a meeting place," Covain assured her.

Tina, who was spending the summer going to the town pool, going shopping with her foster mother, honing her natural cooking talent, practicing her softball skills with her friend Kristin, seeing her boyfriend Josh too often for her foster father's over-protective taste, and meeting with her mother every two weeks, was overjoyed at hearing that she would get to see her beloved grandfather. But during the same call from Jim Covain breaking the news about her grandpa, he also told her about the likelihood of a trial for Simon Texiera starting later that year or early the next.

"Mom," she said to Roberta, "I never seem to get just good news. Even the news about my grandpa isn't that good. I might never see him again. How am I going to go to Puerto Rico? How long will he live, he's so old already. I don't even want to think about a trial."

Wiping her hands on her apron, Tina removed the remains of the raw matzo balls she was learning to make. She stirred the pot a little, and hummed a Spanish salsa tune.

"You know, when I grow up, and if I have kids, they are going to be so loved and protected. I'll be the best mother."

"I think you will," Roberta answered, "I'd bet on it."

Tina smiled, "How much?"

"The ranch."

Tina looked puzzled and asked why she would bet a ranch if she didn't have one.

"Oh Tina, it's just a saying. It means I'd bet everything I own that you're going to be a great mom. If I owned a ranch, I'd bet that for sure."

Tina laughed and blushed.

"Ma, are you serious? Well, anyway, I'll have the only Spanish kids who eat matzo ball soup, and it will be the best. Or, maybe as good as yours. I bet Grandpa would love my soup. He loves soup."

"I'll bet. Maybe when we take you to see him, you can make some and bring it to him. That will be next Sunday."

"He's going to be so surprised. I'm much taller than when he saw me the last time. Can we take him to a Puerto Rican restaurant? He loves Puerto Rican food. Maybe some mofongo. I haven't had it for so long. It's gooood."

"Well, we'll see, but let's get this kitchen cleaned up."

"Okay, Mom. How many days is it until Sunday?"

***

The mini-van pulled up in front of the two-decker house in Smithton. From the front steps, a middle-aged woman stared at the car. The short, tanned, and wrinkled man next to her broke out in a wide smile and waved. Tina opened her door and sprinted toward the porch.

"Abuelo," she boomed, "I am so glad to see you."

The little man was engulfed in Tina's exuberant embrace, totally hidden from the view of the remaining occupants in the car. The woman standing next to them, Valentina's Aunt Isabel, warned Tina to be careful, that Grandpa Diaz was not as strong as he used to be. When Tina finally loosened her arms, she took a step back as if to memorize the scene.

Harold Allen stepped out of the car and walked over to Aunt Isabel.

"We appreciate your help in getting this arranged. This is all Tina's been talking about."

"Yes, my father, too," she answered in a slightly accented, low voice, "he is an old man with only two dreams left. Seeing his favorite granddaughter one more time and going back to that steamy island to die. One I can understand. The other is foolish. He has nobody there but some old cousins who can't remember his name."

Hal nodded as if he agreed with her sentiment, and quickly changed the subject. "We're dropping them off at Ponce, you know, the restaurant on Grove Place in Halstead. We're giving them about three hours and then we'll have Grandpa back here."

"Okay. I hope Tina can handle him. He's so depressed around here. It gets on my nerves, you know."

Before Hal could say anything, Roberta opened her window and told them to move along because time was wasting. Tina took her grandfather, whom she towered over by at least six inches, by the arm and helped him into the back seat. He leaned forward toward Tina's foster parents and broke into a wide smile, greeting them with a gravelly *"Muchas gracias."*

\*\*\*

Valentina walked back down the steps from her aunt's porch after hugging Grandpa Diaz for what would be the last time, the bittersweet nature of the parting seemed to be overshadowed by Tina's excitement over the last three hours. They had talked and laughed over every memory. She told the Allens that her grandfather was the only man she felt she could really trust, the only one who seemed to be connected to only good memories.

"And he ordered the best food. If I lived with him, I would be so fat. I don't know why he's so tiny, the way he eats. But, man, we just had the best talk. My sides hurt, he tells such funny stories. I should be real sad to see him leave, but it's what he needs to be happy, and I understand. Maybe I can go there to see him," her voice trailed off.

*\*\**

Luz didn't have to wait for the police to contact her. The week after her visit to the police station, a fellow worker she had known for years at the fast food place where she was now working part-time showed her an article in that morning's newspaper. According to the local Assistant State's Attorney, a Lillian Morten, police in Puerto Rico had been told of the whereabouts of one Simon Texiera, wanted by Blue Hills police in connection with possible child sex abuse charges of an extreme nature. He had fled the jurisdiction at the time that the reports of the abuse surfaced, but was now in custody at the maximum security holding facility in Winding Brook. He was being held without bail because he was a clear flight risk and because of the seriousness of his alleged offense. A jury trial could be expected to start by the end of the year or early the next.

The last paragraph caused Luz to catch her breath. "Mr. Texiera's wife and baby daughter are expected to arrive in the state to support him. According to local sources, Mrs. Texiera was not aware of any issue regarding her husband's past and is determined to stand by him as he defends against the charges, the detailed nature of which have not yet been disclosed."

"Goddamn, married," she said aloud.

"What's that?" her co-worker asked.

"Nothing. I gotta think. Look, there ain't anyone here. I gotta take my break now. Gotta figure this out."

Once outside, she lit a cigarette and inhaled quickly several times. Married, she thought, why did he get married? He loved me. He just thought he couldn't come back here and took up with someone because he was bored. That's it. No way he goes to prison.

She went back inside and told the manager she felt sick and needed to go home. He grunted an okay and mumbled how hard it was to find reliable help. Luz left as fast as she could and went straight back to her apartment. Nobody else was around. She poured herself a beer and stopped to look at herself in a mirror.

"I bet I look better than her. I'm more of a woman. He needs me to help him. He'll come back to me," she said. She emptied the can and went for another. She paced for a while until she heard her mother coming in with Juanita.

"Luz, why are you home?" her mother asked.

"Didn't feel good. I have a headache. Did you hear about Simon?"

***

"Hi Ma," Tina greeted her mother as Jim Covain shut the door behind her and took his usual seat at the far end of the table.

Luz barely nodded. The last few meetings had seen a bit of fence mending, small steps, as Covain had reported to Lydia Hernandez. He didn't see Luz's lack of enthusiasm today as promising.

"Ma, what's up? You okay?"

"You and me we gotta get some things worked out."

"Yeah, I know, that's why we have these meetings."

Luz waved her hand, "Yeah, I know, but this isn't just about us. I got to make damn sure you don't get hurt."

Jim Covain cocked his head. This was the first time he'd ever heard Luz talk about her daughter's welfare with such conviction.

"Ma, what are you talking about?"

"Valentina, do you know about Simon? Do you know there's going to be a trial?"

"Yes. I'm glad they caught him. He belongs in jail."

Luz held herself back, fully aware that the caseworker was showing interest. "Well, I hear he might have changed, has a family. He wasn't bad all the time."

"Ma," Tina said in shock.

"Tina, okay, he did some bad things, but if they put him on trial, you will have to testify. What good will that do? It's just gonna make you crazy. I'm worried about you. I don't think you should do it."

For the first time since Jim Covain had known her, Tina lost her temper.

"Ma, what the hell are you talking about? You're crazy. He's a terrible person and he deserves whatever happens to him."

"Calm down, okay. What if they make me go to jail, too? Have you thought about that?"

"I will not calm down. You always care about yourself. I told you plenty of times about Simon. You never did anything until it was too late. What about me, Ma?"

"Stop it," Luz growled.

Jim Covain walked between the two Diaz women who had risen to their feet, pointing at each other.

"The meeting's over. Mrs. Diaz, you have to go." Jim opened the door and asked their security guard to escort Luz out of the building.

He watched Luz leave and extended his hand to Tina. That the girl was too mad to even cry surprised him.

"Tina, I don't know about these meetings."

"Jim, I don't want to talk to her. I hate her."

"Tina, she needs help."

"I'm the lucky one," she replied, "because Sellie and Juanita are stuck with her. She's sick. Take me home, please. I want to see Mom and Dad."

# CHAPTER ELEVEN

*Winter 2003 and Spring 2004*

Assistant State's attorney Lillian Morten, who had been selected to prosecute the case against Simon Texiera, didn't look the part of a two-fisted fighter, but in her case, appearances can deceive. Mid-fortyish and with a slight paunch that she didn't try to hide under her casual attire of slacks and various old-fashioned blouses that we got to see all too often, her manner bordered on shyness. Her long brown hair was always pulled back in a ponytail, her blue-rimmed glasses slightly askew and constantly sliding down toward the end of her nose when she wasn't twisting them in her hands.

Before we met Lillian for the first time, we already had formed a favorable impression, courtesy of Tina, who had met with the prosecutor along with Jim Covain and Diane Pacquin.

"Mom and Dad, that lady is so smart. She knows everything and she is really nice to me. I was so afraid of the trial. She made me feel okay. I'm nervous, but it doesn't scare me anymore," Tina declared.

As Valentina's foster parents, my wife and I were late additions to the prosecution support team. At the first meeting, the group had decided that Bobbie and I should be actively involved because Tina would need a lot of our support during the preparation for the trial and the trial itself. And Tina would have to sit in the courtroom with Simon only yards away.

The rest of us were gathered around a conference table in the courthouse where the trial would take place in Glenwood, when Lillian, as she asked that we call her, came into the room with a young man who she said would be assisting her at trial.

"Hi, for the benefit of Mr. and Mrs. Allen, I'm Lillian. This is Mark Goldblatt. Mark is an attorney with our office. He'll be doing a lot of the heavy lifting, prepping witnesses, working with our paralegals to make sure any exhibits are properly sequenced and indexed, that sort of stuff. You might be hearing from him from time to time."

Goldblatt, only a few years removed from law school, smiled and greeted us each by name, just to let us know that he was already on top of this particular cast of characters. His precision was matched by his properly creased grey suit pants, blue shirt sleeves rolled up just so in an "I'm here to work" look, and a red and blue striped business tie.

"Okay, then," Lillian said, "let's go through this."

Her voice was so quiet that I had to lean forward to make sure I didn't miss anything. I wondered how the heck she could command a jury.

"Tina is our complaining witness. She'll be on the stand for quite a while. As we explained to her last time, she can expect a difficult cross-examination, maybe even enough to make her cry or become angered. Crying is okay. Anger not so much. If she gets angry, we hope she can hold it back, and maybe it will spill out back at home."

She nodded toward me and Bobbie, "Do you understand?"

"Of course," we answered together. Bobbie added that everyone could count on us to give Tina all the support she needed. Jim and Diane also spoke to helping us and Tina.

"All right then," Lillian said.

After leaning over to say something to Mark, she turned back to us. Lillian pointed at a two pitchers and a stack of Styrofoam cups. "Sorry, I get ahead of myself sometimes. Coffee and water right there. Feel free. Now, Mark is going to run through a list of possible witnesses on both sides of the case. We need to know of any reaction you have to them. Anything at all that you can think of might be useful to us."

Her voice was still quiet, but now I thought it was her way of making sure she had everyone's attention.

Mark Goldblatt went over to an easel that held a large paper pad. On the top sheet, he had listed several names, including Tina's.

"Last time, we went over the main facts that Tina can remember regarding Simon's abuse. One of our problems, and at the same time one of our strengths, is that Tina was very young when the abuse started and when it ended. So it is natural that there will be details, even whole events that are cloudy or even forgotten. That's where we need corroboration, you know, someone who can confirm facts or independently testify. The most obvious ones are the first two."

He pointed to the names Luz Diaz and Selena Diaz. Just below was the name Juanita Diaz.

"Not Juanita."

Everyone turned toward Tina.

"I kind of want to go through these in order," Goldblatt said.

"It's okay, Mark," Lillian Morten directed, peering through her glasses at Tina. "I want Tina to speak up when she needs to. Glad for it. Why not Juanita?"

Tina seemed embarrassed that she had spoken out, but Lillian again asked her to go on.

"Well, the main reason is that for some of the things she wasn't even born. For the rest of it, she was too little to understand, even if she remembered anything, and I know she never saw anything. It's different for her. Simon is her real father, although she hardly remembers him now. She's still a little kid."

Lillian actually allowed her reserve to drop and clapped her hands. "Tina, I'll let you in on a little secret. We were not planning for real on using Juanita, she's just on the list of a big range of people, but I love how you think about things and even better, how you express yourself."

Tina blushed and said, "Seriously?"

"Quite seriously. Oh, and while we digress, I almost forgot. Tina, you look older than your years, and some of what makes you look older might have a negative influence on the jury. When you come to court, you are going to have to wear outfits that make you look younger and that hide your figure. The jury will be seeing you as you look now and anything that makes them forget just how little you were when these terrible things happened might hurt our case. We don't want that. Okay, then, go on, Mark."

First on the list was Selena. Tina had explained at the first meeting about her sister having been her confidante. Also, that she had witnessed one episode, actually the critical episode. There was some discussion about Sellie being pretty emotional, maybe even volatile. They didn't spend too much time on Sellie because, as Mark explained, Sellie would be going through extensive interviews.

Luz was another matter. Mark told us that Tina and Jim had given them the details of Tina's last meeting with her mother at DOF. While Luz was obviously aware of the final incident that led to Simon fleeing to Puerto Rico and was angry with him, it was also clear that she still had a strong attraction to him, to the point even of desperation. Lillian stood up and threw her arms out wide, now twirling her glasses that dangled from her left hand.

"She could be a major problem. If we knew for sure that she wouldn't waiver about Simon's conduct, she would help, and not calling her at all for our side could hurt. The other problem is that she never directly witnessed the abuse. She can be challenged by the defense on that score. And, there is every chance that she will plead the Fifth Amendment, because she's afraid of incriminating herself. One reason we haven't gone after her is because we really want her to cooperate. There is also a chance that if she isn't called to appear for us, the defense will try to use her. We'll be trying to interview her and then get down to some hard thinking."

Jim Covain raised his hand.

"No need to do that, just jump right in," Lillian said.

"Thanks, well, I agree totally that Luz is a loose cannon. I think in her own way, she loves Tina, or at least thinks she is required to love Tina, but she puts herself first and she is totally hooked on Simon so far as I can tell."

"Yes, thanks. We think we can make a strong case without her, but we'd be better with her. Anyway, let's consider the rest of the list."

Among the other names were the school nurse who had examined little Tina after Aunt Carmen had called, and Carmen's name was on the list, too. The prosecution was aware that the nurse was now retired and had moved away, but found that she was probably willing to travel back to the state to testify. As for Carmen, Tina spoke up again and expressed some concern about how much her mother hated Carmen and thought it could cause problems in the family.

Amazing, I thought, she's thinking about the family even now after that mother of hers helped to blow it apart. I nudged Bobbie, who gave me a grimace.

Mark explained that Carmen was important because, as Tina had told them, Aunt Carmen was one of the few people who Tina had told about the abuse and was the one who reported Simon to the authorities.

The list also included some possible expert witnesses on child abuse and its affect on the victim and many people close to them. Some other family members, such as Isabel, Ernesto and Grandma Diaz were also on the list and were the subject of discussion. These people would be available to cover certain loose ends if needed. Bobbie and I mostly just took it all in, and as she commented to me on the way to the car, the stress that Tina was under must have been overwhelming.

*\*\*\**

As difficult as those days had to be for her, Tina somehow managed to display a formidable outward resilience. She'd be up in her room singing along with Mariah Carey on her walkman, giggling on the phone with Kristin, or waiting for Josh to come around for a walk or to go to the movies. She continued to do well in school and thought that the voice lessons I had suggested would be worth looking into.

Singing had become her passion, even surpassing her constant interest in art. Her voice, a rich contralto, only needed refinement and technique to become superior. If only the trial weren't hanging like a two ton weight around Tina's imminent future, we would have arranged for voice lessons right away.

The trial couldn't happen soon enough. Just after dinner, almost a week after our meeting with Lillian Morten, the phone rang. "I'll get it," Tina yelled from above the noise of the dishwasher. "Josh's supposed to be calling."

Bobbie was still wrapping leftovers while I sipped tea and motioned for Tina to go ahead.

She flew to the phone, a smile a yard wide. She lifted the receiver and said, "Hello." She paused for several seconds, the smile having turned into a taut line, and said, "What are you talking about?"

She listened again, and, from what she said next, it was obvious that Selena was on the other end.

"Why would Ma do such a thing? Were you there when she did it?"

Another pause and then, "This is too much. Yeah, I love you, too. How do you stand it?" followed by, "I guess so, I know you live with her, but that was your choice. Anyway, I'm glad you let me know. Bye."

"What was that all about?" I asked.

"My mother is impossible. She found out where Simon's wife is staying and tried to call her. Someone from her new church, she's going to church with Grandma, knows the lady Simon's wife and baby are staying with, and told someone who told Ma. Ma got the phone number and left a message on the lady's message machine. Sellie overheard her. She said something like, 'When I help Simon get free, he's gonna leave you. I know he still wants me, so don't mess with me, or you'll be sorry'."

"Is Sellie sure that's what she heard?" Bobbie asked.

"Sellie says she confronted Ma and Ma just told her to keep her mouth shut and mind her own business. Selena knows how bad Simon is and how nuts Ma can be. I'm just afraid Ma's gonna do something really bad and that poor Sellie is gonna have a big problem dealing with her. Maybe bigger than mine."

We sat around the kitchen table and didn't say a word. The phone rang again, this time, thankfully, it was Josh. Tina turned to Bobbie and asked if it was okay if Josh came over even though she had school the next day. "I'd like to walk with him, okay?"

"Sure, it's fine," Bobbie approved, "I think, Dad and I need a little air, too. We'll take our own walk."

Roberta looked my way. I took her by the hand, grabbed my Red Sox hat and led her out and down the front steps.

*** 

We had another prep meeting at Lillian's office with the same cast of characters. As usual I strained to hear when she told us that Simon was to be represented by two lawyers from the Public Defender's Office. The list of potential witnesses had been refined, but Luz was still an undecided wild card. Mark said that she would probably be on the final witness list and could be a late decision whether or not to use her. The big news was that the date for the beginning of jury selection had been set to start the first week in December, just a few weeks away, with the actual trial to begin at the end of March, 2004. Tina would have turned sixteen by then. The precise trial date was March 25th. Spring, a time for blossoming and fresh starts.

***

Life went on as normally as it could while we were waiting for the trial process to start in earnest. With her sixteenth birthday due in little over a month, Tina had lobbied Roberta to start learning how to drive and planned to take drivers ed in the spring. I suppose I should have expected it, but when Bobbie mentioned it to me as we got ready for bed the night after our last pre-trial meeting, I realized that I'd become so focused on helping the girl get through the trial that I had assumed that Tina would have nothing else on her mind.

"Crap," is all I could muster at first.

"I know, I know," Bobbie actually laughed at my reaction, "I thought that when Joey left the nest, these days were gone for good, too."

"And my heart and patience aren't what they used to be. It could still snow around here any time now. Maybe we should wait."

"Harold, come on. It will give Tina, and us, too, something besides that damn trial to think about. She's a very responsible kid."

"Well, don't we need DOF permission?"

"I hope you'll forgive me, but I already checked with Jim Covain. He not only said it would be okay, but the state will even pay for all of the related expenses, like driver's ed, the license and our added insurance cost."

I nodded, not at all surprised that Roberta had already had ten toes in.

"Honey," she went on, "I think this weekend would be a good time for you to start taking her out, maybe to some empty parking lot like you did with the boys when they were learning."

"Great, Bobbie, you take the jump, but I get to risk my neck? Why don't you take her out?"

"Hal, you are joking, I assume. Frankly, I never thought you trusted me behind the wheel, and now you want me to do the teaching. I certainly don't mind, but really?"

"No, no," I mumbled, "I'll do it. I was sort of joking."

Bobbie rolled her eyes and waved her hand. "My hero," she teased.

Deliver me, I thought.

***

Saturday came and there was absolutely no chance of snow. More like 12 inches of bright sunshine had fallen just to endanger my life on the roads with another new driver.

"When can I drive, Dad?" was just about the only thing Tina had said all day from the moment I came down for breakfast. I think she'd been up for hours.

"Not until we get to the commuter lot," I must have repeated fifty times.

"Okay, but can we just go now?" she pleaded, impatient with the unusually slow pace of my breakfast.

Finally, I pushed back from my chair. Tina jumped up, handed me my overcoat and the car keys, bolted toward the garage and pressed the overhead door opener. Bite the bullet time. Roberta, who had been suspiciously quiet throughout most of this little battle, gave me her sweetest smile, patted me on the cheek and told me to enjoy myself. It was my turn to roll my eyes and wag a finger. But I did manage to smile.

Once inside the car, I made sure that Tina observed everything I did, from buckling my seat belt, to inserting the key in the ignition, making sure she knew it was called the ignition, to how I had to judge each side of the car to see how much room I had, before I even started to back up. The student told me she already knew all that stuff.

As we drove the mile or so to the parking lot, I explained how to watch for other drivers and pedestrians, when and how to brake, how to turn a corner under control, all the things drivers eventually do without thinking too much. This time, she didn't claim advanced knowledge. Finally arriving at the parking lot, which thankfully had only a few weekend cars scattered widely about, we began the lesson in earnest.

We switched seats and she immediately remembered lesson one.

"Fasten seat belts, Dad."

"Next."

"Put the key in the ignition, but it's already there."

"My bad. Next."

"Start driving."

And with that, she stepped on the gas, the engine made a loud complaint and we went nowhere.

"Oh my god, Dad, did I break the car?" she said, clearly shaken.

"Well, you didn't break the car. You kind of did the opposite. You forgot to shift the gear out of park."

Now she laughed her belly laugh. "Oh my god, I'm so stupid."

"No you're not," I assured her, "you're just a beginner and even with my experience, I do that once in a while. But remember, when you shift out of park and into drive, first keep your foot on the brake and then press on the gas very lightly until you get used to the car moving."

Tina stared at the shift lever, looked back at me, took a deep breath and shifted out of park. She followed my first direction very well, depressing the accelerator with a very light touch, rolled forward about thirty feet, then slammed hard on the brakes.

"Whoa, what was that all about?"

"Wasn't I going too fast?"

"No, you were doing fine. Just try and keep the car under control, say about twenty, and then brake gently if you think you're going too fast or if I tell you to slow down."

Another deep breath, this time by me, as Tina started the car forward again. At four, I stopped counting the abrupt stops, trying to remember if I'd had to visit the chiropractor after my sons' first time in the same parking lot. Finally, on the next try, she seemed to catch on and steered a straight path through the aisle between empty car spaces. As we neared the end of the row, I told her to take a gentle right turn and then right again between the next row of vacant spaces. The first turn, made cautiously, went fine. The next turn, was, to put it mildly, cut a little short. I explained that had a car been parked in the first space, she would now be sitting in the front seat of that car.

Again it was her turn for some deep breathing. "Dad, this is hard."

"Oh, you'll get the hang of it," I said. Or we'll die trying. I thought to myself. "Anyway, enough for today."

***

Thanksgiving had been bittersweet. None of the boys had been able to come into town on the day itself, going to in-laws instead. I spent most of the day watching football and mid-afternoon, Tina, Bobbie and I went out to a turkey dinner at the Ye Olde Colonial Tavern, as close to a traditional holiday locale as there was in the area. The boys called that evening, but it was still pretty empty. Only Tina's recounting of our experience at the restaurant, the turkey, stuffing, sweet potatoes, pumpkin pie, and especially the serving staff decked out in pilgrim and Native American costumes kept the evening from being totally dismal.

On Friday, Jeff and Jane dropped by before heading back south. The other boys promised that the next year would be different, as they had promised last year.

Starting two weeks later, with a few driving lessons in between and Bobbie thankfully taking a turn, the trial events went into full gear. Jury selection began. Toward the end of that week, Lillian, through Jim Covain, let us know that the state had decided that it was more likely than not that Luz would be called in order to explain what happened the night that Simon went on the run. Jim asked if we wanted him to tell

Tina, but we told him no, we would handle it. I wondered if the look on my face was as distressed as the one on Roberta's at the news.

"Should we wait until morning?" Bobbie asked.

"There won't be a perfect time. Call her down and we'll tell her now. I'll do it. I'm used to giving bad news to my clients."

Bobbie went upstairs and escorted Tina into the family room. By the look in her eyes, I knew she expected bad news.

"What is it, Dad?"

Trying to be as soothing as I could be, I relayed the information. Tina just sat there. No emotion, no anything.

She looked at both of us then spoke, but it was as if she was disengaged, or even rehearsed. "Don't be worried. I know she's unpredictable, but there isn't too much she can do that hurts any more than anything she's already done. I was already thinking this would happen. Besides, this is in court, with all those lawyers, and cops and a judge. They'll be in control, not her."

"So long as you're okay with it, then so are we," I lied. I imagined Luz, whom I'd never met but knew Tina resembled, losing it on the witness stand, accusing Tina and everyone else of lying and having to be restrained. Tina, sitting there in horror while the defense team slapped each other on the back, celebrating the prosecution's blunder. I was ready to call Lillian and ask her to reconsider, trying to convince her that they could get a conviction without Luz. But I didn't, because I knew they knew how to do their job. Or I hoped so.

***

A few days later, it snowed. The storm went on for over half the day, leaving the ground covered by almost two feet of the white stuff in its wind-driven wake. Schools across the state had been canceled, and despite her protests, Roberta wouldn't let Valentina go out into the drifts while the storm worked its way slowly past.

"But Mom, my mother never let us go out, not even once, to play in the snow. Please, can I go?"

"We'll see later, honey. If it's not too cold after the snow stops."

At least once an hour from nine in the morning until almost four that afternoon, Tina pleaded her case. Finally, just before nightfall, the sun broke through the thinning clouds.

"Now, Mom? Please."

I had just come down from our bedroom where I'd been doing some homework on what had been an unusual snow day off for me.

"Why not, Bobbie?" I asked.

"Hal, I was about to say okay."

"Okay? Are you serious?" Tina laughed and dashed for her boots and winter coat.

As she pulled on her gloves, she made a strange request. "Mom, do we have any food coloring? I need some, right now."

"I think so, but why in the world do you need food coloring?"

"Oh nothing. I just need it."

While Roberta went rummaging through our cluttered spice cabinet, Tina kept repeating how she couldn't believe she was finally getting to play in the snow. This teenager, who looked more grown up than not, was like a kid let loose in a toy store for the first time.

"Here, all I can find is green," Bobbie said as she handed the small brown bottle to Tina.

Tina had barely grabbed the dye before she ran for the front door.

"Be careful, we haven't shoveled yet," I shouted after her, but she had already disappeared out the door and onto our white-blanketed lawn.

From inside, we could hear her squealing with joy. Roberta wandered over to the front window. "Hal, quickly, come here, you have to see this."

I walked over to in time to see this child-woman lying in the snow, and making the most beautiful snow angel I think I'd ever seen. Roberta and I watched until she finished. Slowly, Tina got up, savoring the feeling it seemed, and then reached for the food-coloring bottle she had placed next to her in the snow.

Bobbie shrugged at me as Tina struggled to unscrew the cap. There was just enough light left for us to see that she was bending over and doing something with the dye just above the angel. When she stepped back, there it was, bright green on the white backdrop, in a script as clear as could be, "I Love You, Mom and Dad."

\*\*\*

January, February and most of March, seemed to pass in slow motion, but finally March 24th arrived and the trial just a day away. Mark Goldblatt had seemed reasonably happy with the jury, with women outnumbering men eight to four. He told us that the jury as a whole was at least outwardly open to the idea that monstrous things can happen to the most innocent among us, even if it seemed unimaginable.

This day was the first time that Valentina openly admitted to being worried. She hardly ate and told Josh and Kristin, who by this time knew bits and pieces about her past and that Tina would be testifying, that she needed to be alone and appreciated that they wanted to keep her company. When she wanted to talk at all, it was to Bobbie, and I think I understood.

I hated Simon and detested Luz's weakness. And now, Valentina was going to have to live through it again, face the predator she had thought to be her father. Rely on a group of strangers to ensure that justice, whatever that was, would be done.

By late afternoon, the only person other than us that Tina was willing to have around that day, arrived. Diane Pacquin, today dressed in faded jeans, a loose sweatshirt and with red braided hair, was Tina's favorite person among her official support cadre when it came to confiding her feelings. When the doorbell rang, Tina came down the stairs and hugged our guest.

"Diane, I can't do this," she stated.

"Tina, dear, it's okay for you to feel that way. I know you can do it. You're a brave, strong, young woman."

"I'm only sixteen, and I don't feel so brave. Simon, I think, might do something to me."

Diane stood straight, putting her hands on Tina's shoulders.

"Tina, he'll be guarded the whole time. He can't hurt you anymore. It's your turn to be in charge now. I've been through this sort of thing with many young people who have had to testify. You are as strong as any of them. It'll be hard, but not harder than what he put you through."

"I feel sick," Tina said.

"Just remember what Mark told you at the last meeting. Speak slowly, and if you feel like crying, go right ahead. You'll see, the judge will even give you time to get yourself together. You can be so eloquent. Just say what you know, that's all it takes. And you will be going first, so you'll be over and done before you know it."

"I wish it was over."

"I know," Diane replied, "and it will be very soon. And then your life will start to get back to normal."

"My life isn't normal."

I looked at Bobbie. It looked like she was going to lose it.

Diane stayed another hour, doing her best to boost Tina's confidence even if she wasn't having much luck in lifting her spirits. When she finally left, the three of us were exhausted and the main event hadn't even started.

"We all better get some sleep," I said. "It'll take us an hour to get to Glenwood and we have to meet with Mark and Lillian before court opens."

Tina started to say something, then said to never mind, but changed her mind again. "Mom, I hope this isn't too weird. Will you stay in my room with me tonight? I don't want to be alone." It was just like the day she visited us from the shelter, just before she tried to run away.

Bobbie struggled against her trembling lips. "It's not weird at all," she answered quietly, "Of course I will."

\*\*\*

They had managed to do it. Tina was dressed in what I can best describe as a Mary Jane outfit. The dress had the desired effect of making her look several years younger and not nearly so well developed. It was a rather drab brown with a wide white collar and white trim. Her relative silence from the day before had disintegrated into a stream of nervous chatter. I was glad of it, too, because it made the time go faster. Once in the car, she talked almost non-stop all the way to Glenwood.

That morning was cold. March was ending more like the lion than the lamb. We bundled up against the wind in the walk from the parking lot to the courthouse. There was a small knot of people standing on the front steps, most drinking coffee from the catering truck parked along the curb. One of them gestured our way. I heard another one of them, a man, say "I think that's her," and a woman standing next to him scowl and say something in Spanish. I would later recognize the woman as Simon Texiera's wife, a fixture in her gallery seat throughout the trial.

\*\*\*

He looked nothing like what I'd imagined. No leering face. No towering menacing body. None of that. It took me a moment to realize that the pathetic person walking into the courtroom accompanied by a well-dressed man and woman, each carrying a brief case, was Simon Texiera. I wanted him to visibly have horns and a spiked tail. No, he was shorter than I'd expected, and if he'd ever had swagger, the weight of his prospective loss of freedom had crushed it out of him. Despite that Tina had told me that he was handsome, if it had been so, it was now masked behind dark-circled eyes and a slight double chin, under taut, down-turned lips. I prayed that the enormity of his depravity had finally dawned on him.

Simon was dressed in a suit, the court having agreed that to force him to appear in his regular garb of an orange prison jump suit would be too prejudicial. It took all of my own legal training to dismiss the idea that all the prejudice in the world was too little for him. As he took his place at the defense table, he turned to wave at his wife and then looked hard at who was sitting in the front row behind the prosecutors. If Tina was aware of his stare, she didn't show it, facing forward and waiting for the judge and jury to appear.

Finally, the jury filed in and the bailiff announced His Honor Bennett Johnson. The judge sat and the rest of the room followed suit. In a high pitched voice, the clerk read the name of the case, "State v. Texiera," and announced the charges as sexual assault in the first degree, rape in the first degree, reckless endangerment in the first degree, and a few other lesser charges. If convicted, Simon faced a substantial term away from society. The judge went on to indicate that a Spanish interpreter was on hand so that the defendant could understand the proceedings, thus stretching the process out.

Tina sat between me and Bobbie. Jim Covain sat on the other side of me, with Diane Pacquin on the other side of Bobbie, fulfilling their promise to be there when Tina testified.

Judge Johnson took care of some housekeeping instructions and then spent some time going over the procedure, what the responsibility was of the jury, what the charges signified and that the jury would have to refrain from discussing the case with anyone during the course of the trial, which would last a least several days. The first morning would be spent by the lawyers for both sides making opening statements. Expectations were that testimony would commence sometime that afternoon. Even though Lillian had explained the opening procedure to her, Tina, now sitting in the same room with Simon and having to wait for several hours to start telling her story, shrank down in her seat and gripped my hand even tighter. She must have squeezed Bobbie's hand just as hard because Bobbie seemed to jump slightly.

Hearing Lillian lay out the information she planned to produce and watching Simon's lack of reaction made me wonder if he understood what was happening, even with the translator speaking Spanish a mile a minute. It was a devastating presentation, made even more so by the young age of his victim at the time which the abuse was alleged to have started. As each element of the case was presented, the difference between Simon's extreme composure and the sobbing and murmurs of denial coming from his wife made the whole scene surreal. Tina was not the only victim of Simon's perversion.

The woman who led the defense team emphasized that Simon denied doing anything wrong, that the alleged victim had been so young during the alleged abuse that any recollections had to be viewed as unreliable or even fantasized, that Simon was now a married family man, loved by his wife and whatever wild oats he might have sown as a young man were part of his distant past. She pointed out that Simon left for Puerto Rico when he did, not using the word "fled" that Lillian had used in her opening, because he realized from his companion, the alleged victim's mother, what the little girl was claiming and felt that his chances for a fair hearing as a Hispanic man was unlikely. He left the mainland an innocent but desperate man.

As soon as the attorney, I hadn't gotten got her name, was done, the judge announced the lunch recess and that the first witness would be taking the stand. The five of us, along with Lillian and Mark, decided to skip the court's cafeteria and walk to a small luncheonette up the street, mostly so Tina could get away from the courthouse for an hour. Despite being urged to eat, Tina only had a soda and nibbled at the fries on my plate. Mark, who would be doing the questioning, went over some of the important facts again. Tina told him that she knew what she was supposed to say, and that she was impatient to get it over with.

"Tina," he told her, "remember, I probably won't finish with you today and when all is said and done, the other side might not be done with you even tomorrow. You just have to hang in."

"I know, you've told me a hundred times," she snapped.

"Tina," Diane Pacquin said, "it won't be so bad. Remember, I've seen lots of kids, some younger than you, get through this. It's hard, but it will go by so fast, you'll see."

Tina apologized to Mark who walked around our table and took her hand. "No need to apologize," he said, "I'd be nervous, too, but," he added, "I'm nervous that you'll be so good, that the jury will think you're the lawyer and I'm the witness."

It was good to hear Tina's boisterous laugh.

"Right," she said, "I'm going to be a star."

Mark smiled back and mentioned how pleased he was with Tina's outfit, then said that we should head back. On the walk to the courthouse, Lillian pointed out that both sides were involved in using some psychological games with the jury. In particular, that it was a tactical choice to have Mark question Tina and most of the witnesses because they wanted the jury to see that the male on the prosecution team was representing the State's interest in convicting a male sex offender, even though there was a female prosecutor sitting at the table.

"But remember," she went on, "that the defense is doing the same in reverse. They're having the female attorney be the visible voice in the defense of a male accused of horrible sex crimes against a young girl, even while a male attorney sits by her side. They want the jury to think that there is no way a woman would defend a man guilty of such things. Of course, the jury should just be looking at the evidence, but you never know what will sway them. One thing's for sure, they're going to try and play up Tina's youth at the time as a reason to discard her recollection. It's why Sellie's and the school nurse's testimony become so important. And if Luz will stick to the facts of the night Simon fled, we have a very strong chance to convict. They will try their best to portray Simon as a family man who loves his young daughter."

"It's creepy," Bobbie interrupted, "that he has his own daughter now."

"Creepy, yes, uncommon, no," Jim Covain said. "Many predators father their own victims and it's quite intentional. The new Mrs. Texiera, and more so her daughter, will someday thank their lucky stars if we're successful in putting her man behind bars where he can't harm little girls again."

***

I don't spend much time in court, and it struck me how relatively empty the gallery was. Being so close to the case, it seemed like the most important event on the planet. Apparently it was just another case, no big splash in the press, no prurient gawkers jamming the courthouse hall. Which was probably all for the good since it would seem less to Tina that she was performing in front of an audience. In any case, I don't know if I was the only one in the room who felt as if Tina seemed alone in a vast room when she was called to the stand. I watched the eyes of the jurors, already forming impressions, follow the tall figure in the plain dress as she took the stand. Tina looked straight ahead, purposely, as she told us later, to try and avoid looking at Simon. Even now, she said she still often thought of him as her father and it made her sick.

The judge started the proceedings by indicating that the complaining witness would only be identified as "Miss F," for female, in order to respect her privacy. She was sworn in and the judge asked the prosecution to proceed.

Mark smiled as he stood and moved toward his witness. Tina seemed frozen in place. Then Mark began by asking her to describe her relationship to Simon. She explained how she thought that he and her mother were married and were the parents of both her and her older sister as well as little sister Juanita. Keeping her composure, she testified that it wasn't until after Simon was gone a few years, maybe when she was nine or ten, that she understood that Simon was not related to her and that her natural father, also Selena's father, had had almost no contact with them after Tina was born.

One of the men in the first row of the jury box leaned over to whisper something to the woman next to him. Judge Johnson asked the jury to refrain from conversing with each other. Tina took a sip of water from the glass in front of her. For the moment, the box of Kleenex next to the glass was full.

"Let's go on," Mark said, turning momentarily toward the jury, "please tell us about your feelings toward the defendant."

"I loved him," she answered too softly for anyone to hear.

"Miss F, I know this is hard, but you'll have to speak up," the judge said.

"I'm sorry," Tina replied," trembling noticeably.

"Take a breath," Mark said, "and then repeat the answer."

Tina took a deep breath and repeated loud enough for everyone to hear, "I loved him." For the first time, she reached for the box of tissues and dabbed at her eyes. "I thought he was my father and sometimes he did really nice things."

"Do you remember when you first noticed that he might be doing something wrong?"

"Objection," the female defense attorney said, "calls for a conclusion."

"Counselor, I'll allow her to answer," the judge answered, and we'll decide if the answer can stand."

"I'll rephrase," Mark said. "Miss F, was there a time when the defendant touched you in a way that made you feel uncomfortable?"

"I don't know if I can explain this, but by the time I was old enough to remember, I thought what he was doing with me was what was supposed to happen. I didn't know exactly when he started. But I only know that what he did hurt. It hurt a lot."

Tina sounded more angry than sad. Without Mark saying anything, she continued, "What I remember was that I was in, I think the second grade, and he came into my room like he used to do. I was seven years old. He came into my room a lot. He would wait until my sister was asleep in the next bed. This time, she woke up and he made her watch while he had sex with me. Now I understand that it was rape."

"Objection."

'The jury will disregard the characterization used by the witness."

Tina looked confused, but Mark explained to her why the judge wanted her just to describe what happened.

"Well, he held my sister's arm while he had sex with me. I was crying because it hurt. It woke my mother and she came in. Everyone was yelling and Ma hit Simon. But then she told him to get out before the cops got him." Tina started to cry in earnest.

"Would you like a moment?" the judge inquired. Tina nodded.

Three of the women and two of the men on the jury also dabbed wet streaks from their cheeks.

After Valentina settled down, Mark asked her if she had ever told her mother about Simon's actions before that night.

"I did, but she said she didn't believe me."

"Did you tell her each time?"

Tina took a sip of water and continued.

"No, not every time. I think when it started, I was too little to tell, but by the time I was in kindergarten, it was the first time I remember saying something. But after that, I told her most of the time for a while, but then I stopped."

"Miss F, how old were you when you first told your mother and then tell the court why you stopped telling her."

"I remember I was five years old because it was the day after my birthday." Tina smiled a little and added, "Ma even bought me a birthday cake."

She looked over at the jury, as if worried that she had said something she shouldn't, but Mark noticed and quickly interrupted, "Please, go on."

"Okay. So, I was five and it was a few years before the night Simon left. Every time I told my mother, she would tell me I had a wicked imagination. Sometimes, she would hit me. So I stopped telling her."

Now most of the jury were taking notes. A few simply stared, trying hard not to give away any emotion.

"I even told my older sister and she told Ma."

"Objection, hearsay."

"Sustained."

Tina looked bewildered again.

The judge told her that usually, she could only tell what she said to someone or what they said to her, not what someone said to somebody else.

She said she understood and would try her best.

Mark walked up to Tina and asked her directly, "Did your sister ever tell you that she spoke to your mother?"

"Objection."

"Overruled, the witness may relate what her sister told her."

Tina looked at Mark who reassured her that she could answer and she answered that her sister had told their mother everything that Tina had told her.

"Now, Miss F, after the night that you described, the night that Simon Texiera left, did you have occasion to be called to the school nurse?"

"Yes, I did."

"Do you know why?"

"I had to be examined by the nurse to see if I had been, I mean, if someone had relations with me."

"We know what you mean," Mark replied.

The male defense attorney, who had been silent up until that point, jumped to his feet and fairly shouted, "Objection your honor, counsel is—"

Judge Johnson cut him off. "Yes, he is. Objection sustained and no more editorial comments Mr. Goldblatt. The jury will disregard counsel's comments."

Bobbie poked my arm. "Disregard huh? They were thinking rape without any prompting. Look at them, they're in shock."

I nodded and told her I thought it wouldn't be a matter of whether guilty, but how long he was going to be put away. I looked at my watch. Valentina had been on the stand for well over two hours.

"Please, Miss F, go on," the prosecutor said.

"Well, the nurse, she examined me, but I think there are some things she's not allowed to do. She said I would have to see a doctor. Then the next thing I knew, a man was there from the state and they said I couldn't go back home, that I would be safe."

"And then what happened."

"I was sent to the hospital. A doctor looked at me." She hesitated.

"It's all right. Please explain," Mark said.

Valentina drank some water and blurted as quickly as she could, "The doctor looked inside of me."

"Thank you. What happened next?"

"I got dressed and was sent to a foster home and so was my sister."

"Thank you. No more questions."

The judge looked over at the bailiff and then the clock on the back wall.

"It's been a long day for this witness. We will adjourn until ten tomorrow at which time the defense may start cross-examination."

He banged the gavel; we all stood and filed into the hall where we were joined by Tina, Mark, Diane, and Lillian. Lillian hugged Tina and told how her proud she was.

"But I cried. I didn't want to cry. I wanted to be strong, to show Simon I was strong and he couldn't hurt me. Now he knows he hurt me. He's probably laughing at me."

"I promise you he isn't laughing about anything," Lillian said, "In fact, he's scared to death of you. He's scared to death of the jury and he wishes he'd never met your mother. And don't worry about crying. It makes the jury feel your pain. You know, tomorrow will be harder because the defense will try to make this look like you made it all up. Believe me, the jurors know that you're telling the truth and they know that Simon is guilty. But it's his lawyer's job to try and protect him, so just answer what you know. Mark and I will do our best to make sure it isn't too rough."

She turned to me and Bobbie. "Please get this young lady to bed early. Hopefully she'll be rested and ready to go. And remember, while we can't change what's happened, we can all make sure Simon can't hurt anyone else."

We turned to leave, and once again I spotted Simon's wife, this time sitting on a bench at the far end of the hall, her face buried in her hands. I wondered what she really knew about her husband, of Luz, Tina and the whole Diaz family. I felt sorry for her. The guy's great skill was in damaging females.

***

When we arrived home, it was Tina's good fortune to have Kristin sitting on the front porch. Before we could open the car doors, the kid raced over to Tina's side and motioned for Tina to hurry up.

"Hieee, Tina, come on," she yelled, loud enough, I was sure, to bring Ollie Kintro running.

Tina climbed out of the car. "What's up, Kris?"

"Oh, I was just worried. I almost gave up. I walked all the way here, but my Mom is coming to get me. I thought maybe, but maybe not, you were …"

"I was what?"

"You know, in court and got stuck there and you were scared, that terrible man being there and all."

I couldn't help laughing despite Roberta's dirty look in my direction. But even Valentina grinned and gave her friend a kiss.

"Are you serious? I mean, I was scared, but I was safe, all those police with guns."

"Security officers," I corrected.

"Yeah, well anyway, I'm glad you came, Kris. You make me smile. Ma, can Kristin stay for supper?"

"Yes, of course," Bobbie answered, "but I thought her mother was coming to get her now."

"Oh, my mom won't mind. I mean, I think she won't mind."

Roberta took Kristin's phone number to try and reach her mother before she left home. There was no answer and it was just a few minutes before Kristin's mom arrived. It was the first time Roberta had met her, although I'd seen her at a softball game that had been one of the few that fit her work schedule. Kristin and her mother couldn't have been more alike.

"Well, Mrs. Allen, oh right, you said I could call you Bobbie. Well Bobbie, sure she can stay. If she stays, when would you like me to pick her up?"

"Oh, we can bring her home," I said.

"That would be nice of you, so I think maybe it would be all right. Tina is such a great kid. I'm so glad they're friends."

"We are, too," Bobbie answered.

"Well, yes, well, I guess I'd better be going. She needs to be home by nine, get her beauty rest. Okay?"

"She'll be home before that. Tina has another big day tomorrow," Bobbie said, as the woman settled behind the wheel.

It really was a blessing that Kristin had come by. She took Tina's mind totally off of her next day in court, at least for the couple of hours that she was with us. Of course, it took my mind off of things, too. Kristin was so totally stream of consciousness when she got warmed up that it left very little room for other thoughts to fight their way into the conversation. The two friends helped with the dishes and then went off by themselves for an hour or so before Roberta took Kris home. As soon as her friend left, Tina announced that she couldn't hold her head up another minute and said good night. I hoped it would be a peaceful one, because the next day of cross-examination was likely to be painful for her.

***

Painful. The word doesn't capture that day. The drive to the courthouse was uneventful. Tina, dressed again in her Mary Jane outfit and her hair tied back in a ponytail, actually dozed, waking only moments before we arrived in Glenwood. Bobbie and I were mostly silent, making only occasional small talk. But when I turned the car into the parking lot and had my first glimpse of the courthouse, my stomach turned. Sitting on the steps with a towel pressed against her forehead sat Mrs. Simon Texiera. Several feet away, two police officers were escorting a handcuffed woman to a paddy wagon.

"Aii, that's Mami," Tina shouted, "The cops, they have my mother."

She jumped from the car and started running toward her mother. I scrambled out and ran after her, but was too late to stop her from gaining her mother's attention just before Luz entered the van.

"Ma, what happened?" Tina shouted again.

Luz looked at her daughter, and handcuffed as she was, still managed to make an angry step forward and yell something in Spanish that immediately caused Tina to lose all control. Gesturing wildly, almost pleading, she begged Luz to tell her she loved her, only to receive a derisive scowl in return. The police gave their prisoner a last push and she disappeared inside.

Roberta rushed over to console Tina. In the meantime, I approached another police officer, noticing as I went, that the towel Mrs. Texiera was holding was bloodstained. I asked the officer what happened and he explained that Luz apparently had been waiting outside the courthouse for the Texiera group to arrive and, according to one of the people accompanying the victim, the woman the cops had arrested just walked up and punched Mrs. Texiera twice in the forehead before they could grab Luz and subdue her.

"Nice woman, that one," he said. "I gather that's her daughter over there?"

"Yes," I replied and briefly explained why we were there and who I was.

"Did you understand what she said to her daughter?"

"No, my Spanish is pretty weak."

"Well, I speak Spanish and I can tell you that she told her daughter that she should rot in hell for what she was putting everyone through. She said she was a little whore."

"Oh my God, that woman is even sicker than I thought. The poor kid has to withstand cross-examination today, which was going to be bad enough. I don't see now how she can manage. I have to run."

"Good luck, really," he said as I headed over to Tina and Bobbie.

"Dad," Tina, now calmed down, said, "can you believe her? Do you know what she said to me? I'm mad, I'm sad and it will be too bad for her if anything I say puts Simon in jail. I don't care."

I'd never heard Tina sound so hard. All I could do was nod. Getting through cross-examination might be easier for her than I'd imagined.

"We need to go inside and see Lillian and Mark," Bobbie said, "I wonder if they know about this?"

"Yeah, let's go and get this over with," Tina agreed, and led the way up the stairs.

*** 

Lillian threw her arms out in exasperation. "Mark, I don't know. She defines 'loose cannon'," she said and then shot a worried glance toward Tina. "I'm sorry sweetheart," she said, "it's just that we have a little problem with your mother as a witness."

As it turned out, we were the first people to tell the Texiera prosecutors about the incident at the courthouse entrance. Although trial work wasn't my bailiwick, I knew enough about the business to know the problem Luz presented.

"Yes," Mark added, "we already knew she'd be difficult, but now she's so obviously obsessed with Simon that we have to decide if she's needed at all, or maybe we treat her from the from the start as a hostile witness. Big can of worms."

"But she's in jail," Tina said.

"Oh, she'll be out in a case like hers probably before the day is over. Anyway, being behind bars doesn't stop someone from being a witness," Lillian said as she reached for her legal pad and scratched some notes, "but anyway, if she is to be a witness, I would prefer that she be our witness, even if hostile. We can control her better. The thing is, we want her to corroborate the events of the night Simon left the apartment to run away. You, and even Selena, were so young, that having an adult to buttress the case could be important. We certainly don't want her to sit there and try to testify that Simon never did anything wrong and that you made these things up."

"But that would be a lie," Tina said.

"Yes, we know, and we have ways to deal with that. But having her be so obviously hung up on Simon doesn't help. Anyway, that's a problem for Mark and me to handle. In the meantime, let's get you ready for today. You did fine yesterday and you'll do fine today. I can tell that the jury believed you. Simon's lawyers will try to shake your story. They might even try to make it seem like you were too young to remember or even that you made it all up. Don't let it bother you. It's what they're supposed to do and the judge and we are there to make sure they follow the rules, okay?"

"Okay, I guess. I just want to get this over with. I wish I'd never been born."

"No, Tina no," Bobbie interrupted, "this whole trial is just a step in you getting control of your life. Awful things happened to you, but you're a blessing to us and everyone around you."

"Thanks Mom," Tina even smiled, then frowned, "but I guess I wasn't such a blessing to my mother. Why do I find it normal to call you Mom and feel weird now when I talk about my real mother?"

Lillian wrote another note, and looked up at her star witness. "Tina, dear, for all that you've been through, you're as normal and good as it gets. Believe me, I've seen it all. Maybe, at the end of the day, Luz will come around. Keep your chin up. Come on all, we have to head to the courtroom."

***

From my angle, I couldn't tell if the jury members were staring at Tina or at Simon; probably some of each. Whatever it was, all of them looked grim, as I supposed they should. I wondered if they were aware of the morning's extra-curricular events. They weren't in isolation, but they might not know of any connection between the attack and the case. But there was Mrs. Texiera, apparently determined to stand by her man, sitting there with a rather large bandage above her right temple. I think I was a little bit in awe of the loyalty this guy commanded. My own attention was then pulled away from the gallery and directly to the witness stand as Judge Johnson told the defense that the witness was theirs.

Tina, already settling back in her chair, fiddled with a strand of hair. The attorney who would be leading the cross-examination, whose name I'd learned was Jill Labon, thanked the court and stood in front of her seat. Her smart, two piece blue suit, feminine, mature and businesslike, stood in contrast to the witness's childlike appearance.

"Now, ma'am," she started.

"Ma'am," I thought, "how ridiculous." I even saw a woman juror cringe. Maybe Ms. Labon was trying to destroy the illusion that Tina's outfit was meant to convey.

"Ma'am, you said you were about two years old when these alleged assaults started, correct?"

"Yes."

"Can you describe the first attack? Or the attacker?"

"Well, I was only two, so I only know what people told me."

"Your honor, please instruct the witness to answer yes or no."

"Of course, but you asked two questions."

"Sorry, your honor. But I think we can just take her answers as a no."

Mark rose to object but then sat back down, even as the judge seemed to wait for him.

"Now, you're how old, sixteen? And you say you were seven when my client left the apartment to travel to Puerto Rico."

"Yes."

"That's about nine years ago. Do you fantasize about having sexual intercourse?"

Mark jumped to his feet. "Objection, your honor. Relevance?"

"Just trying to establish the likelihood that the witness has always imagined having relations, especially with my client."

"I'll allow the witness to answer," Judge Johnson ruled, "but be careful where you're going with this."

Valentina looked over at Lillian and then at Simon. If you understand the often-startling combination of innocence, maturity, lack of facility of Tina with words, oddly coupled with her ability to speak poignantly, you never know exactly what to expect from her. And here she was under so much pressure. The room was totally quiet. You could see her struggle to keep from crying.

"How do I explain this?" she took a deep breath as she answered. "I'm a normal girl, and I imagine many things about life. I think I've had a tough life, so sometimes I daydream about being rich, being really loved, and having a lover. I think everyone thinks about those things. But I know one thing. Even though I was just seven at the time Simon left our apartment, I did not make up what happened to me. Maybe I was too little to understand that what he was doing was wrong, but it happened. I'll never forget that night as long as I live."

Tina stopped to take a sip of water. She dabbed at her eyes. Her eyes weren't the only ones that had welled up. I think Ms. Labon probably regretted opening this door.

Tina continued. "People have to understand. I thought that Simon was my real father. He'd been with us from the time I could remember. He didn't just do bad things to me. Sometimes he did nice things. I thought everything he was doing was just what every dad did. One thing I'm lucky about. From where I'm living now, I understand that most dads don't behave that way. Simon has no idea how to love."

I sat there, both touched by her obvious reference to me, and proud of her. If I thought Simon's case was indefensible to begin with, I was convinced now. I couldn't wait to see how Ms. Labon would recover.

"Miss F," Jill Labon went on, her back to the jury as if afraid to read their faces, "if we suppose that your memory of events that took place nine years ago is so clear, how about a year ago? That should be very clear. Isn't it true that you had sexual relations with a man almost twice your age? That you sought him out? That all you ever think about is sleeping with men?"

Tina started to answer, the color rising even against her dark complexion. Before any words came out, she was interrupted.

"The State objects most strenuously, your honor." This time it was Lillian. "Not only is the witness's recent private life irrelevant, but it has no value whatsoever regarding the case before the court."

"I agree. This line of questioning will not be permitted," the judge ruled.

I leaned over to Bobbie. "See, Labon is struggling to make the jury dislike Tina because she knows she can't change the facts. Simon's a dead duck."

"Just one more question and then I'm done with this witness. It's true, is it not, ma'am, that every memory you claim to have of this alleged night with the defendant was put there by other people? That you basically don't remember anything about being seven in any detail at all?"

Mark leaned forward and waited for his witness to answer the defense attorney.

"How could I possibly forget that night?"

"You are trying to have the jury believe that nobody has tried to refresh your memory or put into your memory events that you don't recall?"

"Yes, we talked about it, but I know these things happened."

"Who are the 'we' who talked about it? The attorneys for the State? Your sister? People who have something to gain by filling your head with whatever information will suit their purposes?"

"Objection," Mark said.

"Well, Ms. Labon, will you rephrase that last sentence?"

"Yes, your honor. I just want to make the point with this very important witness that her memory of events is not based on her direct memory."

"I'll allow the question as limited in that way."

Tina, although admitting later that she was intimidated by the jousting of the lawyers, managed to maintain her composure and then answered in the way she was directed to proceed.

"I think I remember everything about that night. The only thing the people you mentioned did was to get me to think about it. Just my sister reminded me of some stuff."

"For the record, your honor," the defense attorney said, now facing the jury, "the witness has admitted that at least some of what she has testified to was not entirely based on her direct recollection. Perhaps none of it. I'm done with her."

Judge Johnson dismissed Tina. The jurors each watched her walk back to the gallery. Roberta asked me if I thought the defense had scored some points with that last question.

"Possibly, but I wouldn't worry," I answered. But I worried. I thought the jury didn't look so embracing of Tina as they had earlier in the day. Maybe I was trying too hard to see things.

"I see we have a little time. I want to recess at twelve thirty," the judge said, "let's get going with the next witness."

Mark turned and asked a bailiff to get his next witness into the chamber. As agreed regarding any witnesses whose names might help to identify Tina's real name, this witness was given a pseudonym. In her case, it was to be Miss Z. Miss Z, otherwise known as Selena Diaz, strode past our row and into the witness box.

I had been present when Lillian and Mark were preparing Sellie for her testimony. Sometimes volatile, and almost always earnest, she had challenged the seasoned prosecutors' patience. She seemed to balk at almost every question or suggestion. It looked as if she couldn't grasp that the people in that meeting were only preparing her for attempts by the defense to discredit her, and they did not question either her memory or her honesty.

I fell again into jury watching, a habit I didn't break throughout. The prosecution hadn't been quite so careful in dictating Selena's court outfit. Although not inappropriate, Sellie wore a sweater that emphasized how buxom she was, and her rather heavy makeup and her figure, bordering on stout, made her look closer to twenty seven than seventeen. From the moment she took the stand until she left the courtroom for good, I never saw anything close to a look of sympathy from even the women jurors. Even though Selena was not the complaining witness, I imagined that it couldn't help if the jury subconsciously transposed some of Selena's characteristics onto her younger sister.

Mark smiled at the witness, I'm sure doing his best to hide the concern he must have felt about how she would perform.

"Miss Z, can you tell the court your relationship to Miss F?"

"She's my little sister," she said, in a voice noticeably more accented than Tina's.

"How much older are you?"

"About eleven months. Ma was busy that year."

Even the judge couldn't help from laughing before he banged his gavel and asked the room to come to order. I think her answer made Mark relax.

"Could you describe your sleeping arrangements with your sister?"

"Yeah. We were in the same bedroom. I don't think I ever had my own room until the State took us away."

"And during the time that you shared a room with Miss F, how would you describe your relationship with the defendant?"

Sellie pointed at Simon. "That son of a bitch, I loved him, I thought he was my dad."

"Young lady," Judge Johnson jumped in, "please watch your language. This is a courtroom, not your backyard."

Selena apologized and Mark went back to his table to pour himself water. He took a swallow, cleared his throat and continued.

"Yes, please just say what you know. Please describe your relationship with the man you thought was you father."

"Like I said, I loved him. He was pretty good to me."

"So you had no reason to be mad at him or to be afraid of him?"

"No."

"Did he ever do anything with you that you regarded as strange or improper or sexual in any way?"

"I don't think so. No, he didn't."

"Now, on the night that the defendant left your apartment for good, can you tell the court what you remember? And as you tell us, can you please first inform the court if anyone, including me or your sister or anyone else you know, had to refresh your memory."

"I don't need no help from nobody. I told you, don't you remember? I ain't going to forget that night ever."

As careful and as articulate as I could recall Sellie ever being, she recounted her terror that night when Simon had yanked her out of bed and forced her to watch him abuse Tina. She caught herself before almost slipping to give Tina's real name. She described how she had been threatened and the scene when her angry mother threw Simon out. Even though the jury had already heard Tina's version, in a way, this telling was more powerful. It took me a moment for me to realize how hard Bobbie was gripping my arm.

"Thank you for being so honest."

"Objection, your honor. He has no business characterizing the witness's testimony."

"Sustained. Please strike counsel's remarks from the record. Watch yourself Mr. Goldblatt."

"Yes, your honor. Now, Miss Z, would you please tell the court if you are aware of any other occasions where Mr. Texiera behaved inappropriately with your sister."

"She told me almost every time. Like plenty."

Jill Labon jumped up again. "Your honor, that's all, hearsay, the defense objects."

Before Judge Johnson could rule, Selena blurted, "Jesus, I mean, what that guy did. My sister ain't a liar."

"Your honor," an exasperated Ms. Labon objected.

Some of the jurors whispered to each other and Mark, clearly no longer relaxed, chimed in.

"I apologize you honor. This is such an emotional time for everyone."

"Emotional or not, the court cannot allow this witness to go on this way. Do you understand that young lady? Mr. Goldblatt? Obviously, Miss Z's outburst will be stricken and the jury advised to disregard what she said."

"I'm sorry, really. Sometimes I get excited," Sellie said.

Mark walked over to Lillian where they conversed for a moment.

"Your honor, we have no more questions of this witness at this time."

The judge looked at his watch. "It looks like we've already gone a little beyond half past noon. We'll recess until two and start with the cross-examination."

The male defense attorney stood up, I still hadn't gotten his name, and told the court that they did not expect a lengthy cross-examination and wondered if court could adjourn for the day when they were done for reasons he could explain in private before court reopened. Judge Johnson looked over at the prosecution table.

"Well, we do have a witness we could start with, but let's hear the defense if it pleases your honor."

"Fine, my chambers at one fifty. The court is now in recess."

# CHAPTER TWELVE

*Spring 2004*

Several police officers stood in front of their Glenwood station, keeping the curious away from the entrance so that the ambulance could move in as close as possible. Lights flashing, the red and white van pulled up and the emergency team ran inside.

The initial shock of discovering the woman dangling from the knotted folds of her slacks, the other end tied to a heating pipe above a chair, faded into a mad scene of efforts to save the prisoner's life. Among the first to reach her once the cell had been unlocked was a young officer who untied the knot around the limp woman's neck and was able to determine that she was alive. Another officer arrived from the station's medical storeroom with an oxygen tank and fixed the mask over the unconscious woman once it was clear that CPR wasn't needed. It took only a few minutes for the ambulance to arrive and the patient was soon moved onto a stretcher and out the door.

Eileen Simms, the officer who'd brought the oxygen tank, had had a little difficulty catching her own breath, nervous sweat discoloring her blue shirt.

"I don't get it," she said to the small knot of people standing in the hall outside the cell. "I mean, she would have been bailed out of here in no time. I never thought I'd see anything like this happen here."

A detective, who'd been on his way to interrogate a suspect in another investigation when the commotion started, nodded. "Yep, but you never know. That woman, her name is Luz Diaz. Her whole family, most of 'em anyway, are nothing but trouble. Drugs, assault, you name it. Between the Blue Hills force and us, they give us plenty of work. What was she doing here? Any idea why she tried to kill herself?"

Officer Latham, who'd cut Luz loose said that he'd heard her shouting from her cell, "If he wants that bitch, he can have her. I fuckin' hate him. No, I love him, I fuckin' love him."

"I guess you didn't know," Latham went on, "I think she had a thing with a guy who's on trial for some sort of child sex abuse. The guy's married and the Diaz woman attacked the wife this morning in front of the courthouse. That's why she was here."

"Sick, all the way around," Officer Simms murmured, "I don't know if I'll ever get used to these kinds of things."

***

At the Glenwood Community Medical Center, Luz Diaz had regained consciousness and was struggling against the restraints that the doctors and police all agreed were needed to keep her from trying to hurt herself or flee.

"I wanna die, just let me die," she moaned in a whisper that was all her throat could muster. "If I can't get rid of the bitch, I just wanna die."

A nurse adjusted an intravenous line and added a stronger sedative. Before long, the patient was quiet.

*** 

One of the prosecutor's clerks delivered the message to Lillian Morten a few minutes after the court had adjourned for the lunch recess. Lillian sought out Mark and found him speaking to Selena. Motioning for him to come over, she suggested to Sellie that she catch up with Tina and the Allen's for lunch. Mark gave Lillian a puzzled look, but his boss's pursed lips told him he needed to hold his question until Selena was gone.

"Lil, I really need to calm her down about cross."

"Cross isn't going to be her big problem. I just got word that Luz tried to hang herself at the lockup."

"Goddammit, the crazy woman."

"We're going to have to tell Sellie and Tina, and before anyone else does if we can. You and I are really going to have to figure out how to proceed, too. Maybe before we go into chambers. I wonder what's up with the defense? Anyway, first things first. Let's find the girls. I think they're in the cafeteria."

Mark and Lillian stepped around the crowd that was waiting for the elevator and took the faster route down the stairs and into the basement lunchroom. The sisters had just returned to a table, while Hal and Roberta Allen were at the cash register.

"Mark, go sit with the girls. This is just as well. I want to tell the Allens first."

Lillian walked toward the foster parents who both gave her a wave. But from Lillian's face, they knew something was wrong. As soon as the lawyer told them what had happened, Mrs. Allen leaned hard against her husband.

"I feel like I got hit by an elephant," she said. "Do the girls know?"

Lillian took a deep breath, "That's next."

"Maybe I should tell them then," Mrs. Allen offered, looking up at her husband for support.

"I agree, but do we know anything about Luz's condition?" Mr. Allen added.

"My information is only that the attempt was unsuccessful and she's under sedation at the hospital."

"Okay, well, that's enough to reassure the girls," he replied, "but Bobbie, I think you should do the talking."

Without waiting, she headed to the table where the girls were eating and asked Mark if she could have a moment alone with them. He excused himself and went to join his fellow prosecutor while Hal Allen replaced him at the table.

"Ma, what's the matter?" Tina asked.

"Well something's happened that you need to know." Although the cafeteria was crowded and noisy, Roberta was sure the whole room was listening. She lowered her voice and leaned across the table. "Let's start with the good news, I think she's going to be all right, but your mother is in the hospital."

"Ma?" Selena shouted, "Oh my god, what happened?"

The sisters held each other and it struck Hal how odd it seemed that the girls were so distraught over bad news concerning this woman who had been pretty much nothing but trouble.

"This is hard, girls, but you're going to hear it sooner or later. She tried to kill herself at the jail," Roberta told them in a voice so broken that she had to repeat herself.

Both sisters screamed so loudly that a woman who was walking past the table turned to see what was happening, bumped into the back of Selena's chair, and sprawled next to Tina, her full lunch tray crashing to the floor, spilling iced tea on Selena in the process. Selena scarcely noticed. Before anyone could stop her, the girl sprinted away and toward the exit.

Tina started up to help the fallen woman, but suddenly clutched her stomach and vomited into her own tray. Hal ran after Selena, while Roberta tended to Tina as a security guard helped the woman to her feet. The two prosecutors, having been a distance away, were too late to do anything but help comfort Tina.

Mark looked at his watch. "Lil, we're supposed to meet with the judge in twenty minutes. Our witness is gone, and this other mess is happening."

"Look, I'll handle the judge. I think he'll understand. See if you can find Mr. Allen, and send word to the police to watch for Sellie. I'm sure she's headed to the hospital. She'd be arriving there in ten minutes or so."

Mark nodded and went toward the exit while he dialed the police.

In the meantime, Tina was arguing with everyone that she be allowed to go to the hospital.

"I know, I know, she's out of her mind, she's mean, but she's my mother. She needs me. Let me go. If you don't take me, I'm gonna find a way."

"Tina," Lillian said, "I know how you must be feeling." She put her arms around the girl in silence for a moment, then continued in a voice even softer than usual, "We'll get you there as soon as we can. Right now, you probably won't be able to do anything but look at her. The doctors probably have her sedated and sleeping."

"It doesn't matter. I can't explain, I just have to see her. Somebody has to call my Aunt Isabel. Carmen, too. And Grandma. Oh, she's gonna be crazy. I'm going."

Tina looked at Roberta, hoping for support. Roberta took the cue and asked Tina to give her a moment with Lillian. Tina promised to sit at their table and not to try and leave. Roberta took Lillian to the far end of the table and stood with her back to Tina as she whispered to the prosecutor.

"Lillian, I don't like the idea of her seeing her mother, and certainly not under these circumstances, but maybe if we just let her go and see she'll calm down enough so we can all get back to concentrating on the trial. Let me call Jim Covain and see what he wants. It really needs to be his decision anyway."

"Well, maybe. I don't like it." Lillian massaged the back of her neck, thinking for a moment. "I don't know. Maybe I'm just upset generally, not only for Tina's sake, but how we deal with the corroboration we might need Luz to testify about. Maybe this takes us off the fence. Okay, yes. Call Covain, we'll go along with him. Look, I have to get to the judge's chambers."

She turned to Tina. "Mrs. Allen is going to call the state to see if they have any problem with you going to see your mom. Promise you'll wait?"

Tina shrugged and gave them a noncommittal nod.

Lillian turned to leave for the conference just as a flushed Harold Allen came back into the lunchroom.

"Couldn't find her. She probably went to the hospital. I just don't know my way around here. Stop and ask anyone for directions and they act like they're stone deaf."

"Yes, likely the hospital. Mark has the police looking," Lillian said, "just get a hold of Jim and keep Tina company until we get out. You guys don't have to be up there anyway. I don't think there's any way the court will proceed, at least not today. I'll get word to you down here."

Roberta watched Lillian go around the corner, then dialed Jim Covain.

***

Jill Labon and her co-counsel, Paul Cofrancesco, both stood before Judge Johnson with their palms extended.

"Judge," Cofrancesco declared, "you have to declare a mistrial. They can't find their witness, apparently not even at the hospital. And remember, the reason we wanted to meet with you in the first place was to discuss the mother. She's on both lists. Now she's gone off the deep end. How we keep the jury from knowing without sequestering is beyond me. We certainly have nothing to proceed on today and our guy is stuck in jail."

"Your honor, the State doesn't see any basis for a mistrial," Lillian responded. We haven't found Ms. Diaz, but I'm sure we will. She's bound to show up somewhere, I still think at the hospital. We can just adjourn for the day."

Judge Johnson leaned forward at his desk, chin resting on two closed fists. "Well, there'll be no mistrial today. But I'll give the prosecution until the end of tomorrow and if no sister, there will have to be a mistrial. But don't go away thinking I'm going to dismiss these charges. As for the mother, look, I can't decide for you what to do with her. If we go forward, she's your problem. She's on the stand, some way or another; she's going to say what she's going to say. I don't need to remind you not to ask her any questions that you know she will deliberately lie about, no matter how much it might help you. Does anyone even know if the woman is in any condition to take the stand any time soon? Anyway, well let the jury know that we're adjourned for the day. Lillian, you and Mark better get to it."

***

"Roberta, I really don't think it's a good idea."

Bobbie held the receiver away from her mouth to tell her husband that Jim Covain wasn't so sure Tina should be allowed to see her mother.

"Hello, Roberta?"

"I'm here."

"Can you stay there for a while? I want to come down and talk with Tina. I'm going to see if Diane Pacquin can leave work early to join us. Takes me about a half hour to get to Glenwood."

"Okay."

"Where's Tina? I want to talk to her."

"We left her sitting at Mark's desk. Just about everyone here is involved in trying to locate Selena."

Roberta called Tina to take the phone. It was clear from hearing Tina's end of the conversation that Jim was giving her a pep talk and getting

Tina to agree that it was good idea for him to come down. After a few moments, she handed the phone back to her foster mother with the comment that she would wait, but she would do what she had to do to see her mother.

*** 

Grandma Diaz was surprised to find the door to the small apartment unlocked, certain she had left the place secure before heading to the market. She nudged the door open with her back while she dragged her wire carriage, with its load of grocery bags piled three high, into the living room and had to catch herself from stumbling backwards over a couch cushion thrown haphazardly on the floor. Immediately afraid, she turned and faced a room that looked like a tornado had plowed through her home. She moved back into the front common hallway, one hand on the doorknob ready to slam it and run.

"Hello, is someone in there?" she yelled.

No reply.

She repeated her demand, this time even louder, and heard some footsteps, accompanied by deep sobs. Now petrified, she pulled the door shut tight and prepared to run when the familiar voice of her granddaughter Selena, now full of anger, replied "Grandma, wait, it's me, Sellie."

Grandma swung the door open and saw Sellie, carefully applied makeup now streaked and wet, and a hair clip dangling next to her ear.

"Selena, what are you doing here? You're supposed to in court today. Why did you wreck the apartment? Calm down. Sit. How did you get here?"

"I hitched."

"That's stupid. Something bad could happen to you."

Sellie put the couch cushions back in place and sank into one corner, trying with some difficulty not to let her jangled nerves completely take control.

"Nani, I guess you don't know yet."

"Don't know what?"

"It's Ma. She's in the hospital. She tried to kill herself."

The old woman gasped, trying to catch her breath. She slumped on the worn easy chair and fanned her face with a sweaty hand.

Sellie pulled herself off the couch and knelt next to her grandmother. She took her hand then held her close, both of them shivering.

"Sorry, Nani," Selena said quietly, "I thought those jerks would have called you. I don't know how bad she is, I just hate her."

The girl became agitated again. "She messes up everything. She don't care about Valentina and her trouble, she don't care about me. She don't care about nobody but herself. I can't take her no more. I'm sorry I messed the place up. I'll fix it. Just, her and everything gotta be so neat, so perfect, I just wanted to make the place look just like her, messed up. That's how it should look."

Grandma didn't answer. She stood with a great deal of effort and walked to the phone, intending to call the Glenwood hospital. Before she could pick up the receiver, the phone rang. She put the phone to her ear and heard a male voice on the other end announce himself as someone named Kirsch from the prosecutor's office, who proceeded to give her the news on Luz.

"You're too damn late. You guys too busy to tell me my daughter almost died?" she shouted, "My granddaughter had to come all the way to Blue Hills to tell me?"

"I'm sorry, ma'm. What's that about your granddaughter?"

"That's goddamn right, she had to come all the way to Blue Hills from Glenwood. Could have been killed herself."

"Ma'am, is your granddaughter Selena Diaz?"

"Yeah."

"Ma'am, look I'm sorry for the late call, but most of us have been spending a lot of time trying to find Selena. She was supposed to be on the witness stand and she took off when she found out about her mother. When she didn't show up at the hospital, we didn't know where she'd turn up. Could you wait a minute? I have someone here who needs to speak with your granddaughter."

While the caller was away from the phone, Grandma Diaz handed the phone to Selena. "Somebody there wants to talk to you. Then I have to call the hospital. I gotta get there. Damn, your mother has the car. I don't have money for a cab. Soon as you get off, I'll see if Carmen is around."

After almost two minutes, Mark Goldblatt's voice inquired, "Selena, you still there?"

"Yeah, I'm here."

"Selena, you can't just take off like that. I know what a shock the news about your mother is, but you have to understand how important you are to helping us put your sister's abuser away."

"I'm sorry, really sorry. I'll be ready. It's just too much. My mother is so bad. I think she's even worse than Simon. I mean, he isn't our real father. She's supposed to keep us safe, and all she does is hurt us." Selena's sentences were punctuated by increasingly uncontrolled sobs. She handed the phone back to her grandmother.

"Mr. Kirsch, will they let me see Luz? I want to come down. I want to see her, too."

"Mrs. Diaz, this is Mark Goldblatt. I'm truly sorry about your daughter. I think they'll let you see her, but I don't know how she is other than she apparently is going to survive this. Tina is pretty upset, but she wants to see Luz, too. We're trying to figure out if DOF will allow it. So, yes, I think you can come down. Oh, I understand that Selena was too upset to talk, but please, I can't emphasize enough that she definitely has to be in court on Monday or else the judge might throw the case out."

Grandma assured the prosecutor that Selena would be there and the call ended. She dialed Carmen, who, after getting over the shock of the news, agreed to come over and drive her mother and niece to Glenwood.

*** 

By the time Jim Covain arrived, the courthouse side of the building was empty except for the cleaning crew. The Texiera jury had been sent home with instructions not to watch TV, listen to the radio, or read any local newspapers. Judge Johnson had considered ordering the jury to be sequestered, but after interviewing each member, and admonishing them that a failure to follow his instructions would compromise the trial, he allowed them to leave.

Over on the other side of the old building, the only people left were Lillian Morten, Mark Goldblatt, Harold and Roberta Allen, and Valentina Diaz. Diane Pacquin was unavailable. When Covain entered Lillian's conference room, Tina was sitting alone in a corner, twisting her blouse bottom into a wrinkled mess and rocking back and forth. Roberta Allen rose to acknowledge the caseworker, gestured toward Tina and pleaded with her eyes that they needed someone to reason with the girl. Covain walked over to Tina and rested a hand on her shoulder, intending to reassure her, but it only made her start, as if she had been alone and unaware of his presence. She looked up at him, and even gave him a weak smile before managing to say, "I want to die. I'm trouble for everyone."

With the others in the room as silent observers, Jim Covain pulled a chair alongside the girl and spoke to her in tones too low for the others to distinguish any of what he was saying. For over ten minutes they sat there, with Tina occasionally nodding, once in a while allowing herself a brief reply, frequently dabbing at her eyes, and once leaning over toward her case- worker to grasp his hands as if never to let go. Finally, she stood and addressed the others.

"This is hard for me. I don't get it, why I feel so attached to her, why I should feel guilty for things that aren't my fault. Just, I think she would be so happy if none of us kids were around to spoil her life."

Roberta began to speak, but her husband nudged her arm and told her to let their foster daughter go on.

"Jim is right; I know this isn't my fault, any of it. My mother needs help, I guess, so I feel sorry for her. I'm stupid, but I can't help it. So, I still want to see her, I mean, she tried to kill herself. But we'll find out if she wants to see me, and if she does, I'll go for a little while, and if she doesn't. I can't promise I won't be hurt, but I'll know just how bad off she is."

Roberta leaned over to Hal and said, "How pathetic. I want to rip my hair out. What this child is going through because of that woman."

Before her husband or anyone else in the room could stop her, Roberta stood up and walked around to Valentina and held her close. The others, all too worn out to do anything but stare and wish that this day would end, gathered their belongings to start for home

\*\*\*

Grandma Diaz, Carmen and Selena stood at the nurse's station on the second floor, the intensive care wing of the hospital. The no-nonsense veteran nurse who they'd spoken with said that unless both doctor and patient agreed, and the patient was deemed able to receive visitors, then and only then would they be allowed in. The three Diaz women had been waiting for over twenty minutes for an answer and were beginning to believe that they'd been forgotten, when the nurse finally returned.

"Okay, here's the situation. The patient is sedated, but awake enough to talk. The resident says he has no objection to a very brief visit from anyone the patient wants to allow in. Brief means maybe ten minutes. She needs rest."

"So that means we can go in now?" Selena asked.

"Well, that's the other thing. She says she'll see you and your grandmother, but not you, I'm afraid," she said gesturing toward Carmen.

Luz's sister drew her hands down the length of her face, almost amused that even now, Luz could manage to hold on to her jealousy.

"I understand. It's okay. You two go on ahead, I'll grab some coffee. I need it anyway," she said, suppressing a yawn.

Her mother muttered something in the way of an apology, having to apologize for Luz had become something she'd been doing since she could remember.

The nurse walked the two remaining visitors toward Luz's room and instructed them, "Usually we would only allow one visitor at time, but we want to keep the time short, so you will go in together and then we will ask you to leave after ten minutes. Maybe in the next day or two she can have longer visits. Her follow-up treatment after she's been released hasn't been decided. You understand that given what she tried to do to herself, something needs to be done for at least a little while to try and get her in the right frame of mind."

Selena was tempted to say, good luck with that. But only said, "I don't know if I want to see her by myself, anyway."

Like the other ICU rooms, Luz's room had a sliding glass door, often kept open. A central control station with a variety of patient monitoring devices sat in the middle of a wide hallway of the semi-circular bank of six rooms. The nurse led the visitors past the station and to the open door of the unit on the far right side. "Remember, ten minutes is all, and then out," she commanded and left them alone.

Selena trailed behind her grandmother as they walked into the room. The girl half-expected to see a corpse, and despite her bitterness, was glad to see her mother lying there with her eyes open, looking almost herself despite an intravenous tube extending from her arm and another monitoring device running from an index-finger to a machine flashing various numbers depicting the patient's heart rate and other vital information.

"My baby, why?" the matriarch said and leaned over to kiss her daughter on the cheek.

"Mami, I can't stand seeing Simon with no other woman. I know, he sometimes done some bad things, but, man, I love him like it drives me nuts."

The heart rate machine beeped several times, and the monitoring nurse came in just to make sure all was okay, explaining that she had to reset the device. She disappeared in a moment.

Luz continued to complain about her long separation from her lover, making no reference to the trial.

Grandma took a deep breath, put her hand on her daughter's arm and said the only thing that made sense to her, "Look, how you feel you can't help. But there ain't no man worth killing yourself over. And that guy, look what he done to your family."

Luz pushed her mother's arm away and growled, "Whatever he done, he don't deserve to be locked up. He needs me to keep him straight."

The volcano that had been bubbling in Selena's stomach erupted without warning.

"You are so fucking stupid, Ma, the most stupid, fucking mean woman in the world. I don't know why I fucking came here," Selena shouted, completely oblivious to her surroundings.

The nurse at the monitoring station came running in, the nurse from the nursing station down the corridor not far behind. Two visitors in other units stepped outside to see what was happening.

"Get offa me," Sellie complained to the older nurse who was pulling her away and down the corridor.

"Oh god, I'm going, I'm going," Grandma said to the younger nurse, hiding her face with her hands so nobody could get a good look at her.

"Your granddaughter cannot come back here," the older nurse said, still moving Sellie quickly to the exit.

"Don't worry, I don't want to see her. She should have killed herself."

"Selena, calm down," Grandma said, "and shut up. Don't you say that no more, she's still my daughter."

Just as they reached the elevator lobby, Carmen came in from the other side. Before she could express her surprise at seeing her mother and niece so soon, her mother told her that they just needed to leave and she would explain it all later.

***

"No, I'm sorry, that isn't possible right now. Not tonight anyway. We'll have to see about tomorrow."

"Why not now, I need to explain to her daughter," Jim Covain said to the resident on Luz's floor after having originally been denied by the senior nurse on duty before asking to speak with a doctor.

It was less than a half hour after the chaotic family scene in Luz's room that Covain placed the call to the hospital. At first, the resident, as the nurse had done few moments earlier had done, told him only that the patient was still agitated and couldn't receive visitors. The caseworker explained how important it was for Valentina to visit her mother, given the trial pressures and related family circumstances. Unlike the nurse, the resident decided to fill Jim in on what had transpired.

"I see. Well, I can see your problem. All I can say is that this girl is nothing like her sister. For some reason, she's much more conflicted about her mother than her older sister is. She would never create a scene."

"I'm sorry, but our responsibility is toward the patient. If it helps any, you can tell her just what I said before, that her mom is still agitated and we have to keep her sedated. Tell her that her mom is in no danger of dying. She just needs some rest and some psychological support. Call back tomorrow and we'll see."

Covain walked back into the conference room and gave the word privately to Tina first and then to the others. He would wait until after Tina left with the Allens before giving the prosecutors all of the details concerning the disastrous hospital visit that they would want to know before court convened again and Sellie went back on the stand. Tina, for her part, was resigned to, if not satisfied with, the answer, still hoping that the next day she would get the visit she felt she needed to have.

# CHAPTER THIRTEEN

*Spring 2004*

Our house looked totally neglected. Getting Tina ready for the ordeal of the trial had pushed all of our usual springtime chores into a corner. I'd been too stubborn to heed Bobbie's suggestion to hire a landscaper, assuring her that I'd have plenty of time to get the lawn and garden ready and the leftover leaves of fall hauled into the woods. As soon as we pulled into the driveway after the trauma of the whole day at the courthouse, the sea of dandelions and emerging crabgrass were an immediate reminder of just how different our lives had become. I imagined Ollie Kintro complaining to the neighbors about the eyesore next door. The idle thought crossed my mind that anything that drove Kintro crazy was not necessarily a bad thing. Anyway, I made a note to get the weed killer spread the next morning, just to get us feeling some sense of routine again, if nothing more.

Tina went straight to the refrigerator and started a binge that lasted an hour. The only thing she said during the tense ride home was that all she could think of now was food. She never mentioned Luz, never mentioned the trial, not a mention of anything but food. Bobbie and I left her alone. She needed to let her get the events of the day out of her system however she wanted. From our bedroom, we could hear Tina pacing below, and after a while, climb the stairs and shut the door to her room.

***

The next morning, the weather turned unseasonably hot. Tina was still asleep at ten when I headed out to do the yard work. Despite the immediate stream of sweat soaking my Red Sox tee shirt, it felt good to forget about things for a while. I even managed to acknowledge my wonderful neighbor, who, I guess to his credit, was in the never-ending process of tending his garden. He even smiled, evidently pleased that the value of his home was increasing by each pass of my lawn spreader.

By noon, I was exhausted and several pounds lighter. I opened a beer, drained it almost without taking a breath, and headed for the shower. When I emerged, my wife was sitting on the edge of our bed holding the phone to her ear, nodding once in a while, before hanging up.

"Hal, that was Lillian. She's actually in the office today."

"And?"

"And she has some news that Tina won't want to hear. Her mother refuses to see her. Lillian is also pretty near deciding not to call Luz as a witness even though her testimony is important. She thinks Luz is too unpredictable and too in love with Texiera to tell the truth. She thinks the other side won't call her either, mainly for the first reason. Far too unpredictable."

"Well, hopefully we can give Tina some excuse she can accept. She'd be too hurt."

"Who'd be too hurt?" Tina's voice sounded from the hall. I hadn't heard her open her bedroom door. She came into our room, all ready for the heat in short shorts, a tank top, and her hair piled on top of her head and away from her face and neck. "What's the problem, Dad?"

"No, sweetie, I said 'she's too hurt'. Your mom is too hurt to see visitors. You'll have to wait a while. Actually, it's not that she's hurt, she's just too depressed. I hope you understand."

Tina slumped next to Roberta, who took my cue and told her that "in time" her mother would probably want to see her.

There are phrases in the English language Tina doesn't understand. But in this case, the implication of Roberta's choice of words seemed to cut Tina with the precision of a surgeon's scalpel.

"When is it my time and not hers?" she asked.

***

Having been advised that the missing witness had been found and would be back in court, Judge Johnson started the next Monday with another chambers meeting among the lawyers. As Mark told us before the opening gavel that day, the judge warned everyone that they had to keep everybody under control. He added that both sides indicated that they were keeping Luz Diaz on their witness list, although I had the feeling that she was the last person Mark wanted on the stand.

At 10:00 sharp, the bailiff began the proceedings as the judge entered from his chambers. It promised to be a very uncomfortable day, not just because nobody knew what to expect from the witness, Miss Z, but because the air-conditioning was down on this strangely sweltering day. The courthouse staff had recovered three old-fashioned rotating fans from storage. One was set close to the judge and the witness stand, the other two near the two attorney tables and the one closest to the prosecutors also rotated toward the jury. The judge, the witness box, the lawyers and the jurors were all well-supplied with water. The gallery was out of luck. Judge Johnson indicated that they regretted not being able to allow the spectators to bring food or drink in, but assured that there would be a large supply of water in ice chests in the hall outside available to anyone. He pointed out that the courthouse had a first aid room with a nurse available at all times for anyone who was adversely affected by the heat. The hum of the fans promised to make it difficult for the lawyers and witnesses to be audible, and one of the fans rattled constantly despite efforts by a maintenance man to correct the problem. The whole scene reminded me of one of those Hollywood courtroom dramas set in the 1920s South with everyone wiping their necks with soaked handkerchiefs and women cooling themselves with palm-shaped fans.

I daydreamed enough to miss the court re-calling Selena to the stand. Her white blouse was already sweat-stained and she swallowed a whole glass of water before the questioning began.

The judge reminded Miss Z that she was still under oath. Based on the chambers meeting, nobody mentioned why the witness was unavailable at the end of the previous week other than Judge Johnson saying that he was "glad that she was feeling better." It seemed pretty clear that the judge and the lawyers were aiming to keep the jury unaware of the suicide attempt.

Jill Labon, suit jacket removed, walked to a spot where the jury, the judge and the witness would be able to hear her above the din. I wondered how she really felt about the case. She was straightforward, never dramatic. With her hands clasped behind her back, she began her cross-examination.

"Miss Z, you indicated on direct testimony that you shared a bedroom room with your sister during the time when the alleged incident occurred. You also indicated that my client never touched you. Is that correct?"

"Yes, I said it because that's the truth."

"Isn't it true that you fantasized about him? That you fantasize about men, and that you sometimes even fantasize about your little sister with men?"

"Objection," Lillian said, jumping to her feet.

"How can you fuckin' say that," Sellie shouted, losing her cool, forgetting every bit of coaching by the State's lawyers.

"Miss Z, I told you before to watch your language, and simmer down," Judge Johnson said, "and the objection is sustained."

"Please your honor, my questions goes to the credibility of this witness," Jill Labon argued. "I intend to show that her supposed corroboration is the product of her own vivid imagination and a reflection of her own inability to behave like a proper young lady."

Selena kicked at the witness chair, chest heaving. The judge looked down at her angrily and she sank back into her seat. He turned his attention to the attorneys.

Calling both teams of lawyers to the bench Judge Johnson shook his head from side to side, his face a deep red. The rattle of the old fan was the only noise in the room. From the expression on their faces, Simon Texiera's attorneys seemed unhappy. After a minute or so, the lawyers dropped back to their battle stations and the judge addressed the jury.

"I apologize to you, as does the witness, I'm sure, for her outburst. Nonetheless, the question posed by the defense will not be permitted. Miss Labon, you may proceed."

"If it please your honor, I have just a few more questions of this witness. Miss Z, on the night in question that my client left the apartment, you were, I believe, eight years old. Is that correct?"

"Yes."

"What experience did you have with sexual intercourse?"

Sellie looked over at Mark and her face colored. "I didn't have none."

"Did you know what it was at all? Yes or no."

"Not exactly, but—"

"Your honor, please direct the witness to answer yes or no."

Selena must have been worried that the wrong answer would harm the case, and her eyes pleaded again with Mark for direction. From my seat behind him, it appeared to me that he was making a point of not returning her gaze.

"Please answer the question Miss Z," the judge directed.

"No, I was just a kid."

Miss Labon was probably delighted that Miss Z hadn't stopped at a simple "no." Lillian leaned over to Mark and whispered something in his ear.

"No further questions of this witness, your honor."

Lillian stood up. "Redirect your honor. Miss Z, what did you think you were witnessing?"

"My dad, that's who I thought he was, was very excited and being very rough. When he was nice and hugging and stuff, he never looked like that. Ti ..., I mean my sister, she never cried if he was just hugging. I was really scared."

Lillian paused for a moment, walked over to her seat to look at her notes, pulled her glasses off and twisted them while looking at Selena. "No more questions your honor."

Selena stepped from the stand and headed to the exit, intercepted briefly by Mark, who, it seems, told her to wait in his office. Several people in the gallery followed her into the hall to take a cold bottled water. Bobbie asked me if I wanted to step out as well. I shook my head no and told her to go ahead if she wanted. She didn't bother to respond, just got up to stretch and sat right back down.

"We still have some time, are you ready with the next witness?" Judge Johnson inquired of the prosecution.

Luz, Luz Diaz should have been the next witness, I thought, sweating in this building with the rest of us, itching to put that molesting son of a bitch away, standing up for her little girl, my little girl.

Mark Goldblatt, along with Lillian, having decided to go ahead without Luz and call her only as a last resort, penetrated my private rant when he stood and replied, "Yes your honor. We call Regina Boughton."

Regina Boughton, the school nurse who had examined Tina the day after Simon's last attack and concluded that she likely had been sexually assaulted, came in from the rear entrance. As I understood it, the doctor who'd examined Tina would have been preferred, but he had died a few years ago and while the medical record existed and would later be introduced by a hospital record keeper, Lillian felt that having live testimony would have the desired impact on the jury. As for the nurse, certainly this was no pleasure for her, having to fly for several hours, giving up a few days from her dream retirement, probably enduring many sleepless nights and readily agreeing to testify on behalf of a child she barely knew but whom she couldn't forget. Luz popped into my mind again.

As the stout, sixtyish woman was being sworn in, I looked over at Simon Texiera, hands clasped on the defense table, head bowed and being cooled by the swishing fan a few feet away. Funny, but he almost seemed irrelevant to the case. I couldn't help feeling that Valentina was on trial. Whether or not the man understood enough English to follow the proceedings, I hadn't the slightest idea. I hoped so, because I didn't want anything to be lost in translation.

The young prosecutor led the witness through the morning of her examination of the child. While the nurse was describing her opinion that had been reported to school and police and confirmed by a physician, that that there were outward signs of abuse, the jurors were busy writing notes. Mark repeatedly mentioned Tina's age at the time, and every time he said "seven" I hoped that any small doubts raised at the end of Sellie's testimony would be erased. When the nurse finished describing the bruises and small cuts she had found, Roberta let out an audible sigh. She spoke for just about everyone in the room, maybe even the defense.

As Mark finished with the nurse, Judge Johnson indicated that the lunch recess was approaching and inquired of Jill Labon what her intentions were with the witness.

"Your honor, we have only one or two questions of this witness. I would prefer to proceed now."

"Go ahead, but be prepared to be interrupted if this takes too long."

"Yes, your honor. Mrs. Boughton, the injuries you described, do you know who caused them?"

"Well, I suppose by the defendant."

"Your honor ..."

"Yes, I know Ms. Labon. No conjecture from the witness, please, just state what you know and the jury will disregard the last response."

"Sorry, your honor. No I can't say that I definitely know who caused this injury."

Jill Labon glanced at the jury, certain that she had scored at least a small victory. "And one last question. Is it not possible that the injuries you described could have been caused some other way, even been self inflicted?"

The nurse glared at the lawyer. "In my experience, highly unlikely."

"Please answer, possible or not?"

"Possible, but from a seven year old, highly unlikely."

"Please, just answer, possible, yes or no?"

"Yes, possible."

Another glance at the jury.

I worried that small doubts could become reasonable doubts and once again, Luz was there, and I could see her lying in self-pity in a hospital bed. When I focused again, I saw that the witness chair was empty, and everyone was filing out of the stifling room.

*** 

We spent a part of the ninety minutes lunch recess back in the prosecutor's conference room. The first ten minutes or so were taken up by both Mark and Lillian getting the still angry Selena calmed down. She was having the hardest time accepting the fact that the defense lawyers were only doing their job and they had to try and discredit prosecution witnesses. Beyond that, her disgust with her mother punctuated the discussion.

For her part, Tina was mostly silent and exhausted, scarcely any expression in her normally animated eyes. Bobbie spent a few minutes massaging Tina's shoulders and at Lillian's urging, Bobbie and I and the sisters headed for the cafeteria. On my way to the door, I quietly asked Lillian how much she felt not having Luz corroborate the events of that last evening would hurt.

"Exactly what we'll be discussing while you're eating. Maybe we need her."

"Need her?" I said perhaps a little too vehemently, "Jesus, she should be on trial. Why isn't she on trial?"

Lillian put a hand on my shoulder with that calmness that made her seem to be always in control, and simply said, "If we can't use her as a witness, she may have hung herself in more ways than one. And that gives me a great idea."

\*\*\*

In that afternoon's proceedings the hospital records of Tina's examination were introduced without challenge. Then Mark put a PhD. on the stand who was an expert on child abuse, particularly sexual assault cases. Jill Labon spent a few minutes challenging his credentials, but ultimately acknowledged his expert qualifications. I found his testimony too clinical, even if thorough. It was almost as if abuse happened in the abstract. Maybe I was just too close to the case. I wanted Texiera to bleed with every word and hoped that maybe the Spanish translation carried more emotional impact, but Simon just sat there as if he was attending some required college lecture.

Throughout that afternoon, Lillian Morten had been absent, finally entering the courtroom just minutes before the defense was finishing a perfunctory cross-examination of the PhD. Lillian seemed more animated than usual, engaging with Mark in a whispered conversation that drew glances from the judge. They broke their huddle just as Jill Labon finished with the witness. Judge Johnson turned his attention to the prosecution table.

"There seems to have been a little party going on over there," he grumbled, "but for the record, you seem to have run out of witnesses. Are you ready to rest?"

"Your honor," Lillian said, "sorry for the distraction. But no, we are not ready to rest, we have one more witness to call, but we need an extra day before proceeding."

"Tell me more, Ms. Morten."

"Your honor, the prosecution intends to call the mother of the complaining witness to the stand. As you may know she needs some extra time to be ready, and we are advised that the day after tomorrow should be appropriate."

Roberta nudged me hard, her mouth wide open. Tina, who had seemed bored all afternoon, fanned herself with an open hand. The defense team jumped up to support the request for an extra day, and for the first time, Simon Texiera seemed not to have to wait for translation as he turned and shot a glance toward his puzzled wife.

Judge Johnson, fully understanding the potential legal, if not physical chaos that promised to unfold in his courtroom, leaned back in his seat. Then before addressing the attorneys, he asked that the jury retire for the day, and that they should wait in their room before departing to get instructions on when to return to court. After they had filed out, he took a few seconds collecting his thoughts and then asked the lawyers to approach out of everyone else's hearing. Later, Lillian filled us in on the side bar.

The judge had started off.

"As we discussed in chambers, this is your call. First of all, I want to be sure that only one extra day is enough. What information does the prosecution have that this witness is well enough physically and mentally to testify so soon?"

Lillian told him that she had spent all afternoon at the hospital first talking with the doctors, especially the shrink, and then Luz. She had told the judge that, "Physically she is in decent shape, better than many witnesses I've seen in my day. Mentally, the psychiatrist says that Luz knows fact from fiction. As far as emotional stability goes, frankly, I'm praying, but I don't know if that woman has ever been emotionally sound. The doctor says a lot of what drives her is the need for attention and love, but obviously suicide is a rough way to get attention." She indicated that from her meeting with Luz, she seemed almost too willing to testify.

Then Judge Johnson asked for the defense to speak. Jill Labon told him she had approached the case both with and without Luz's testimony, possibly even as her own witness, and would proceed as the Court required.

Lillian told me and Roberta after court finally adjourned that day that they saw several benefits to using Luz, that even an outburst wouldn't be all that unwelcome, and if she lied or was uncooperative, that wouldn't be so bad either because they thought the jury would see through it. The real prize would be to get her corroboration on the record. It would be beneficial in resolving any issue in the jurors' minds regarding faulty recollections of the sisters, or any inability to conclusively identify Simon as the perpetrator.

Judge Johnson threw them a curve when he said that he wanted to speak with the hospital psychiatrist directly before exposing his courtroom to this witness so soon after her suicide attempt. He also admonished both sides that if and when the witness testified, they needed to be certain to avoid as best they could allowing the witness to knowingly perjure herself. In order to maintain Tina's anonymity, Luz would be called Mrs. A.

After several minutes, the judge sent the attorneys back to their tables and went on the record.

"Court will stand in recess until Thursday at 10 a.m., at which time we will proceed as will be discussed in my chambers at 3:30, the day after tomorrow."

So the judge was taking one day more than requested before resuming the trial. The whole experience was so tiring; I wondered how anyone could stand going through a trial that lasted months, even years, when our mere few weeks drained us so. It was a wonder how Valentina was handling all this, but if she was anything at all, she was a survivor.

***

As much as the relatively rapid pace of the trial seemed like an eternity, the two-day hiatus awaiting the judge's decision regarding Luz created a snail's-paced reality of its own. I took the opportunity to go into the office, but I can't say that I was any good to anyone. Meanwhile, Bobbie decided that Tina should go to school and do some catching up in person, as diligent as she had tried to be with assignments she had been given ahead of time by her teachers. For her own part, Bobbie spent her time shopping and cooking a few of the types of full dinners we'd had few of on trial days.

On the first evening of the two days, Valentina maintained her silence, at least regarding anything connected to the trial. Between bites of baked chicken, she did manage a few questions about her math homework, but it was one of those times, becoming more frequent, that making conversation seemed like a chore for the girl. Shortly after putting the last plate in the dishwasher, she called Kristin to cancel a tentative visit that night and announced that she was heading for bed.

The next day seemed to drag by even more slowly, with the time appointed by the judge for giving the lawyers the word on Luz set for late afternoon. I made it at the office until noon before deciding that waiting at home was preferable to putting my staff on edge by having to put up with my own case of nerves. All I could imagine was Luz sitting in the witness chair, making Simon Texiera seem like a saint and her daughter some sort of troubled kid.

Watching TV seemed more annoying than distracting while I spent the afternoon waiting for Roberta to get back from another shopping excursion. I found myself drawn to an hour and a half of those courtroom shows where a publicity crazed judge brow beats some hapless, lawyerless, litigant in a case worth $200. Maybe some psychologist can explain why I would be drawn to court room dramas under the present circumstances, but at least it passed the time.

Bobbie arrived home at a little after two and Tina about a half hour later, surprisingly with Kristin in tow.

I wasn't sure that I wanted her around with the expected ruling maybe a few hours away, but if Tina wanted company, that's all that mattered. I don't know how well Kristin entirely understood what her friend was enduring, but she certainly knew her friend was suffering and was intent on getting her mind off things.

"Hey, Tina, ya wanna throw the ball around?" she asked.

"No, it's too hot."

"Hey, Tina, ya wanna listen to the radio, maybe dance a little?"

"No Kris, I don't think so."

"Whatever you want, girl," Kristin sang, "but I'm gonna rock and you can just watch if you want."

Kristin pulled Valentina out of our kitchen and up the stairs to Tina's room. I could hear the radio blasting and at first just Kris, but then both girls, singing at the top of their lungs. The music continued for quite some time and was loud enough that Tina didn't hear the phone ring at a little past four.

Roberta answered and told me to pick up an extension. Lillian had Judge Johnson's decision.

"We're being allowed, for better or worse, to call Luz," she said, "The judge told us that the doctors advised him that physically Luz is able, and mentally, while depressed, there's nothing in her current state that should prevent her from understanding and answering questions. Luz has been consulted and is even anxious to take the stand. Not only that, but she's being released as we speak. I don't know. The more Mark and I discuss it, the less confident I am that this is a necessary or wise move. It's just that when you take Tina and Sellie's testimony, and their youth at the time, coupled with the absence of testimony affirmatively identifying Simon as the culprit, I'm worried that this jury will find enough doubt to find him not guilty, even if in their hearts they know he's guilty of this and lord knows what else."

"So, have you decided?" I asked.

"The tilt is toward calling her. If not, we rest and the defense goes ahead. We're having her come to the court house and she'll be waiting in my office. It's kind of unusual for a witness, but given her attack on Mrs. Texiera and her suicide attempt, we're arranging to pick her up and sneak her in a side door and away from everybody. Right now I think we need her testimony. If she lies, then we think we can make it clear enough that she's lying to have her actually help us to convict. One more thing; we don't want Tina in the courtroom during her mother's testimony."

"Thanks for that," Roberta said.

"Yes, she doesn't need to go through that. We're going to have Tina wait in a room where she and her mother are not likely to see each other. You can stay with her."

"Roberta will stay, I'm going into the courtroom," I said.

"Be my guest," Bobbie answered.

A short time later, Tina and Kristin came downstairs when Kristin's mom arrived to take her home. When Tina walked back inside, Bobbie broke the news.

*** 

Possibly the only good thing about the next day was, that despite the continuing heat wave, the air conditioning was now working in the courthouse. The creaky fan was gone, but the courtroom was more crowded than it had been throughout the trial. Before the opening gavel, the din of anticipation from the gallery was in stark contrast to the original, quiet days at the opening of the trial. There had been some brief hearings on other cases, and it seemed that the Texiera case, through local press coverage, was drawing some interest. The gallery now included curious Glenwood and Blue Hills residents as well as several of the five or six attorneys who had been present for the early docket, apparently with some time to kill and drawn to the drama of the case. The crowded room seemed almost as warm as the last day.

Valentina and Roberta were waiting nervously in a conference room, with no telling how long Luz would be on the stand. I kept checking my watch, as if it would make ten o'clock arrive sooner. A few minutes after the scheduled opening, all of the lawyers and then Simon filed into the room. His wife and her companions were already seated, Mrs. Texiera surely not knowing what to expect other than that her attacker would be taking the stand. Then the bailiff asked us all to rise and the judge called the court to order. Looking weary, he asked the prosecution if it was ready to proceed.

Mark Goldblatt stood and said, "We are your honor. The State calls the witness to be identified here as Mrs. A."

Slowly, Luz Diaz struggled up the aisle and through the gallery gate to the witness stand. Although there was nothing wrong with her legs, there was little doubt that Luz intended to play the victim. She was dressed very simply in a white blouse buttoned to just below her chin, evidently to hide the abrasions left by her suicide attempt, and a loose fitting blue skirt. Her hair, cropped short by the hospital staff, seemed unbrushed and she wore no makeup. Tina resembled her so much that were it not for twenty five pounds that I gathered were added over the last few years and the fact that she was a few inches shorter than her daughter, they might have been twins.

In the row behind me, I heard a reporter say to another, "Hey, that's Luz Diaz. I know her from some problems she's had in Blue Hills." It looked as if the attempt to keep Tina's identity confidential might be doomed.

The bailiff attempted to swear Luz in but she failed to respond. A short dialog ensued among the judge, the interpreter and the witness. The witness, it seems, claimed that her ability to converse in English was limited to common words, not courtroom vernacular, and so everything had to be translated, even the swearing in. From what I knew, I thought Luz was just posturing. The judge ordered the interpreter to administer the oath and Mrs. A was ready to testify.

Mark reminded the witness that she was sworn to tell the truth and she nodded after the translator was done.

She started by identifying herself as the mother of the complaining witness. After a few more preliminary questions, Mark cut to the chase.

"Mrs. A, were there any occasions where your daughter, Miss F, told you that the defendant had touched her inappropriately?"

A pause for translation, another while the witness answered in Spanish, followed by the translation to English.

"I do not remember such a thing, but she always told stories, so maybe."

"Do you recall how old your daughter was when she first told you such a story?"

"I told you, I don't remember such stories, so how could I tell you how old she was?"

Mark glanced back at Lillian and paused for a moment before resuming.

"Okay, so you don't remember. Do you remember an evening where you were awakened by screams coming from the bedroom Miss F shared with Miss Z?"

Mark looked again back at Lillian, then at the defense table and then Judge Johnson. The judge sat impassively, but worried that the witness was about to make a shambles of the truth.

Luz cleared her throat, and then spoke rapidly in Spanish. I thought I heard the name "Valentina" and the interpreter paused and asked to speak with the judge. Judge Johnson asked him to wait a moment and called the attorneys to the bench. They all nodded and the judge asked the interpreter to tell the witness not to use her daughter's name. The interpreter then repeated the witness's answer.

"Well, there was a lot of commotion and Simon was struggling with my daughter. Maybe she was not behaving, I don't know. She was sometimes a bad girl. My Simon, he loved her, but I let him punish her if she was bad. I don't know, but the neighbors, they hear a lot and I was afraid they would think Simon hit her too hard and I told him he better leave, but he didn't hit her. She was crazy crying, such a bad girl."

Mark walked up to the witness box, as close to Luz as possible and stared intently. Then, scowling, he turned to the judge.

"I request the court to allow me to treat this witness as hostile."

Jill Labon rushed beside Mark and told the judge that she objected.

"The witness is answering as best she can."

"She certainly is answering," Judge Johnson responded, "but the motion is granted. Ladies and gentleman of the jury, as you've been told, when a witness is declared to be hostile, it means the witness is seen to be answering against the case being presented by the calling party. The attorneys who called the witness may treat them as if they had been called to the stand by the other party, meaning they can ask cross-examining type questions. I am asking the interpreter to explain this to the witness."

Simon Texiera allowed himself a smile even as his young wife fidgeted in her seat. I was glad that neither Tina nor Bobbie was in the room to hear Luz try to free her daughter's attacker.

Mark bore in.

"Isn't it true that you were angry because you caught your boyfriend sexually molesting your seven year old daughter?"

"You're lying. He was punishing her."

"Isn't it true that you told him to run so he wouldn't face exactly what he is facing in this courtroom? Because you knew he was molesting your daughter?"

"I would hate him if he did that. He is a good man. My daughter lies."

"How do you explain that the school nurse and the hospital doctor determined just the next day that she had been sexually molested, in fact raped?"

She shouted an answer. Spanish speaking people in the gallery murmured. Once again the translator looked for guidance. He was told to translate exactly as the witness had answered.

Your honor, she said, "She fucking did it to herself, the little bitch."

Wagging his finger toward Luz, the judge demanded that the witness be warned to watch her language or he would find her in contempt.

Mark, nearly shouting, followed up. "Isn't it true that you really don't need translation, that your English is quite good and that you understand every word I'm saying?"

Jill Labon complained, "Your honor that question is out of order. We all agreed to the translation."

Mark retorted, "Your honor, that agreement was for the purpose of making sure that the defendant was being allowed to understand the proceedings. My question is for the sole purpose of showing that this witness is adept at deception and lying when it suits her, and this is one of those occasions."

Before the judge could respond, Luz tossed her head back and snarled in clear, but accented English, "Goddamn right I understand. I understand that my sweet little Valentina Diaz is a liar. Simon never touched nobody. I'm telling the truth."

The judge slammed down his gavel. "Recess and counsel to chambers. Jury to their room. Nobody else is to leave this room, no one."

The jury filed out, then the judge started to step down.

For a moment Luz seemed confused, but seeing her chance, she dashed to the defense table and tried to reach Simon who shrank back as a bailiff grabbed Luz from behind and dragged her kicking and screaming through a side door. Lillian chased them, yelling for the bailiff to keep her in an adjacent room. Throwing up his hands, Judge Johnson stalked into his chambers.

In the row behind me, through the chatter of the excited spectators, I heard the Glenwood reporter ask his Blue Hills colleague if the name the witness used was Valentina. Losing all of my composure, I turned and told the both of them that if they printed that kid's name in the papers, I would ruin them, though I had no idea what I could do to stop them. One of them growled back, "Who the hell are you?"

I thought the better of retorting, and regained control of myself enough to end the confrontation with just a nasty stare.

While I was so occupied, Lillian rejoined Mark and they and the defense team headed through the door to the judge's chambers. Almost a half hour passed before they emerged and the court was called to order. The jury remained excluded.

Leaning forward and staring down from his chair behind the bench elevated two feet above the floor, and spitting each word, Judge Johnson pointed a finger at the gallery. "None of you are jurors, but you are all witnesses to these proceedings. All sides in this case have gone out of their way to protect the anonymity of the complaining witness. Now, at the moment, I'm not in a position to judge the value of the current witness's statements in court, but I sure am going to tell you that for purposes of this trial, under pain of contempt of this court and incarceration, none of you will disclose the name of the complaining witness. Nor, will members of the press report the name."

I wanted to applaud the judge, but instead, turned to the reporters behind me, and simply said, "There."

The Blue Hills reporter said, "We'll see about that."

Why a two-bit reporter from a small town rag could be so defiant was beyond me.

The judge wasn't through. "Mrs. A is going to step back on the stand. The jury knows nothing of her actions at the beginning of recess, and she has been told that if she does not behave as required and refrain from uttering that name, she will also face consequences from me. I believe that we have reached a solid understanding. We will continue with the translations. And this courtroom will be totally silent. Now recall the jury."

The jury came in and the judge advised them that he had called the recess because the complaining witness's mother had apparently not fully understood the need to keep the name of the alleged victim confidential. He told them not to mention the name to anybody under pain of dismissal and more severe consequences.

At last, Luz Diaz was ushered back into the witness box and reminded that she was still under oath.

Mark Goldblatt turned toward the jury as he asked the next question.

"So, we are to understand that not only was Miss F imagining an attack, but so was her sister, Miss Z."

"She was too little to know what she been looking at."

"And Miss F was not too young to understand what it took to make herself look sexually abused?"

Luz hesitated to allow the interpreter to finish his translation as if she really didn't get the gist of the question then shrugged. "No, man, I don't know. You know kids, they hear stories. They know a lot."

Mark told me afterward that he was convinced at that point that Luz's lies were so obvious that he needed no more from her, but he'd decided to close one last hole.

"Mrs. A, do you recall making a phone call to an establishment in Blue Hills known as the San Pedro the day after the attack? That you were calling there because you knew that is where the defendant was likely to be, so you could warn the defendant that the police were after him and to flee? That you did so not because you thought him to be innocent, but you knew him to be guilty and were also afraid that you would be arrested, too?"

"Yes, I called him, but like I been telling everyone, I was scared that my man would not be treated right, that nobody would believe him. The cops would frame him and just like this, there wouldn't be no fair trial."

Mark faced the jury again and said, "I have no more questions."

Now it was the defense's turn and I was anxious to see how they would handle the witness. It was one thing for Luz to have lied as a hostile witness, but a big problem for the defense to knowingly permit her to perpetuate the lies. However, they did not want to eliminate the chance that the jury would accept Luz's testimony as having some element of truth.

Jill Labon walked next to Luz, and said, "I have just one question. Do you love your daughters?"

"Oh, I love them so much, but when they been bad, I gotta keep them in line."

"No more questions."

Luz was excused, repeating the slow walk back down the aisle toward an officer who would bring her back to a heavily guarded cell until the bail that might have been posted days earlier, but neglected, could be made. As Luz passed by, the defendant and his wife each pondered what their future might be.

Judge Johnson nodded toward the prosecution table. "Any more witnesses?"

Mark stood and announced, "The State rests."

***

Court was recessed for the rest of the day with the defense set to commence its case the next day. I filled Bobbie in on all of the events, perhaps ignoring Judge Johnson's rules, but I thought she needed to know just in case someone else broke the order.

Roberta growled, "She used the poor kid's name. That witch knows just what she's doing."

We decided to shield Tina if at all possible. Although she now accepted the fact that she had done nothing wrong, Tina still felt embarrassed and ashamed. Petrified that the details of the trial would become public and known even in our town, far removed from the events and places of her childhood, she felt she couldn't face Josh or Kristin or anyone else if the whole story became identified with her. So far, the trial had been nothing more than just another case, drawing scant attention. But Luz's performance, coupled with the presence of so many spectators, not to mention the reporters, threatened to change all that, notwithstanding Judge Johnson's order.

That evening, Valentina pried to hear about her mother's testimony. Her original concern that her mother's mental health would be too much for her to handle testifying, shifted to intense curiosity about what had actually transpired.

"Dad," she begged over dinner, "tell me how she fixed Simon for good. I know, she's confused by her feelings, but she threw him out once she saw what he was doing."

"I haven't a doubt that her testimony helped the prosecution tremendously," I half-lied, because I agreed with Mark and Lillian that the woman's lies were transparent and not believable. Tina's tenacious desire to be loved by her mother despite everything she knew touched me, and in truth, infuriated me.

Roberta nodded in agreement, "That's exactly what Dad told me and the same for Lillian. Now get some rest because tomorrow Simon's lawyers get their turn and I guess you'll be back in the courtroom. It could be another long day."

"I just want to be back in school."

"It will all be over soon," Bobbie said and walked upstairs with her daughter.

***

I had begun to regard the telephone as my enemy because it hadn't been bringing much good news these days. My sons each called every few nights and for some reason, I sensed a reserve from each of them, that they still disapproved of Tina's presence in what they still thought of as their home. Or maybe it was my imagination, but I didn't look forward to their conversations the way I used to. Other than that, all too often in the last few months phone calls brought some sort of depressing information. When the phone rings at seven thirty in the morning, it's never good news, and when the phone rang at that hour the next morning I cringed before lifting the receiver from the bedside phone.

"Hal, it's Jim Covain. Maybe it could be worse, but it isn't very good."

"What is it, for God's sake?" I said.

"Who is it?" Bobbie asked, propped up on an elbow.

"Shh, it's Jim. What could be worse?"

"The Blue Hills Times ran a story this morning naming Luz Diaz and identifying her as having attacked the wife of sexual predator defendant Simon Texiera and then later attempting suicide in the Glenwood jail. It went on to say that she testified at the trial of the man described as her former live–in boyfriend."

"That bastard," I said as I repeated to Bobbie what Jim was saying. "I hope the judge throws the book at him. He thinks he's found a way around the gag order, but damn sure it won't take very long for anyone who knows Luz and Simon to know that this trial is all about Tina."

"Hal, what can we do?" Bobbie asked, "I have visions of our whole high school, our whole town, knowing about Tina. She won't want to show her face. It's not fair."

On the other end, Covain could hear Bobbie and he told me that he was about to leave for Glenwood so that he could speak with Lillian Morten as soon as she arrived. I told him that we had to bring Tina to court because she needed to be there to hear the defense witnesses, and we were back to trying to find a way to shield her from all of the nastiness.

Fatigue was becoming a problem. I remembered being so resistant to the whole idea of taking on the responsibility of this girl, and now I found myself searching for every means to keep her safe, to give her a normal life, and it was becoming an exhausting battle. This should have been a private matter, but maybe it was foolish to think that it could be kept that way, certainly with the trial. And now the damned newspapers.

*****

Lillian and Jim, together with Mark Goldblatt, and unexpectedly, Diane Pacquin, were waiting for us when we arrived back at the Glenwood courthouse. My fear that the offending reporter would be lurking outside hadn't materialized, so at least Tina was unaware for the moment of the potential for her name to become public knowledge. Trying to make it look like there was nothing unusual happening, Lillian stood to address the group, but looked straight at Tina.

"Another day closer to the end. The other side doesn't have many witnesses, just some supposed expert on child sexual fantasies, which, I assure you, Tina, we can deal with very easily. Not much chance I can see that they put Simon on the stand. There are some boring things we have to clear up before court opens, so, seeing that Diane was able to be here, maybe you and she can chat in my office or go to grab some breakfast downstairs."

Valentina shook her head. "I'm not bored. I want to know everything. I don't even know what my mother said, and it's killing me."

Roberta's lips tightened into a straight line when Jim Covain walked over to Tina and said, "It's foolish to think we can keep everything from Tina. She's handled a lot in her life, and this isn't nearly so difficult as most of that."

"Right. I'm not a little girl. I've been raped, I've been tortured, I've lived in so many places, had to deal with so many kinds of people, what is it that you think I can't handle," Valentina shouted, "it's my life and my family. Even here, I'm a nobody, they don't even use my name. I'm not Miss F. Do you think I care? Use my name. Valentina Maria Diaz. Tell my story. Let me tell my story. What is it you're all so worried about?"

"Honey, we just don't want to put you through any more pain," Bobbie said.

"Mom, I feel pain all the time, but you help me through it. Sometimes it feels weird when I call both of you Mom and Dad, because I imagine what it would have been like to be your real daughter. I know it's just my fantasy, but then sometimes, it just feels right."

She took a deep breath then laughed. "Geez, you guys look like I just shot you. Please, tell me what's going on."

Odd, but I relaxed, and I think everyone else did, too. Jim looked at Lillian who merely said, "Why not?"

"Okay, Hal, you've sat through all of it. Why don't you go ahead," Jim said.

Roberta and Diane both moved next to Tina, who by this time probably expected worse than we were going to give her, but she laughed again and told them it would be all right.

I thought for a moment about how to put things and then ran first through Luz's performance pretty much blow by blow. Tina let me finish and merely said, "Is that it? Why do I feel sorry for her?"

Mark added only that if Tina worried that her mother's testimony would help Simon, he thought that she had been so clearly lying that he would be very surprised if the jury saw her as only confirming what both Tina and Sellie had reported.

Now for the matter of the newspaper. I think I was more angry with that reporter than I was with Simon. To my way of thinking, Simon was plain perverted. The reporter, on the other hand, was out to make a name for himself in some insignificant news rag by playing around the fringes of the gag order no matter how hurtful it might be to the victim of a horrible crime.

"Tina," I said, "we're concerned that your name is going to become very well known," then proceeded to tell her about the news story. I didn't tell her that other newspapers could pick up the story where it might reach our town. This time, she was less quick to respond, thinking it over it seemed.

Several seconds passed before she began to talk, at first slowly and then gained momentum.

"Dad, everybody, please. This is not fun, but like I already told you, I can deal with these things. If I'm famous now, maybe I can help other kids. I'm telling you, show me that news guy and I'll walk right up to him, write my name down and make him tell the truth about what these guys do. I hope Simon's name is famous, too."

Notorious, Tina, I thought, would be a better word for Simon.

"Well, Tina, you are an amazing young woman, but that reporter did the wrong thing and I hope he pays for it," Roberta said, and emphasized her feelings with a slap on the table.

"Oh, don't worry about that, I've already sent a message to Judge Johnson about our friendly local Pulitzer Prize candidate," Lillian told us, "and I wouldn't be surprised to see the guy squirm today if he has the guts to show his face around here. Anyway, I second the sentiment, Bobbie. Valentina, I've handled lots of cases kind of similar to yours, but you stand out. You are remarkable."

"Famous, right?" Tina beamed.

"Famous,"Diane said, and leaned across the table to shake Tina's hand.

Mark reached for his briefcase and reminded us that it was time to head to the courtroom and the defendant's turn to run the show.

*** 

The Blue Hills reporter didn't have to wait long to enjoy the show, although "enjoy" probably isn't a word he would choose in his report that day. Before Judge Johnson turned the floor over to Jill Labon, he asked if the reporter who had filed the article about the incidents related to a witness in the case was present.

"Yes, your honor," a reply came from the gallery.

"Please step forward, we need to have a word."

"Yes, your honor," the reporter said and walked through the gate to a spot as far away as he could manage from the judge.

"I showered this morning, young man. No reason to stay there. Please come a little closer to where these old eyes can get a better look."

The judge scowled when most of the gallery laughed, but there was no doubt at all that he enjoyed watching the guy's apparent misery.

"There, that's better. You look like a bright young man. Was there something I ordered that was confusing about reporting the complaining witness's name? Let me clarify. You will spend this evening in the lock-up and you will pay a three hundred dollar fine. You will apologize to this court and directly to the young lady you so gallantly tried to assassinate."

"Your honor, with all due respect, I never reported the witness's name."

"Young man, what is your name anyway, no matter, we'll try to protect your anonymity," the judge mocked.

"Your honor, my name is Richard Grey, and I don't believe I violated your requirements."

"Don't get cute with me, Mr. Richard Grey. You gave out all the information anyone with a mind to do it could use to identify the witness. And you need not bother waving the First Amendment at me. I don't even want to hear why you thought it would be a great contribution to our information base to expose the young witness to whatever the consequences might be of your hot reporting. Get this person out of my sight and into his accommodations."

"Your honor, I'm sure our lawyers will be in touch," the reporter blustered as he was led away.

*** 

The rest of the day was anti-climatic, if such a thing was possible. There was no chance that Luz would be called as a defense witness, so Jill Labon called on two experts. The first was a man who explained how a child's sexual fantasies could lead to both false memories or false accusations, the alleged perpetrator becoming the victim. On cross-examination, he admitted that certainly sexual abuse does occur and that he had not ever examined the complaining witness in this case to try and figure out if she was fabricating her claims. The second witness, a bookish looking young woman, holding a doctorate in something she described as related to the psychological transference of physical abuse to sexual touching, was earnest, but in my mind, strange and unconvincing. The defense was trying its best to create a scenario where Tina's memory of sexual abuse was actually a repressed memory of being beaten by her mother. The jury seemed bored by both witnesses.

When the young woman was excused, it was early afternoon. At lunch, we sat with the prosecutors who predicted that Simon would not be called in his own defense. They were right. But just after court reassembled following lunch, a clerk handed the judge and Lillian a notice that had caused Lillian to engage Mark in an animated discussion. Then, she rose and asked to approach the bench along with the defense team. Whatever it was that Lillian said, the judge nodded in agreement, and the lawyers all retreated. The judge announced that court would adjourn for the day so that the prosecution could get ready to examine a new defense witness just added to the list. Julia Texiera, wife of the defendant, would be allowed to testify as to the character of her husband, all with Simon's agreement.

*** 

"Will today will be the last day of testimony?" Roberta asked as we left home the next morning.

"Unless the wife takes more time than we expect, I think so. Then comes the summations and the charge to the jury. When that's done, we wait for the verdict," I answered.

She sighed and sank into her own thoughts.

***

"The defense calls Julia Texiera," Jill Labon announced. The woman from Puerto Rico, thrust into a situation she could not have imagined when she married her man and soon after provided him with a daughter, seemed timid and embarrassed as she was sworn in. She still sported a bandage from Luz's attack, but if Simon were to be convicted, her wounds would be far deeper than anything Luz had done. Pleasant looking, and at least outwardly not flashy the way Luz had apparently been in her younger days, Julia's eyes were red from too many sleepless, teary nights.

Jill Labon's first question, "Describe the defendant's relationship with you, how he treats you," elicited an immediate objection by Mark on the grounds of relevance. The judge allowed the question, and the door was opened for the morning for the jury to see an apparent different side of Simon Texiera.

The translation process was very slow and the witness had to be reminded constantly to speak up. She broke down frequently. Speaking from the heart, she said that her husband was always kind to her, having rescued her from a life with her family where the father was an abusive drinker and the mother had her hands full trying to maintain an impoverished family of seven.

"Did he ever beat you?"

"No."

"Was he verbally abusive?"

"No, he was always kind and gentle."

"For the record, the State objects to this whole line of questioning," Mark interrupted.

"Mr. Goldblatt, I've already ruled. Never mind. Objection noted for the record. Will the defense please proceed."

"Thank you, your honor. Mrs. Texiera, have you any children by the defendant?"

"Yes, a beautiful daughter, just over one year."

At that moment I recalled the chilling bit of information that I'd learned, that it was not unusual for a sexual predator to purposely father their own victims.

"And will you describe your husband's relationship with his daughter?"

"He is gentle and loving. She is his joy."

"Just wait until she's a year or two older," Bobbie whispered to me.

Tina was covering her eyes. I remembered that Simon had apparently not molested his other daughter, Tina's little sister Juanita.

All the while, Simon sat almost impassively, smiling once when his wife described how he loved being the one to bathe his little girl.

"Is your husband a church-going man?"

"Your honor, the State objects." This time it was Lillian.

"And this time, I'll sustain."

"Well, then, we have no more questions."

Mark walked over to the witness and asked her if she needed a moment. I thought I heard her say before the translation, "Okay."

After a brief pause, Mark said that he had just a few questions.

"Mrs. Texiera, before your husband was arrested, can you tell us what he had told you about his background?"

"He told me that he was born on the island, but went to the mainland when he was about twenty after his mother died. He didn't know his father. Simon said he went there for work but came back when the work dried up a few years ago."

"Did you know anything about the people you have seen testify? The mother and her two daughters? That there was a third daughter fathered by your husband?"

Julia became totally distraught, sobbing uncontrollably. She managed to say a few words, translated as, "Lies. All lies."

I wondered how many lives a loser like Simon could destroy. It was more depressing than infuriating. As Mrs. Texiera started to settle down, my heart was heavy for her.

And then, with no further drama, the testimony in the State vs. Texiera came to an end. Court adjourned for the day, with summations and the jury deliberations to start the next day.

\*\*\*

"Who fucking gave that story to the papers?" the angry voice at on the other end of my kitchen phone demanded. It was later in the evening on the day the defense rested.

"Luz, please, calm down. I don't want you calling here," I answered.

Fresh out on bail and already out of control Luz went on, "You trying to embarrass me? I know you hate me. My daughter, some daughter, she's trying to ruin me. You ask that reporter to put my name all over town? I can't even goddamn go to buy cigarettes."

I lost it. "You damned thoughtless bitch, you're lucky you aren't on trial, too. I'd have locked you up years ago. Look in the mirror and accept responsibility for what you've done, what you've let be done to your daughters. That bastard raped your little girl and you still want to sleep with him. In case you haven't figured it out, you got your own name in the papers, and if that keeps you locked behind your own door, that is too good for you."

"You too good for me? You think you're better than everyone? Take money from the state, turn my kids against me? I give those kids everything. And look how they thank me. My life is ruined."

My right eyelid started to twitch, an uncontrollable response when my temper rises. I was deciding between slamming down the receiver or continuing to vent. I did both, first telling her to stay the hell out of our lives and then jolting the receiver on to the cradle so hard that it flew right off and the expandable cord flipped the phone into the air and then banged it down onto the tile floor.

From somewhere upstairs Roberta shouted, "Hal, did you fall, are you okay?"

I grunted something and gently set the receiver back in place. Roberta had started down the stairs just as I was headed up. "What now?" she asked.

"It's Luz. Mad as a hornet about the news stories. Too bad for her, the slut."

"Hal, not so loud. Tina'll hear you."

"What, you think she doesn't know." I said, having trouble keeping my voice down. The damned eyelid wouldn't quit.

"Hal, please. We'll tell our friends at the prosecutor's office. Lillian and Mark and Jim Covain, too they'll handle Luz."

"Yeah, I suppose. Just, oh never mind. I need a cold shower," I answered and stalked upstairs.

\*\*\*

The courtroom was jammed with many familiar faces and a few new ones, including a new reporter from that Blue Hills rag. There'd been a debate about whether or not Tina should be there, and Lillian had decided that she should be and visible to the jury. This would probably be the last time before deliberations that the jurors would see Tina and the prosecutor wanted to play every card that might drive any doubt out of those twelve minds. Valentina was wedged between Bobbie and me. No Luz. The only drama would be in the courtroom.

We all rose for the judge for one of the few remaining times in the trial. He said a few words to the jury and opened the floor for the defense to give its final argument.

Jill Labon, businesslike as always, rose, straightened her skirt and approached the jury. Her client, expressionless, almost withered looking, sat with his hands folded on the defense table. His lawyer made a brief gesture toward him, as if inviting the jury to see how harmless this man looked, and began by talking about his wife and young daughter. How dedicated this man was to them. Not a man who could harm anyone. She went on for over an hour, describing the evidence, or lack of it, against her client and how the information provided by the two sisters was not reliable and failed to give proof of guilt. The jury listened to her politely, seeming to pay attention, committed to doing their job. She finished by telling the jury that not only was there reasonable doubt, but that there was no proper verdict other than not guilty. Thanking them for their time and service, she turned, smiled at Simon, and sat down next to him.

Now it was time for the prosecution to make its last pitch at the panel, and again, Mark would handle the chore.

In his argument, that lasted almost two and half hours, he painstakingly reconstructed the case and testimony. Occasionally, he turned in Valentina's direction, the jury following his lead. Maybe it was my imagination, but I thought that the eyes of many of the jurors hinted approval of my foster daughter. If Tina noticed, she didn't say. She said scarcely a word all morning.

As he recreated testimony of first Tina, then Selena, and then the nurse, Mark slowed his pace, as if to drag out the pain that Tina felt. "A small child, a toddler who was just learning to speak when this unspeakable abuse started," he reminded the jury, "and by the time the horror with the defendant ended, she was still a young child. A victim of a man so ruthless that he forced another young girl to look on in horror."

Quickening his cadence as he reached the end of each point, he dramatized as best he could the desperation that the victim had to have felt. As well as I already knew the story, the recreation was draining me. When he'd finished talking about Tina's testimony, she rested her head on Roberta's shoulder.

Mark ended by asking the jury to find the defendant guilty on all counts, suggesting that there was no other conclusion they could reach under the facts and evidence presented. From her seat, Julia Texiera uttered something in Spanish, but settled down when the judge motioned to her. His concentration broken, Mark turned to Lillian, then caught himself, remembering to thank the jury as had the defense, then turned again toward Lillian before taking his seat.

Judge Johnson looked at his watch. "Well, I let this go a little long past lunch. Thank you, counsel, for moving the proceedings along. We'll take an hour break, return at 2:30 sharp. I'll be charging the jury and then send them off to deliberate. We stand in recess."

***

Roberta, Tina and I left the courtroom to head to the cafeteria. Valentina asked us to hold on, and ran ahead to where Lillian stood, engrossed in a cell phone call. Lillian turned toward Tina, shook her head in the affirmative and went back to her call.

"Mom, Dad, you go ahead. Lillian said I can call Sellie. I just need to talk to her right now."

This was one of the occasions when I felt like a total observer to Tina's life. Bobbie and I could do some things for her, but we couldn't be her flesh and blood. We could never be total insiders. Bobbie told her that she should do what she needed to do and we'd save her a seat.

"Okay," she said, her back already turned, as she hustled down the hall to Lillian's office. She never made it to lunch and was sitting on a bench outside the courtroom when we arrived back upstairs. For the time being, she didn't volunteer what she had spoken to her older sister about, but she seemed more nervous than at any time during the trial.

"Do we have to stay?" she asked me.

"I suppose not," I replied, as much to my wife as to Tina. "Jury instructions aren't all that exciting anyway. Let's wait until Mark or Lillian comes back and I'll tell them we'll wait to hear from them on the progress of the jury. Earliest decision would be tomorrow."

# CHAPTER FOURTEEN

*Spring and Summer 2004*

From the ride home, including a quick stop at a fast food place so Tina could finally eat something, and through the late afternoon and into the evening, she asked only about what would happen if the jury decided this way or that way, questions asked and answered many times already. She never brought up her call to Selena, nor did we ask. She wouldn't come to the phone to talk to Kristin, claiming she had a headache, and went to sleep early.

"What do you think?" I asked Bobbie.

"Don't know exactly, but I wouldn't be surprised if Luz is worrying her. Why else would she need to call Sellie, and then be so nervous afterward? I supposed it could be the tension of the verdict, but I don't know what Sellie could have said about the trial or even why Tina would feel such a need to call her sister right then and there."

"I think you're right. I got the feeling today that she was seeing us through a window, only her foster family, and she needed to connect to her own."

Roberta sighed. "It hits me a lot, you know. That awful woman is her mother, and I am not. And in the long run, that's what counts. I think Tina does love us but as bad as Luz is, and as much as Valentina knows it, I always sense that Tina would do anything to make things different."

"Well, we'll know pretty soon what happens to Simon. Luz is going to be unhappy one way or the other. The guy is either married and back to the island or married and in prison."

"Uh huh, and whatever that means for Tina, it probably can't be good."

\*\*\*

The call came shortly before noon the next morning. We had headed for brunch about halfway to Glenwood. Tina's appetite was getting back to normal, so we planned to eat on the road so we wouldn't be too far away should the jury return quickly.

I was still adjusting to having a telephone ring from my pocket and jumped a little when it sounded. Mark was on the other end telling us the jury had a verdict and to hustle down.

Bobbie and Tina knew from my end of the call that Simon would soon get his verdict, but I announced anyway, "They're in. Very fast. I think the sucker is going away for a while."

Tina shot up from the table and ran ahead to the car before I could ask the server for the check. When I got outside, she and Roberta were standing there waiting. Tina was a bundle of energy. If the verdict came in not guilty, it would be horrible, but I think one way or the other, a big weight was lifting off of the girl. For the moment, it seemed none of us was thinking about Luz.

\*\*\*

Even though I'd practiced law for years, trials weren't my thing, and certainly not criminal trials. My image of these things was informed by TV lawyer shows just like most people. We sat in the gallery as we had for weeks. The now famous case had jammed the seats. Tina was constant motion. Two rows back and across the way, Mrs. Texiera and company sat, conversing quietly. Simon and his defense team seemed not to be saying much to one another. Lillian and Mark talked and Mark turned once toward us, giving a reassuring smile. My own heart was racing.

Announcing the opening of court for last time for this trial, the clerk had us rise. Judge Johnson came in, we all sat, and he directed the bailiff to have the jury brought in. The only sound left in the room was the shuffling of the jurors as they found their seats. They all looked grim.

TV wasn't off the mark. "Ladies and gentlemen of the jury, I have been informed that you have reached a verdict. Is that the case?"

The foreman stood, "Yes we have, your honor." He handed a slip of paper to the bailiff who handed it to the judge. The judge opened the sheet, studied it briefly and then asked the defendant to stand.

Simon, surprisingly, stood straight and seemed calm. His attorneys stood on either side.

"Mister Foreman, how finds the jury?'

Tina held both Bobbie and me by the arm.

"In the case State of Massachusetts versus Simon Texiera, on the first count of rape, and on the second count of rape, and on the counts of reckless endangerment we find the defendant guilty, guilty, guilty, guilty."

Mrs. Texiera lost all control, trying to rush to her husband. Several jurors smiled at Valentina, who for her part, was holding on to Roberta and letting all of her emotions flow. The judge banged his gavel, restored some order, set the date for sentencing for the next week, and dismissed the jury after thanking them for a job well done. Simon still seemed impassive, almost removed, not even reacting when the bailiffs took him by the shoulders, handcuffed him and led him away.

Lillian and Mark each hugged Tina and thanked us all, inviting us to return for sentencing. In the relief and exhilaration of the moment, Luz had almost slipped my mind.

I motioned for the prosecutor to follow me to a quiet corner and laid out the fears we had about what Luz might do. I explained Luz's threatening phone call and the guesses we had made about Tina's call to her sister.

Lillian Morten, plain and blunt as ever, said, "We'll make sure someone has a little chat with Luz about the threatening stuff. Of course, the DOF folks, especially Jim Covain, need to have their own conversation. That's some young lady there. I've seen other cases, some almost as bad as this one, and I'll tell you Valentina really stands out. Take care of that one."

"Thanks, thank you both. Yes, quite a kid. Say, any guesses about Texiera's jail time?"

"Well, we're going to ask for the max, consecutive, maybe the 50 year total range. As steep as any ever got in this neck of the woods. The guy's married with a kid, don't know what His Honor will do, but I think he doesn't care much for Mr. Texiera," Lillian said.

"Yeah, not a guy to have a beer with. Anyway, maybe our lives can start to get back to normal, whatever that means. Thank you both again. We'll see you next week."

***

Sentencing day would be the following Thursday. A full week away. The hard part was over, and our household established some of the old routine of work, school and just plain relaxing. That Saturday, Kristin invited Tina to hang out at the mall and we agreed. When Kristin's mom dropped her back home, Tina was in a great mood.

Things seem to be as settled as we might hope until late Sunday morning. The three of us had been out walking, just enjoying the exercise and a beautiful day. When we got back, the message light on our answering machine was blinking. Bobbie pressed the machine to hear Selena's distraught voice asking that Tina call her as soon as she could. Tina immediately grabbed the phone and dialed her sister's number.

All we could hear from Valentina's end was "Oh my God, when? What are you going to do? I don't think I can, 'cuz of DOF. Okay, yeah, let me see."

She hung up and turned to us.

"Grandma, she's in the hospital with a heart attack and Ma is going nuts. Remember when I talked to Selena the other day? She got me so nervous. Ma was already crazy, thinking that Simon might be found guilty. Talking about how she loves him, how to ruin his wife. Since she heard about the verdict, she got worse and out of the blue, Grandma ends up in the hospital and Selena is alone to deal with Ma. She wants my help."

Roberta had Tina sit beside her on the family room couch. "First off, how is your Grandma?"

"I guess she'll make it, but I want to go see her."

"Okay, I think we can do that. Now, I don't really know what you can do about Sellie or your mother. What about one of your aunts?"

"I don't know, they usually have their own problems. Maybe Carmen. She likes us kids. She can't stand Ma."

"We really can't do much today. No way can you get involved directly with your mother, at least not without DOF saying how and when. Sellie might be a different story," I said, "but we'll have to wait to call first thing tomorrow. Do you know Carmen's number?"

"No. She's probably working down at the furniture store. You can call her there. Oh, my God, I can't believe this."

\*\*\*

Roberta and I decided to take Tina to visit her grandmother. As tough as that might be under normal circumstances, by now we knew that Carmen was going to take Sellie there as well, unfortunately, accompanied by Luz.

Carmen, as usual more than willing to do what she could for her nieces, hadn't been told by Luz about her mother's heart attack, learning about it from my call, and she was anxious to see her mother.

Grandma Diaz had been moved out of intensive care and was asleep in her shared room when we arrived at the Glenwood hospital. There was no roommate at the moment. Tina walked over and put her hand on her grandmother's arm, rubbing it gently. The old woman's eyes opened a bit and she gave her granddaughter a faint smile.

"Oh, *Lo siento mi abuela*, I'm, sorry, Grandma, I didn't mean to wake you."

Grandma nodded and reached out for Tina who took her hand. Tina sat there, happy to be connected, hanging on to a woman who, unlike too many adults in her life, had loved her unconditionally. Bobbie and I retreated to the hallway, now busy in the middle of the evening visiting hours.

Several minutes passed and we could see Tina, still in the same position, maybe pulling some corner of her life together, here in the place where broken bodies were fixed. And then, the rest of her family arrived.

Almost devoid of expression, the three Diaz women walked past us, Sellie pausing only to give us each a peck on the cheek and Carmen acknowledging us with a quiet thanks. Luz, appearing to be as subdued as I'd ever seen her, looked away from us and entered the room first. Tina looked up in time to fend off Luz's attempt to slap her across the face. Understanding far too late what a bad mistake we'd made in believing that Luz would control herself in her stricken mother's presence, I tried to intervene, only to have Luz's closed fist glance off of my shoulder.

Luz, who until now hadn't uttered a word, stopped the physical attack, and said to Tina, "You have broken my heart. I hate the day you were born."

Selena, now weeks removed from her raucous outburst in the same hospital, ran toward her family, yelling at her mother to shut up. Carmen took hold of her by the shoulders and ordered her to control herself.

Grandma Diaz had drifted off, oblivious to the commotion, and Tina was spouting something at her mother in a stream of Spanish that I couldn't understand and was glad I couldn't. Then she turned to Bobbie and said that she wanted her mother out of the room while she visited, out of sight until we left, and she wanted Selena and Carmen to have their time with Grandma. Luz, now anything but expressionless, snapped her fingers at the group of us with contempt and said, "Don't worry. I don't want no part of any of you. I'll be home when I get there, sister dear, I'll hitch a ride. You don't care how I feel, I don't give a shit how you feel," and with that she stormed off without a backward glance.

Roberta took Tina by the hand, but Tina pushed it away. "Don't worry about me. My mother is crazy, she's bad and I'll get over this. I just need a little space. Poor Sellie, you're stuck living there. You were better off when you weren't."

"Aunt Carmen says I can visit anytime I need to get away. But with grandma being sick and all, I don't know. I mean, Ma ain't so bad she can't help, just, since she got home again, she's been drinking and Juanita has been running the streets. She didn't even want to visit Grandma, sayin' she sees her enough. Getting too much like Ma."

Carmen, so different from her sister, shook her head, "Bad over there. Time was, I had more time to pay attention to the girls, but between this and that and Luz not wanting me around, I haven't been there much. For awhile, when Sellie and Tina were both out of there, I felt better about things. But now, Selena is bearing the brunt, and if we lose 'Nita, smart, beautiful Juanita, I don't know."

She wasn't looking for an answer, at least not from me or Roberta.

\*\*\*

In the time left until the final day in court, either Bobbie or I checked in with Sellie once or twice a day. We learned that following the hospital confrontation, Luz didn't return home until the next morning, feeling no pain and keeping to herself. By the day before court, the Diaz household was tense. Selena reported that Grandma would be returning home in two days. Luz, in one of her better moments, had decided not to try to go to Glenwood for Simon's sentencing.

Some dreams come true, and some nightmares never end. Tina felt trapped.

"Dad," she said at breakfast on sentencing morning, "I don't want to go."

Up until then, she hadn't even hinted at staying behind and she took me off guard. I guess the look on my face disappointed her.

"Dad, I've been thinking about this all night. I hate Simon. I'm sad, too. I thought he was my father for a long time. There's no need for me to be in that courtroom. You and Mom can go. I think I'd rather go to school. I missed so much. Besides, this isn't the end of anything. My mother is messed up, poor Sellie is stuck, and now Juanita is acting up." In a crescendo, her voice quivered, "All I want is just to be a kid, that's all, and it isn't happening."

Whatever steel that girl possessed ripped. I tried to console her but she waved me away. Having heard from upstairs, Roberta, still in her robe, came flying down the stairs.

"Tina, what's—" but Tina waved her off too, her body shaking so hard that the table her elbows rested on rattled.

Bobbie and I stood there, helpless. Several minutes passed before Tina calmed down. Finally, she sighed, stood up, said she needed some air, and went out to sit alone on the back deck.

\*\*\*

Valentina left for school before Roberta and I headed back to court. Offering only a terse goodbye after giving us each a peck on the cheek, she opened the door, turned to us and said, "I'll be home right after school. I hope I never see Simon again."

Now, oddly it seemed to me, the strangers, Bobbie and I, were left to witness the final chapter in the State of Massachusetts v. Simon Texiera.

\*\*\*

The parking lot next to the courthouse was fuller than I'd ever seen it. Simon's trial, which had begun with little public notice, was now the center of attention in Glenwood, Blue Hills, and most of the state. TV trucks took up several spaces, camera and lighting crews hurried about, and familiar news reporters from all of the state's TV studios stood chatting with each other, waiting for court to open and the sentence to be rendered.

Thankfully, Bobbie and I were not of any interest to the media, and we walked quickly past the tangle of wires that made the walk up the courthouse steps hazardous. We went directly to the prosecutor's office, which had become so familiar to us. Jim Covain, Diane Paquin, Mark and Lillian were to meet us there, and we were the last to arrive. They all inquired about Tina and seemed to understand her wanting to be absent.

Jim commented that he hadn't known any case quite like this one, not only because of Tina's youth when the abuse had begun, but the drama of Luz's testimony and her overall behavior in court, made more compelling by the presence of Simon's wife.

Lillian concurred, and reiterated how impressed she was with our foster daughter.

Mark looked at his watch and told us we needed to get into the courtroom. Roberta took my arm when we entered the crowded hall. We threaded our way through the horde of spectators being told to move along and went to our front row seats for the last time.

Roberta leaned over to me and whispered, "My stomach's in knots. Hopefully, this horrible part of poor Tina's life can be put behind her. Strange, isn't it, that I feel sadness for the Simon's new family? They're victims, too. I can't look at his wife."

With the opening of court, the last chapter was about to begin. A somber Judge Johnson stepped up to his seat and brought the gavel down. I glanced at the defense table and saw that Simon was now wearing an orange prison jump suit and sat with his hands covering his face.

The judge leaned forward and looked squarely at Simon. Then he looked at down at some notes and went through a short description of the recommendation the jury had made regarding sentencing, emphasizing that they had recommended against leniency. Once again, he shifted his gaze to Simon. A woman's weeping was the only sound in the room for a few seconds.

"Will the defendant please stand," the judge directed.

Simon Texiera rose slowly, his attorneys on either side of him.

"Is there anything you wish to say before I pronounce sentence?"

The translator repeated the invitation, but Simon nodded no, he did not. His lawyers indicated that their client had wanted just to have the sentencing be over with as quickly as possible.

Judge Johnson nodded back and then, in a clear voice said, "I have decided to accept the jury's recommendation. Therefore, it is the determination of the court that the defendant, Simon Texiera, having been determined guilty on each of the several counts, will serve the maximum term allowed on each count, the terms to be consecutive, for a total of 60 years." He banged down his gavel amidst an uproar in the gallery. The weeping woman was now screaming. The judge stepped down, Simon was led away, and it was over.

Roberta was saying something I couldn't really hear. Lillian and Mark motioned for us to join them at their table, together with Jim and Diane. While we, and apparently the whole gallery, understood that they had just witnessed an extremely tough sentence, Lillian seemed especially excited.

"Ladies and gentlemen, you have just witnessed the longest sentence ever imposed on a sexual predator in the history of our state," Lillian exclaimed. "I truly never quite expected that. He deserves every second of it, but there's no doubt in my mind that Tina and Selena had a major impact on both the jury and the judge. Maybe even more so, so did Luz."

I shook her hand, and took Mark's as well, with my wife still firmly attached to my side.

I felt as giddy as a newlywed. "You two and I, we're all lawyers, but I don't know that I could go through this sort of grind all the time. We can't thank you enough, although I must say I hope I never see either of you again."

They both laughed. Mark ventured that if we did, it would be over dinner and hopefully not in a courtroom.

"Okay," I answered, "deal."

"Well, we have to meet the press, a bit unusual out here in the sticks," Lillian said, "and then back to that grind."

"Yeah, the paperwork never goes away." Jim added, "Right now I'm going to call my boss with the good news."

They all said their goodbyes, with Diane accompanying us to the parking lot.

Outside, the press was waiting for the prosecutors to appear. Nearing noon, the skies were dotted with white clouds and the day was becoming steamy. As we walked toward our car, Diane asked us if we needed anything.

"To be honest, I think problems with Luz aren't over," Bobbie said. "Tina knows it, we know it, and DOF knows it. Diane, I have a lot of faith in you. I haven't any idea what will happen or how this sentence will affect Luz, but I won't be surprised if we'll need your wisdom. In the meantime, we want to get back home before Tina gets there and hears the news from someone else."

"I'll always be here for you and Tina. Good luck." Diane hugged Roberta and left us to attend to other business

\*\*\*

Some of Valentina's natural cheerfulness started to show. Almost two weeks had passed since Simon had been sent away for likely the rest of his life. Tina's initial reaction to learning of the sentence was, as Roberta put it, "astonishingly indifferent. A defense mechanism." It had taken a few days before she asked even whether or not Simon could appeal, could be released early, and other questions about the possibility that Simon could ever walk a public street again. Then it dawned on me why she didn't want to be present when the sentence was announced. So much of the misery of her earliest years had been forced out into the open during the trial, that she was afraid that her tormentor might get off too lightly, that he might be vengeful. I mentioned my theory to Bobbie, who then hinted at that with Tina one afternoon before I'd come home. Tina had admitted that she'd had nightmares about it. At dinner that evening, we reassured her that Simon was not going to bother her ever again.

It took a few more days for the ice to crack. On Saturday morning, now over three weeks since the end of the trial, from behind the closed doors of the bathroom, we heard Tina's voice soar into her best Mariah Carey imitation. The first notes she had sung in months. When she came down, late morning as was her usual weekend habit, Tina asked if she could have Kristin come over.

"Anything you want," I answered.

Roberta, whisking eggs at the counter, looked over her shoulder and added, "She can come for dinner, too."

"Are you serious? Can she? I'm going to call her right now," and before we could tell her to eat first, she had started to call her friend.

\*\*\*

"Thank you guys, I mean, it is so neat."

A full day around Kristin—it had been awhile—takes some adjustment. Conversations with most people don't start in the middle of a thought, but her energy is infectious. She makes Tina feel good and quite important, and she makes me and Bobbie laugh for no reason at all.

"We were happy to have you, sweetheart," Bobbie said.

"Awesome. Well, my mom will be here, and so maybe we can sit outside, it's nice out, and wait for her, okay?"

"Okay," I said and held the door for them to go.

Before she stepped outside, Kristin turned to us. I'd never seen her look so serious.

"You guys, sorry, I mean Mr. Allen and Mrs. Allen, I love Tina. She told me all about the trial, well mostly all, I think she left some stuff out, and she is the best. Lots of kids at school, they think life is bad when they can't have the car. I'd die if I had people treat me like that, I mean like what happened to Tina. I'd die."

Tina blushed. "I had to share, is that okay? Mostly just about my mom, and a little about Simon. I don't want people to feel sorry for me. I just need a real friend to understand me. Kristin is the only real friend I've ever had. I love her, too."

Roberta went over and told them they were both pretty special people, that we loved them both.

The girls blushed, I cleared my throat, and could only muster, "Come back soon."

"Sure will," she said, taking her seat next to Tina on the front steps.

***

Later the following week, Tina took a call from Selena. They had talked a few times after Grandma, who was recovering nicely, had returned home. From what Selena had told her sister, Luz had gone into a depression once she'd learned about Simon's sentence. According to Tina, Luz was distraught at the thought of not seeing her old lover, probably never again. Once, she let it slip that she thought Simon's involvement with her daughter was just a way to make her jealous.

Apparently, Luz had not quite gotten over her anger at the news story and didn't want to be seen by anyone until she thought people might forget. That's why the news coming out of this latest call was surprising and even ominous to me and Bobbie.

We always tried to afford Valentina privacy when she spoke with her sister. This time, even though we couldn't hear what Tina was saying, she was exceptionally animated, so we knew something unexpected had happened. Maybe to Grandma again, we speculated.

"Is everything all right?" Bobbie asked when Tina came back.

"Mom, it's my Ma. I don't know what to believe. Selena says Ma suddenly wants to go to church all the time. Like she thinks everything is evil. Like she wants to get rid of the devil."

She sank down onto the family room couch.

"But that's at least something good, right?" I questioned.

"I don't know. I don't trust her. But that's not all. She's going to call Jim Covain. She wants to start meeting me with him. She wants me back home. Soon."

# CHAPTER FIFTEEN

*Summer 2004*

Tina and Kristin walked past the snack bar and over to the bleachers next to the baseball field where Josh and his summer league teammates were preparing to play a team from the next town. Kristin was between boyfriends. Tina, for her part, knew her feelings for Josh were cooling. Josh, who was anxious to keep the flame alive, had insisted that Tina come to the game, even if she dragged the mildly annoying Kristin along. The girls had given up summer softball, Tina because the trial had dampened her enthusiasm and Kristin because her family had bought a summer place on the shore where she would be spending a great deal of the hot weather.

"Watch me, Teens," Josh yelled up to Tina, who had asked the boy a thousand times not to use that nickname. Tina shuddered a little and frowned as Josh stepped into the batter's box for some hitting practice. Josh, though not the best player on the team, was good enough. His consistent contact with the practice pitches clanged sharply off the aluminum bat. After each swing, he turned to make sure Valentina was paying attention, certain that his batting prowess would be sure to captivate her.

The girls sat through the first few innings, paying much more attention to each other than to the game.

Tina yawned, leaned over to her friend and said, "Let's get out of here."

Kristin answered, "Hey, it's only the third inning," but Tina was already on her way to the fence behind Josh's bench to let him know she wasn't staying.

Turning away before Josh could try to convince her to stay, Tina hurried over to where the perplexed Kristin was waiting for her at the bottom of the bleachers.

"Tina, what's wrong? I mean, are you okay? What's the matter?"

A little girl brushed against Valentina's leg, searching for something or other that her older brother had swiped and thrown down. Tina barely noticed.

Several seconds passed before Tina replied.

"Kris, I can't sit still. Let's walk back to my house, I mean my mom and dad's house."

"Why did you say that?"

"What do you mean, Kris? I just need some quiet, maybe we can talk about some stuff."

"No, Tina. Not about the quiet part. I mean why'd you say the thing about the house being your mom and dad's? I mean, first you said it was your house, then it was their house. I mean, whenever I come over I always tell my parents I'm going to Tina's house."

"I'm feeling a little funny, I guess. I know that while I'm living there I can call it my house. But it really isn't. It's kind of like we're playing some make believe game."

Kristin nodded even though she didn't quite understand.

The girls stood at the busy intersection on the block beyond the ball field waiting for the traffic signal to change. The conversation stopped and a somber mood persisted when the light changed for them to cross the street. Neither spoke until they'd walked another few blocks, still another mile to go. Then Tina pointed to a bench at a bus stop.

"Let's sit there for a few minutes. I'm a little tired. Worried, too."

"What's up?" Kristin asked, unusually subdued because her friend never behaved this way around her.

"Like I told you the other day, my mother is pushing hard to have me come home. My sister told me Ma keeps calling the state."

"Do you want to go?"

"I love you, Kris. I love Mom and Dad, too. But there's nobody here like me. I feel weird a lot. Josh really doesn't get me. Both of my sisters are with my mother. The whole neighborhood where they live is Spanish. A lot of students at the school there are kids I've known for a long time."

"You're making me cry."

Tina hugged her friend. "Kris, I'm sorry. I didn't mean to make you feel bad. You'll always be my special friend."

They sat there in silence for a long while until Tina stood, took Kris by the hand and said, "Let's go, girl, we need to get home."

*** 

At her most recent session with Mrs. Bronislaw, Tina spent the whole hour trying to satisfy herself that the meeting DOF had arranged for her with her mother was a good idea.

"What concerns you the most," the psychologist inquired, "you've met with her before?"

"Yes, but the last one ended with a fight. At the trial, she tried to make it seem like I lied. She tried to kill herself over that rapist. Now, a few months later, suddenly she starts going to church and everything is supposed to be different."

"So, do you not want to meet? Or not go back to live with her?"

"Mr. Covain says that if they think Ma is ready to have me back, they could decide to have the court approve a plan to get me back to her. She would have to meet some conditions. It wouldn't be right away."

"Okay."

"But things are so good for me with Mom and Dad. I know my life is probably better with them. I don't know why I just can't be happy with that."

"That's something only you can answer. The meetings with your mother will give you the chance to see if you think the changes are for real. I know Jim Covain will be very careful about any plans to reunify you with your mom."

"I miss Selena and Juanita so much. Grandma, too. I'm just worried Ma will fool everyone. She manipulates people. That's why the meetings worry me. How can I tell? How can the state tell?"

"Valentina, you have excellent instincts, and you understand your mother. Just take it one step at a time. The visits will be supervised. You're scheduled to see me the day after the meeting. You can share whatever you'd like. You're a strong young woman, and I'm confident you'll handle this just fine."

Tina leaned forward and said, "I hope so. I just wish it wasn't so hard."

\*\*\*

Luz was still wearing a plain, pale blue, high necked blouse with a dark blue scarf to cover the rope scar. A large silver crucifix hung from a chain that was tucked under her scarf. Her hair was tied back in a severe bun, and her black skirt was floor length. Luz's appearance startled Tina when Jim Covain escorted the girl into the small DOF meeting room.

"Ma, you, look so different," Tina blurted.

"Valentina, I am different. I've found the Lord. I know I didn't always treat you good. I know I have hurt you and thought only of myself. I'm trying so hard. You'll see. I want you to come back to me so bad."

Luz looked at Jim, seeking direction on how to proceed. He acknowledged her with a tight smile and said, "You two just talk about whatever you want. No real rules except no arguing."

"Okay," Luz answered. "Just tell me, Tina, can you forgive me?"

"I don't know. I mean, I'll try, Ma, but you always confuse me. How do I know I can trust you? There were too many times I needed you and you weren't there for me. Sometimes, a lot of times, you were even against me. I'm your daughter and sometimes I can't help myself, how I feel. I love you and then you make me sick."

Jim Covain rustled some papers, trying not to look up, but anxious to see what Luz would do. She surprised him.

"You are right. I think about what I've done. I talk to my pastor. I get sick, too. But ask Selena. Ask Grandma. I'm learning how to be a good person. I don't drink no more," she even allowed herself a smile, "and I'm trying to quit smoking. That's harder than I thought."

Tina waited a moment before replying, "Ma, I really want to accept you. It's going to take me some time. I mean, the trial. It's only been two months."

"The trial. Yeah. You know, I wrote to Simon's wife. I apologized for what I done. She probably don't know what to do with herself. I don't know if Sellie told you. I got probation. A year to behave and do stuff like soup kitchens. I learned my lesson."

"Yeah, Sellie's told me a lot. She says you been changing. Anyway, how is my little Juanita?"

"That one, I don't know. I mean, she's a good girl, goes to church with us. But a little wild, too. I guess she has some of my blood. I'm trying hard to see that she lives a better life than me."

She's certainly saying all the right things, Covain thought, The home visits should be interesting.

"Ma, you can't let her mess up."

Luz stood up, placed her palms on the table and leaned toward her daughter. "We both need you to come home. Juanita misses you. Grandma misses you. Sellie talks about you all the time. You are the only one missing."

Valentina turned toward her caseworker, silently seeking his help. He pulled his seat to an end of the table.

"I think this is a good time to stop," he said, "Tina understands, I'm sure, what the situation is. This'll take a while. Let's schedule another visit right here next week, same time."

"Can I hug her?" Luz asked, sounding like a small child.

"Tina, it's up to you," Jim replied.

"Come here, Ma," Tina said, and took a small step toward Luz. Before her mother could do anything, Tina took another step, reached out, gave her mother a short embrace, and then stepped back. "See you next time," she said before Luz could say anything, asking Jim Covain to take her back to her foster home.

***

Jim Covain sat down next to Tina, facing Mrs. Bronislaw. Sitting alone in the waiting room for the previous half hour, Tina had been imagining what Jim and her psychologist were planning for her future.

Before Jim had asked Tina to wait by herself outside, Mrs. Bronislaw, Jim, and Tina had gone through, it seemed to Valentina, every second of the three meetings she'd had with Luz during the past month.

The two meetings with Valentina's mother since that first session had been virtual reprises of the first. After the second meeting, Jim and another worker visited the Diaz home and spent a lot of time interviewing all four of the female members of the household. It seemed from what he'd learned that Luz, indeed, had become a faithful churchgoer. She hadn't raised a hand or even her voice toward anyone. There was nothing untoward that he could find. The one situation that gave him pause was that Luz had seemed to have found a new love interest. Apparently the guy was the son of Luz's aging pastor and a devout man himself. Jim and the other social worker had decided that this new man was not like the previous males in Luz's life, and besides, there was no real suggestion that the man would be a problem in any way. Luz and the gentleman had given the state permission to investigate whatever they would like about his background. Aside from a youthful speeding arrest, the man seemed upright and held a good job working for the electric company.

Tina covered a nervous yawn as Jim began to fill her in.

"Mrs. Bronislaw and I agree that your mother seems to be headed in the right direction. I've also spoken with Mrs. Hernandez. We all feel that while it's too soon to move quickly to reunify you with your family, it is time for DOF to go back to court to set up a plan that will get you back home."

"What if I don't want to?"

Her question didn't exactly surprise him. Kids in stable foster homes sometimes resisted reunification.

"I mean, I'm not saying I don't want to go home. It's just, I'm not sure, you know, if I can really trust my mom. Can you make me go back?"

"Well, we could decide that there is no reason for the state to continue foster assistance, but in your case, it's not likely that you'll be put in that position anytime soon," he answered. "The court is likely to want Luz to prove herself over an extended time."

"Am I old enough to decide for myself?"

Jim nodded, "Yes, you can sign yourself out of DOF anytime you want now. But if you feel that way, I wouldn't be too hasty."

"I'm just asking. I love my foster parents. But there's Sellie and Juanita and Grandma. It's not just my mother. Besides, I think I can handle her now and she does seem changed. I'm not stupid, so if I ever do this before you want me to, it will be because I need to do it. I'm pretty worried, too. It's all I think about."

"Well, for now, first things first. We'll be going before the judge in the next few weeks. Your lawyer and Diane Pacquin will be there to make sure your interest is protected."

Tina stood and wandered over to a window. She needed some air.

"I was thinking about my friend Kris. All she cares about is music and boys and fun. She's so lucky. Can we go now?"

\*\*\*

The creaky apartment door had barely opened when Tina found herself crushed in Selena's embrace. Behind Selena, Luz and Grandma stood smiling. Jim Covain waited for Selena to let her sister go before escorting Tina inside.

For over a week now since the home visit had been approved by the Family Court, Valentina had played the scene out in her mind, fully dreading the day, even though her meetings with Luz had all gone well. Now, back here in the building she had not seen in several years, all she felt was awkwardness. Jim gave her a reassuring pat on the back, and she greeted her mother.

"Mami, it's been a long time since I've seen this place."

Luz smiled and hugged her daughter.

"You got a new chair, couch, too."

"Those old ones, they fell apart. Used layaway."

"I'm here too," Grandma Diaz interrupted.

"Grandma, Grandma, I am so glad to see you. Are you doing what the doctor said? No fried foods. Ai, yai, yai."

Grandma laughed and gave Tina her own long hug. "I can't wait until you come back, my beautiful Valentina."

Tina glanced over at Jim and didn't reply.

She turned back to Luz. "Where's Juanita?"

"Oh, that one. She had a little trouble in school. Got detention. I'll handle that when she gets home," Luz's voice rose, "but she better be here before you go. I told her this is a big day."

"Yes, I want to see her. But I want you to show me the place. I was a kid last time I was here."

Luz's face colored, but she didn't say anything as she took Tina by the hand toward the three bedrooms.

Jim Covain remained behind, sitting in a corner on a kitchen chair he had pulled into the room. He observed how neat the home was, so different from the hallways and yard of the apartment building. It seemed as if nothing was ever disturbed in the small living room. If it weren't for some wonderful aromas wafting in from Grandma's oven, Jim felt it was as if the antiseptic place wasn't intended to be enjoyed.

Several minutes later, with Sellie and Grandma having adjourned to attend to the cooking, Tina and Luz returned to the living room.

"Ma showed me the room I would share with Sellie. Juanita and Ma would be in Ma's room and Grandma by herself. It's a nice room. Smaller than my room now, but it's nice."

Luz scowled. "Valentina, please, don't talk about that other place. That's just a place to stay. This is your home."

Tina fought the urge to say something hurtful about why she was even in that other place, and replied, "Sorry Ma. I didn't mean anything by that."

The moment of tension passed when the apartment door opened and Juanita walked in, clearly sulking. Luz took her firmly by the shoulders.

"What do you got to say for yourself? I told you, no more trouble in school. And what, you forgot Valentina's coming to see us?"

Luz saw the caseworker taking in the scene and let go of Juanita. "You gonna apologize to everyone? You know you will be grounded and the pastor will have a talk with you."

"The pastor? You only go to church because you want his son and he's too stupid to see through you. Good, tell the pastor. But you know why I got detention? 'Cuz the kids still make fun of me for being your daughter. They don't forget anything. So I punched one of those girls. I was trying to stick up for you. That's why I got detention. I don't care if I never go to school again."

Luz took a deep breath. "We will talk about this later. You visit with your sister. I want to talk to Mr. Covain."

She motioned to Jim to follow her and led him to her room, which he noticed was also in pristine order.

"I'm sorry about that. I been having a hard time with Juanita. Maybe it's my fault. I'm sorry for things I done, but I'm really changed. Juanita's just mad. Yes, I like the pastor's son. His name is Paolo. But I go to church because it helps me. I'm trying very hard. But like I used to hit Selena and Tina when I got mad, I don't do that no more, I swear. Juanita is gonna be grounded, but I ain't gonna hit her."

"I understand how teenagers are, Ms. Diaz," Jim replied. "I'm glad to see that you're trying. We wouldn't be here today if we didn't think so."

"Thank you," Luz said, "now if it's okay, we'll eat some of Grandma's cooking and have a nice time."

"Okay," Jim said, but he had more doubts now than he did answers.

***

Other than Juanita looking sour the whole time, the visit was pleasant and uneventful. On the drive back to the Allens, Jim asked Tina how she felt.

"I miss Grandma's cooking. Puerto Rican food is the best. She even made me fried food and didn't touch any herself."

"Valentina, you know what I mean."

"Do you think my mother has really changed? I know, she looks different, and she goes to church a lot. She was okay with handling Juanita getting detention, but Ma's not totally crazy, with you there and all. Maybe that's why she didn't hit her."

"If you want, we'll look more into how Luz is handling anger," he answered, but if truth be told, that little investigation was already number one on his list.

"Yes, I do. If I'm going back, I'm going only if the old Luz is gone forever. I need to be sure."

# CHAPTER SIXTEEN

*Autumn 2004*

Autumn. I usually enjoy autumn. Fall is a time of change, and color, although melancholy, as winter approaches. It's hard to go through autumn without competing emotions. Bobbie and I had been spectators to the struggle Valentina was having with the idea of reuniting with her family. She wanted it, but she needed to be sure of it. She didn't want to hurt us, but she didn't want to hurt herself. Her laughter was less frequent and extended periods of silence were becoming the norm.

One day at breakfast, a few weeks after the school year had begun, and not long after her visit to Luz, Tina pushed her plate away and announced, "I feel sick. I have to go back to sleep."

Without consulting me, Roberta answered, "Honey, if you're feeling too stressed, please tell us. Maybe you need a break. Take the day and just rest. We'll check in with you later."

"Oh, I'll be okay. Just not feeling good. You guys go to work. Don't worry about me."

"You sure you don't want to talk to us?"

"No Dad, really. Just go to work. I'm going back to bed. See you guys later," she said and left the table.

*** 

Roberta called in a panic. "Hal, I just got home and Tina isn't here. No note, nothing. What are we going to do?"

"Hold on, Bobbie, maybe she just went for a walk. Wait a little while."

"Okay, I'll wait a little while, but this is strange. I don't like it one bit."

"I agree. If she's not back in a half hour or so, I'll come home and you can call Covain."

***

I arrived home as quickly as I could after Roberta's second call. My own heart was racing. No word at all from Tina and by now Bobbie had been home for over an hour. When I stepped inside, my wife was sitting at the kitchen table, her face buried in her hands.

She looked up at me and said, "I'm scared. Jim called back a minute ago. He's contacted the police around here as well as in Blue Hills. Maybe she headed for her mother's."

I nodded, hoping that was the worst possibility. At least we'd know she was safe. My mind raced to the crazy thought that I would ever consider Luz's place to be a safe haven for Tina.

"Maybe we should split up and drive around ourselves," Bobbie suggested.

"Did you try Kristin or Josh?"

"Of course," she snapped, and then apologized.

"Okay, well, I guess it wouldn't hurt if we looked ourselves. The police can only do so much. But I think one of us should stay here just in case she shows up. I rushed home so quickly that I left my cell phone at work. Give me yours so we can keep each other informed."

"Okay. And I almost forgot to tell you, Covain had another problem to handle, but he should be coming here pretty soon."

Bobbie handed me her phone and I left her to agonize alone.

\*\*\*

I'd been up and down almost every street between ours and the center of town for almost an hour, when the cell phone rang. Roberta's voice did not reassure me.

"Hal, get back here fast. Tina showed up and she's a mess. Thank god Jim was delayed. He didn't need to see her like this."

"What do you mean, she's a mess. Dirty? Bloody? What?"

"Just get here. Her clothes are dirty like she was lying on the ground and she's totally out of it. We might need an ambulance."

"Oh shit. Hang on, I'll be there in less than five," I said and slammed on the accelerator.

\*\*\*

Tina couldn't stop laughing. From the moment I walked in the door she kept pointing at me, then at Roberta, and roared.

"Damn it, Tina, what the hell drug are you on?"

"Hal, she won't tell me. And she won't tell me who she was with. Whoever it was just dropped her here and took off."

"Valentina, if you don't tell me what you're on we're going to take you to the emergency room."

The smile disappeared for an instant, then Tina erupted in another round of laughter.

"Dad, don't, ha ha, don't take me there, ha ...."But before she could finish, she swooned forward and fell to the floor.

As Tina struggled back to her feet, Bobbie grabbed the phone and dialed 911.

"Ma," more laughter, "I don't want the hospital, I'm fine," she slurred and swayed as if about to fall again.

"Tina, you lie down on the couch and shut up."

I'd never seen Bobbie so upset. She dragged Tina to the family room and forced her to lie down.

"Hal, why did she do this? Do you think she's been using drugs all along?"

"I don't know. I don't think so. Maybe she's feeling more pressure than we realize to go back to Blue Hills. I hope she'll do some explaining when she sobers up."

We sat quietly for several minutes, watching Tina occasionally burst into laughter, still obeying orders to stay on the couch. Then the doorbell rang, and Bobbie raced to open the door, expecting the emergency team, but instead being faced with Jim Covain. In the distance we could hear a siren.

"What's going on?" he demanded.

"Tina's home and she's high as a kite on something. I've called 911."

Jim nodded and went to see Tina. We watched as he quizzed her, not having much more luck than we had. In the meantime, the sound of the siren grew louder, then halted.

I went to open the door and two EMTs jumped from their ambulance, oxygen and a stretcher in tow. Next to the ambulance, a police car pulled in. The officer joined the others in the family room. Jim, sitting beside Tina, stood to make room for the crew to tend to the girl.

Pulling me out of earshot of the policeman, Jim said, "I think she's stoned on marijuana. I've seen it many times. I think she's not used to it. She's probably not so bad off as she seems."

"Why the cop?" I asked.

"You called 911, a cop comes along. I'll chat with him. I'm pretty sure he won't arrest her, if that's a concern."

I nodded and we stepped back to watch the team get the oxygen in place and start to move Tina onto the stretcher. Jim spoke quietly with the officer who shook his head in the negative to something Jim said. I heard Jim thank him for understanding.

Tina looked at the policeman from her new spot on the stretcher and pointed. She giggled and said, "You're so hot."

The man just stared back at her, looked over at us and Jim and shook his head again, this time as if to say, what's the use.

"Jim, Bobbie and I are going to the hospital," I said.

"Okay."

"Can I ride with her in the ambulance?" Bobbie asked.

"I was going to, but yes, you can. I'll follow along with Hal. We need to talk anyway."

The team loaded the stretcher into the ambulance and the officer pulled away in his cruiser. The ambulance, with Roberta kneeling next to Tina, backed out. I followed close behind. I don't know if Roberta told Tina I was behind them, but Tina lifted her head, gave a cheery wave through the rear window, and was clearly laughing behind her oxygen mask.

***

"Hal, I'm willing to bet that kid has never used drugs before today. And if I had to guess why she started now, I'd say she wants to piss you off."

"What do you mean?" I asked, not taking my eyes off the ambulance and taking my chances by running every red light the ETMs sped through. "Why would she do that?"

"I've seen this sort of thing before. She wants you to get so angry that you toss her out. I know she's been agonizing about the possibility of returning to her family and she'd rather not make a choice that she thinks will hurt you. She loves you guys."

"So you're saying she's on the verge of deciding that reuniting with Luz is what she wants? So she half kills herself with drugs just so we tell her to leave? That's nuts."

"Nuts to you, maybe. You're forgetting that she's a teenager. I've seen adults use less logic."

It struck me how attached I'd become to Tina. "No, we can't throw her out if this is what today was all about. Certainly Roberta isn't about to make her leave. As much as I might find it distasteful, if Tina wants to go home, we'll find a way to support her, but she has to be thinking straight."

We arrived at the emergency entrance and were directed to a parking area. Jim asked me if I was okay.

"You know, Hal, maybe I'm wrong, which in a lot of ways would be worse, I mean in terms of drug use, but assuming I'm right, just give her the love and support she needs right now and she'll see things clearly. She's good at hiding her real feelings. She's had to just to survive. Once she understands that you will support her no matter what, she'll be okay."

I shrugged, not knowing what else to say and opened the door to the emergency room where Bobbie was already pacing, Valentina already having been taken in for examination.

*** 

Tina turned toward us, her chin resting on the palm of her hand.

"How long have I been asleep? How long do I have to stay here?"

Bobbie stood over Tina and stroked her tangled curls. "You've been out for a few hours. We think you'll be discharged pretty soon."

"Is DOF taking me away from you?"

"Tina, no."

"Ma, I did a bad thing. I'm too embarrassed to go home with you," Valentina whispered.

"Yes, you did a bad thing, but we all make mistakes, sometimes big ones. Dad and I both want you to stay with us, if that's what you want," Bobbie answered.

Tina sat up now and was quiet for a moment. The sudden beep from the monitoring device hooked up to her finger startled her, but she leaned back and was silent again before finally responding.

"Is Jim here?"

"No, he left when he knew you'd be okay," I said.

"Good. I need to talk to you guys alone. I love you. I really do. I don't think I knew how much until I thought maybe I have to go back to my mother. Honest, I think she's trying hard to change, but still, I'm not sure. When we were in Puerto Rico she seemed different, too, but when we came back she was her bad old self again. I love my sisters and Grandma, but sometimes Sellie drives me nuts and Juanita, she's into some bad stuff."

"Sweetheart," Bobbie said, moving closer to take Tina's hand, "I think I understand. You have our support no matter what. Our home is yours for as long as you want. But you have to promise that there will be no repeats of today."

Tina smiled, "You can bet I won't. I don't feel so good this morning. Anyway, I don't know if Jim told you, but he says he isn't pushing reunion so fast. But then I think I just want to get it over with."

A young nurse came in and announced that our patient would be discharged soon. The hospital had already contacted someone at DOF and had been given permission to release Tina back to us.

"Great. Is that okay with you?" I asked Tina.

"You bet. I can't wait to get back to the house. I'm so hungry. I hope you guys aren't mad. Cross my heart, I promise I'll be good."

Tina was true to her word. She behaved like an angel, was doing well in school, and seemed relatively content, if occasionally given to those bouts of silence. Over eight weeks had passed since her drug adventure and fall had arrived in a cloud of several cool, rainy days. My Red Sox were playoff bound, and I was looking forward to them making it to the World Series.

It was on another of those gloomy early evenings that Bobbie arrived home with Tina after the latest in the series of meetings between Luz and Tina. I could tell from the look in my wife's eyes that something was wrong.

"Tina, how about getting some homework done while Dad and I get dinner ready?"

"Mom, I'm a big girl. Let me tell him."

"Tell me what?" I asked, although I was certain this was something I didn't want to know.

"Dad, Jim Covain is going to call you about coming over tonight. The state has decided that my mother has been good enough that they think reunifying should be done now. They plan on going to court."

My stomach began to churn, but I tried not to show it. "Well, I suppose this was something we knew was possible. Isn't it a good thing that your mother has turned a corner?"

Tina sighed, "I don't know what to believe. I mean, she seems better when I see her, but you know I talk to Sellie sometimes. She says she thinks the pastor's son is perverted. He's at the apartment a lot. Sellie told me he does things like tap her and Juanita on the butt, or some creepy way he looks at them. I asked Jim about it, but he says the man has a clean record, a good job and he's been interviewed several times. He's asked Sellie, and you know her. She sometimes exaggerates and her story isn't always the same. Jim says Lydia Hernandez is pushing the reunion."

"What about your lawyer?" Bobbie asked.

"Jim is having me talk to him tomorrow. I wasn't ready for this yet."

Suddenly she slammed her fist on the kitchen table and began crying. She didn't bother to wipe the tears, shouting, "When do I get to make my own decisions? When is my life really my own? Why can they make me go to a place where I don't feel safe? Why can't I be the one to say when my mother is ready or if I ever want to be with her? I still have nightmares about Simon in my room and my mother beating me because I had a little wrinkle on my bed. I don't want any more nightmares. Mom, Dad, is there anything wrong with that?"

Before we could reply, she raced out of the room and up the stairs. Roberta said we should wait a while, let her calm down, before discussing things with her, but I couldn't stand it. I hurried upstairs and heard her door slam as I reached the top. I saw a brief glow appear under her door, but as I reached for the handle, her light went out.

# EPILOGUE

*Spring 2012*

The San Jose Festival had transformed over the years. Rock bands appeared along with Latin musicians. Even the food was more eclectic, as was the crowd. It had become a moneymaking enterprise, and sponsors throughout the region were anxious to set up booths, selling anything from cell phones, to baby strollers, and even insurance. The beautiful young woman of twenty five led Roberta through the throng as I trailed. It would be the first time for us to meet her fiancé, Pete Villas, seated with his parents in front of a salsa band.

It was less than a year since Tina had graduated from the local community college. From the time she had been reunited with her family, almost three years had passed before we had heard from her again. The first time she called us, really out of the blue, she apologized for taking so long. Tina told us that things had been fine at first with her mom, but there was always some problem or other. A little bit of temper now and then, but no violence. Luz had insisted that she not communicate with us, and Tina felt that she had to respect those wishes even though it had killed her.

We were saddened to learn that Grandma had passed away a little less than two years after Tina had returned, and that began a time of bigger problems. Not long afterward, the pastor's son moved in. It turned out that Sellie was right. This time, it was Juanita who was the victim. Fortunately for the youngest sister, Luz had changed enough to throw the man out and press charges. But it also started her drinking again and churchgoing tapered off significantly. A week before Valentina contacted us, Selena had moved out to live with a man who worked in the diner where she waited on tables. At that point, Tina felt she needed our support again, and we, of course, had been thrilled to hear from her.

"Mom and Dad," Tina yelled over the sound of the band, "this is Pete … Pedro … my fiancé. Isn't he handsome?"

Pete grinned and stood to shake our hands. He really was handsome. "We met at school. He's an accountant. So smart."

Pete grinned again.

During the few years since our reunion with our former foster daughter, we heard from her often and saw her occasionally. We were delighted to witness her bulldog determination to improve her life. Tina decided to quit her waitressing job and go back to school full time to get a degree. Even though she'd been uncertain about exactly what she wanted to do, she knew that she wanted to work with kids in some way. Wild horses couldn't have kept us from her college graduation. The joy on her face as she accepted her diploma was beautiful to see. Now on top of that, it looked like she had found a great match in Pete.

The band stopped to take a break, so we could finally hear ourselves think. After a brief conversation with Pedro, I told Tina that we had to be going.

"Before you go," she said to me and Bobbie, "I need you to know something. From the moment I met Mom at school that terrible day, I knew what a wonderful person she was. You both mean everything to me. There are times when I think I understand my mother, and other times when she still scares me, but I can handle it. You've made a profound difference in my life. When you took me in you could have said, 'Maybe it's not for me, I'm busy, I have a job, I have a family, I have hobbies, a house, friends.' I felt rejected. I felt abandoned. Then you came and took me in and I said to myself, will you accept me with all my anger and sadness? Take me to a place where there is love, encourage me so I'll never give up, walk me to a place where I can feel what being safe is like for the first time? You saved my life when I wanted to end it. You brought me hope. Even when I felt lost and broken, you were there for me with your doors wide open. You made me a home when I'd been living out of my trash bags. Your love pulled me through and you gave me the confidence and strength to deal with whatever I face. I can't ever thank you enough."

Giving Tina a hug, Bobbie replied. "No, we can't thank you enough. You taught us courage, you taught us perseverance, but most of all, you showed us that you have a rare spirit. You're one in a million."

"Are you serious?" Valentina laughed, and her eyes sparkled with delight.

# About the Author

Avi Morris holds a B.A. from University of Connecticut and a J.D. from the University of Connecticut School of Law. After many years as a federal attorney and then as a business consultant, Mr. Morris fulfilled a dream to write fiction. *Crocodile Mothers Eat Their Young* is his first published novel. He and his wife, a teacher, have hosted several foster children in addition to raising three children of their own. The family resides in Connecticut.

## ALL THINGS THAT MATTER PRESS

FOR MORE INFORMATION ON TITLES AVAILABLE FROM
ALL THINGS THAT MATTER PRESS, GO TO
http://allthingsthatmatterpress.com
or contact us at
allthingsthatmatterpress@gmail.com

If you enjoyed this book, please post a review on Amazon.com and
your favorite social media sites.
Thank you!

Made in the USA
San Bernardino, CA
21 August 2014